Closure

Closure

A NOVEL

LINDSEY TODD

VERITAS WORDS / LINDSEY TODD

ISBN: 978-1-5136-6344-9

Published by Veritas Words (Lindsey Todd).

Dedicated to T. —
Thank you for helping me
create meaningful art.
"You helped me live and learn."

ONE.

THE SPOTLIGHT WAS WHITE-HOT and blinding, and as the MC introduced me to an expectant audience of 300 people, I pretended to fiddle with the microphone cord, gazing downward to escape the glare of the light and the weight of their stares.

"We have with us tonight a prolific artist from the Philadelphia area. Her album of traditional Christmas carols has sold over 30,000 copies through Lighthouse Media, and her debut country album, *Road Trip,* was recently released on all of the major music-streaming platforms. Please join me in welcoming Morgan Wells to the stage!"

There was clapping and whistling, and I knew that my friend, Mara, was undoubtedly the head cheerleader. I couldn't help but smile as I swallowed deeply and tried to ignore my trembling knees.

"Hi, everyone. I'm Morgan," I said, my voice sounding foreign and far too loud as it echoed through the microphone and bounced off the walls I couldn't see. "I won't lie, I am much more comfortable in a studio than I am on a stage, so if I seem a little nervous, just bear with me."

Deep breath. Swallow. Continue.

"The song I'm performing for you tonight is one of my favorites. It's Ingrid Michaelson's version of 'Can't Help Falling in Love,' and I hope you enjoy it."

More applause. I nodded somewhere to my left after that, indicating that the DJ could start my karaoke track, and the first familiar chords of the song came streaming through the speakers all around me.

"Wise men say only fools rush in…"

My voice felt small and tentative in this grand room, a place I'd never expected to find myself two weeks earlier. The event had been publicized on Facebook—an Open Mic Night, hosted by a local young adult organization in the heart of Philadelphia—and initially, I'd thought: *Of course I can't sing. I become an inept, stressed-out ball of nerves when I open my mouth in front of an audience.*

Performing live had always been more or less out of the question for me, as had Philly itself over the last two years. There was no part of me that had planned on being in this place—in this city—tonight, until Mara told me that she was planning on going, and had invited me along. Something had inexplicably compelled me to get in my car and drive into the city, drawing me in for the first time since the *last time.* I didn't believe it was a coincidence, either, that I was able to find the perfect karaoke track at the last minute for the song I chose.

"Like a river flows surely to the sea, darling, so it goes...some things are meant to be..."

And as I let that note hang in the air, the audience faded away, the stage dropped from beneath my feet, the walls expanded, and I was transported to a different time in my life—to a different era. One where I had recorded this song, and presented it to you as a Valentine's Day gift in your kitchen five years ago by candlelight.

The emotion began to well up in my throat, forming a small lump as I shaped the final words of the song:

"I keep falling in love with you."

I saw you, Wade. In the five-second window after the final note of the song resounded and died, and before the enthusiastic applause commenced, I saw our relationship play out like a film reel in my mind. I saw the easy, carefree way you used to pick me up and spin me around; I saw the way you held me each time after we made love. I watched our screaming match unfold in my driveway that last New Year's Eve when so much of what we'd built came crumbling down around us, and I relived the moment we said goodbye for the last time, though neither of us realized it then.

Far too soon, everything fell back into its proper place in the universe, the way it had all been arranged before I'd begun singing. The applause was deafening, shattering the images of the memories, and I darted offstage without taking a proper bow.

Finally, I could breathe. Finally, the build-up to the pinnacle of the evening had been resolved, and I could sit back and enjoy other people's performances. I headed to the bar for my second glass of wine.

"That was really lovely," one girl remarked as we waited for the bartender.

"Thank you," I said, shooting her a warm smile.

Suddenly, there were hands on my shoulders, shaking me in excitement, and I turned to find a grinning Mara just before she pulled me into a hug.

"That was amazing, Morgan. You sounded so good!"

I hugged her back, still attempting to shake the bittersweet nostalgia that had followed me off the stage.

"Thanks for encouraging me, Mar. Really. I can't explain why, but this was...needed."

"I'm glad," she said, taking my hands and swinging my arms back and forth affectionately. "Except...now *I'm* nervous!"

I shook my head and rolled my eyes at my crazy friend, who'd studied classical voice in college and had toured with an opera company in Italy.

"You're crazy. Get up there and do what you do best."

"You are such a hypocrite," she teased, giving my hands one last squeeze before dropping them to go find her friend, who would be singing a duet with her in the next few minutes.

As the room darkened again and I turned toward the stage for Mara's performance, I noticed him—the boy she'd introduced me to earlier as Kyle. We'd texted about him briefly before I'd arrived; Mara had told me she'd met someone recently who was exactly my "type." When I met him at the beginning of the evening and she'd waggled her eyebrows at me mischievously, I knew immediately that she'd been right. On top of the fact that he was in medical school and was "one of the most authentic people" Mara claimed she'd ever met, he was tall with rust-colored hair, an easy smile, and broad shoulders. He looked masculine—albeit not quite as ruggedly handsome as you'd been—but I was still learning to accept that nobody would ever be you.

One of Kyle's many attributes was that he was musical and played guitar, and he'd performed a song with his band earlier in the evening. As he began to walk by, I shot him a thumbs-up and a friendly smile, surprising myself over the fact that the gesture had come easily.

My boldness paid off. Kyle noticed my enthusiasm, even in the darkness, and suddenly changed course to approach me.

"Hey, you sounded great," he said, stopping at my table.

"Thanks," I replied, tucking an invisible strand of hair behind my ear. I was fairly certain I was blushing, and I was already aware of the butterflies that had begun to form in the pit of my stomach.

"Two albums, huh? That's really cool. You're a songwriter?"

"I am," I confirmed. "I'm a writer in general though, so songwriting has always come pretty naturally." Then, "And you're a good guitarist. Have you been playing long?"

"Eh, since I was about twelve. My dad taught me how to play," he said, his face breaking into the kind of smile that threatened to thaw two years of loneliness.

"That's awesome. I learned a bit when I was younger, but—tiny hands," I explained, holding them up, "so I never could quite master the whole barre chord thing."

Kyle laughed, and I warmed with the sound of its deep and sexy pitch.

"Hey, listen—I'm up again after the next act. I'll catch up with you later?" he half-stated, half-asked, reaching out to touch my arm as he moved past me. I noticed that, pleasantly, the place where his hand had rested on my bicep reacted with an unexpected tingling sensation beneath my sleeve, and I allowed myself to feel more optimistic than I'd been in months.

After you and I had broken up—now more than two years ago—I spent the majority of my time alone. I went on the occasional date, but I've always been a black-and-white, yes-or-no kind of girl. I wouldn't pursue or accept a second date with a man who didn't make me *feel* anything; thus, I earned the reputation of "picky." I listened time and time again to my friends' insistence that I wasn't even giving my potential suitors a fair chance. I nodded respectfully while they assured me that one date wasn't enough to determine anything. Inside, I already knew the truth: a first date would always tell me all I'd need to know about true chemistry. I'd learned that lesson from the way my skin had burned beneath my sweater the first night you took me out.

Now, there was the possibility of Kyle, and he was the first *real* possibility there had been in a long time. Still, what I couldn't reconcile was the fact that, though I was standing in a room full of distractions and had just been touched by a man who made my stomach warm, I was still thinking about you.

"Now, please welcome to the stage: Mara Conn and Max Bleecker!"

The MC's voice was suddenly booming through the mic and through my maudlin thoughts, and I watched as Mara took the stage with Max to sing "The Rose" by Bette Middler. As soon as she opened her mouth, I knew it was going to be good—my friend could easily silence a room with her voice, and the way she effortlessly infused this just-for-fun song with the subtle flavor of her operatic background transformed the version we all knew into something more intense and pulsing and alive.

When Max chimed in on the second verse with his smooth, tenor harmonies, the song shifted again into a different mood, a different tone. The two of them held the audience captive for nearly five minutes with the magic of their blended voices, and as they sang the final note, the applause was deafening.

"Encore! Encore! Encore!" the audience chanted, but Mara and Max only laughed. In fact, Mara was already ducking off the stage when Max said, to appease us all, "We'll be back."

A few good-natured *boos* echoed through the room as I ran to hug Mara in congratulations.

"Amazing. I have chills right now. How do you do that?"

She shrugged. "I thought they'd all be able to tell I was nervous. Glad it wasn't so obvious."

She was crazy humble, which was why I loved the girl.

The rest of the night was a blur of music and philosophical conversation—Mara, Max, and I stayed clustered together, talking about deep and familiar things like God and faith and the future in low voices. I felt wonderfully content with the notion that I belonged somewhere—that I wasn't alone in a world that so often seemed hostile to who I was and what I believed.

When the last act performed and all the lights were switched on, our little trio paraded across the street for rolled ice cream, which I'd never had before but proved to be delicious. It was sprinkling rain and chilly for early September, so Mara, Max, and I split an Uber back to the lot where we'd parked, laughing about our quirky personality types as our driver made his way through the maze of skyscrapers you'd taught me to love.

As the three of us slid out of the car and began the short walk to the parking lot, still bantering and walking in a perfect line so that none of us was excluded from conversation, I realized that that night had been the first time I'd felt young since graduating from college. I'd hibernated for so long in the safety of my little Philadelphia suburb, allowing the painful memories of the city where I'd fallen so totally for you to keep me away. I didn't want to be reminded of you everywhere I looked, but inevitably, I would always feel your presence here. There were a billion other streets for me to walk, beckoning me from every other corner of the world, and yet I was still so besotted with the parameters of your little life. As a result, my feelings for this city were no longer simple—I both loved and hated Philadelphia in equal measure.

Still, as I climbed into my car after waving goodbye to my friends and pulled onto John F Kennedy Boulevard, the gut-wrenching ache I'd expected to feel evaporated with the beauty of City Hall, stretching on for blocks and blocks directly ahead of me. For the first time in years, I had a front-row seat to this architectural gem. The last time I'd seen it this way had been with you, but the knowledge of this didn't make me sad—I simply felt City Hall's stagger-ing splendor, and let it wash over me until I felt restored.

I eventually found my way to the interstate, heading west away from the city, and I allowed myself to glance back at the skyline in my rearview mirror as it disappeared behind me. For so long, that lovable cluster of buildings had been impossible to look at—even in pictures—without falling to pieces. For so long, something I'd once thought to be a symbol of all that awaited the two of us after college, was too much to bear—until this moment. And as I blasted "It's Time" by Imagine Dragons, the rain spilling in soft drops through my open sunroof on a starless night, I real-ized and believed for the first time that God has the power to mend even the most broken of narratives. Finally, I was starting to experience proof of this for myself.

"Now, don't you understand? I'm never changing who I am."

And as the last notes of our former anthem beat through my speakers, I thought back to the beginning of our shared history and smiled as the tears, hot and healing, fell.

TWO.

WHEN I MET YOU FOR the first time, I was just a few weeks into my fifteenth year, and the air was bitterly cold with the chill of late January. Still, there I was in a knee-length, strapless dress, black and adorned with sequins all over, unaffected by the weather and warmed with the anxiety of waiting. I was standing in my best friend, Jenny's kitchen, shifting my weight back and forth from one 3-inch heel to the other.

"What time did you say they were coming?" I asked, scratching my open palm, which was now dampened with sweat.

Jenny rolled her eyes. "Chill out. We have another fifteen minutes or so. And knowing the boys, they'll probably be late, anyway."

It was as though she thought she could calm my nerves by telling me I'd have to endure another twenty minutes *at least* of this torturous anticipation. Instead, I went into full-fledged panic mode, refusing to eat even one bite of the delicate hors d'oeuvres her mother had provided for the evening.

It was my freshman year of high school, and my first high school formal, to boot. I probably wouldn't have gone at all had I not been friends with Jenny—or at least, I was fairly positive I wouldn't have been going with a date. But Jenny had been popular in middle school, and she knew some boys from her old class who were now attending our brother school near Philadelphia. She'd set three of us girls up on dates with them for our freshman formal, but truthfully, this was also my first date in general. As in, *ever*. I had never met this kid, Alan, but Jenny had reassured me that he was sweet and charming, and that we were just *bound* to have fun together! In reality, I knew she'd probably just set us up by height compatibility, as neither one of us was particularly tall, but that was OK with me. I was going to my first dance with a boy.

There came a sudden knock at the door, and Jenny's dogs went berserk as my heart leapt into my throat. I averted my eyes from the entryway as Jenny's mother rushed to greet the first of our dates.

"Dee, so good to see you. Wade, you look great!"

I exhaled a little. So it wasn't Alan at the door.

It was you.

With the momentary relief I felt, I lifted my eyes and peered through the kitchen doorframe into the foyer just as your tall, blond form made its way inside.

In that moment, something small and sure inside of me dipped. The world didn't stop spinning—I wasn't struck by Cupid's arrow—but it felt like you were someone important. Like you would maybe be important for a very, very long time.

Anna, ever the flirt, ran to greet you, in all of her 5'11" glory. She wore a comical grin on her freckled face, and her blue satin dress slid a little further down over her enormous boobs as she extended her hand to you—did you notice?

"I'm Anna," she said, almost gleefully.

You glanced downward as you shook her hand, but not at her cleavage—at your shoes. You seemed to be blushing, but when I looked a little more closely, I saw that your pink complexion could mostly be attributed to your teenage acne. Still, acne or no acne, that moment began an exhausting pattern for the rest of my evening of looking at you and looking away. I think I half-hoped you would notice my shameless glances, but I hardly knew what I would do with myself if you actually tried to talk to me.

My date, Alan, arrived next. He was short, with skater hair and a slight build, and his smile didn't quite reach his eyes as he introduced himself to me.

When Jenny's date finally arrived at the house, our mothers all cooed and fussed over us, fixing stray hairs and helping pin boutonnieres to lapels before the endless snapping of photos started. The six of us stood in an awkward line, as though preparing for death by firing squad, and pasted anxious smiles to our faces.

About twenty minutes later, we all piled into Jenny's mother's van. It was a tight squeeze, especially with you boys and your gangly limbs, but we managed to make it work for the short ride over to the school.

"Have fun, everyone!" Mrs. Scott shouted through the open window as we all tumbled out, we girls making a beeline for the door with our exposed shoulders and legs.

The dance committee at my school, Villa Marie, had transformed the entire front entryway into a cozy winter wonderland. Delicate snowflakes were projected onto the dark walls, outlined in an electric blue, and tables with snacks were decorated with festive, bare-tree centerpieces, glowing bulbs strewn from various branches.

Once I'd taken it all in, I scanned the mob around me consisting of my classmates and their dates, subconsciously looking for you. A few moments later, you emerged, Anna leading you by the hand into the auditorium, almost pulling you. Just as my heart reacted, a warm arm wrapped around mine, distracting me.

"I thought I lost you for a second, there!" Jenny said, laughing. "I already can't find John."

John was Jenny's date, and appearance-wise, they

couldn't be less compatible. Jenny was big-boned and tall, while John was short, like Alan, with an overall small frame for a boy his age and an afro as big as Michael Jackson's circa 1967. All of the boys, really, looked awkward and displaced as freshmen—except for you. You, Wade, looked *exactly* right.

I gave Jenny's arm a little tug and whisper-yelled into her ear, "Bathroom. Need to talk to you."

"Huh?" she replied. The shrieking girls and the roar of their dates' deep laughter was deafening in the hallway.

I rolled my eyes and dragged her into the ladies' room.

"Wow, starting off the night in the bathroom. What's up with you?" Jenny asked.

"Wade."

"What about him?"

"Just…did you have to set him up with Anna?"

"Wait…*what?!*" she squealed, eyes wide. "You have a thing for him?!"

"I mean…it's not a *thing*. I don't know him. I just know he exists, now. Obviously."

Jenny shook her head, incredulous.

"OK, rewind, back up. You're serious? Because we can make this happen."

"Yes. I mean, I don't know. Don't meddle or anything. Don't do anything embarrassing, *please.* I just thought I should give you a heads up. You know—for next time."

I could tell Jenny was thinking something over. A few seconds later, she said,

"Don't tell Anna about this. You just *know* it would turn into a competition."

I did know. Anna was showy, loud, and obnoxiously flirtatious. She was also boy-crazy, and oddly fixated on sex for her age. This could have been a result of all the attention she regularly received over her impossibly-developed figure, or it could have had something to do with all of the salacious magazines her father kept stashed in his closet. In any case, if Anna knew I was even considering you that way, she'd move in that much faster. My feelings for you had suddenly become an unintentional game I didn't want to play. All I really knew was that I had to get to know you, had to get close enough to you to analyze what this shocking and sudden thing was that had overtaken me without my permission.

Tonight was Anna's. Maybe another night would be mine.

I proceeded to watch you, helplessly and hopelessly, the whole night over Alan's shoulder as we danced. Really, he was sweet—it wasn't his fault that he hadn't had the good fortune of being you. What I *will* say is that he tried. He even asked questions that indicated he might be interested in me beyond that night.

"So I hear through the grapevine that you're a singer," Alan prompted during a slow-dance.

"Oh? I mean, yeah. Yes. I just recorded a Christmas album last year."

I was totally disinterested, unaffected by the conversation. I was watching you dance with Anna, your large hands spread wide on her lower back, your face peaceful. I felt my breath catch at the realization that you might already like her before I'd even had a chance to talk to you.

"…iTunes?"

Shoot. Alan was talking to me again.

"What was that?"

He looked at me like I might be a little nuts, so I quickly improvised,

"The music's loud."

"I was just asking where I could access your music on iTunes."

"Just type in my name," I said. Then, "Would you excuse me? I think I need some air."

"I'll come with you," Alan said.

Despite having heard him, I didn't lag as I made my way to the door, a rush of frozen wind greeting me and stinging my cheeks. There was a couple making out in the shadows against the brick wall. I turned in the opposite direction, trying to make myself invisible.

I couldn't feel my skin after a few moments, but I couldn't bear to go back inside just yet. Instead, I looked up at the stars—stars that allegedly showcased the beauty of everything destined, of everything preordained in the universe—and I wondered if this was how it felt to fall for someone, like the teenage protagonists in all the novels I'd read. I blamed the authors of those books for the way I felt in that moment. If I hadn't read quite so many young adult romance stories, maybe I wouldn't be so fixated on a boy I'd met only two hours ago.

I took a deep breath and turned toward the door. I was certain nothing would ever come of these startling new feelings I harbored for you. The stars had grounded me.

THREE.

IN THE WEEKS THAT FOLLOWED my freshman formal, you friend-requested me on Facebook, and I grew overly optimistic. In fact, I proceeded to desperately concoct a reason to reach out to you.

I knew you could play guitar—you played with your school band, and there was a picture of you on your profile at a concert with your electric guitar, your thick golden hair brushed to the left, your eyes wide and blue. So I dug out my own guitar, coated with a thin layer of dust after having been neglected for a year, and left a post on your Facebook Wall asking for advice on mastering a B chord (never mind that this information was readily available all over the internet).

You ignored the post for so long that finally, John—Jenny's date from formal—ended up actually jumping in and answering the question, which totally defeated the purpose. I assumed that this would just be the end of it, so I threw myself entirely into school and extracurricular activities after that, determined to forget about you and the experience that had, impossibly, bordered on love at first sight.

Then one day, completely out of the blue, I received a message from you, apologizing for having never answered my guitar question. You asked me how I was. We exchanged a few smiley-face formalities, and then something kind of miraculous happened: we started talking. You told me about band practice and algebra homework and gearing up for the next football season, and I shared my inspirations for writing songs, and told you stories about weekend excursions with my aunt, uncle, and little cousin.

There were follow-up conversations, many occurring late at night when we both procrastinated sleeping. You confided in me that you still kept in touch with the first girl you'd ever kissed, and I confessed I still talked to a boy with whom I'd had a bit of a long-distance relationship in the past. You and I developed a friendship rather quickly, and it genuinely surprised me how easy it was to talk to you. You weren't just insanely good-looking, masculine, and talented; you were smart, sensitive, and funny—all traits that the stereotypical football player wasn't supposed to possess.

But life has its catches. Just when I thought that maybe all of our conversations and shared interests were leading somewhere, Jenny threw a birthday party at her house, inviting you and some other guys from your school, along with several of our classmates you hadn't met before. That was when you met Lacey.

Lacey was in English class with Jenny, and I was still getting to know her when Jenny hosted the party. She was small—even smaller than I was—with curly, ash-blonde hair and wide blue eyes framed by thick lashes. Her skin was so pale it was nearly translucent, but the light dusting of sandy freckles over her nose brightened her complexion. Before I could process any of it, you and she were a *thing*, and all of our late-night conversations suddenly revolved around Lacey, the object of your affection.

At first, the conversational shift was one big heartbreak of an adjustment, but after a while, I came to reluctant terms with the fact that you would never think of me the way you thought of Lacey. I decided, in fact, that if you had ever thought of me that way, you would have chosen me months before you even knew her name. So, I assumed the supporting role of "wing-woman," offering you my insights into Lacey's personality and acting as an intermediary between the two of you, because you were still immature when it came to expressing your feelings and properly dating a girl. I never tried to sabotage the relationship—I cared too much about your feelings to even consider interfering—but you trusted me with so much. You were vulnerable with me, open in a way that you weren't with most people. You told me I was your best friend.

The end of our freshman year closed with a casual dance at my school dubbed "Aloha." You boys all wore Hawaiian-flowered shirts and leis, and we girls used the occasion to wear the shortest, most brightly-colored dresses we could find. Lacey had invited you, and I went with Jenny and some of our other friends as a group. I watched your smile grow as you danced with your pixie-like girlfriend, and tried to be authentically happy for you.

After the dance, Jenny's mom shuttled the eight of us over to the local diner for a late meal. Somehow, the seating arrangements resulted in Lacey and Jenny sitting across from each other at the far end of the table, with your friends in the middle, and you and me on the other end.

You mostly talked with John and Alan the whole time, until Alan turned his attention to me.

"So, Morgan—what's up with your music these days? Got any talent scouts knocking at your door?" Then, as an afterthought, "Hey, can I be your official drummer if you make it to the big-time?"

"Uh, sure," I conceded, the awkwardness of the forced conversation making me inwardly cringe. Absentmindedly, I reached for the salt shaker to busy my hands and release some nervous energy. I was struggling to avoid staring at you, and every time you talked, I was grateful for the excuse to look at you, however briefly, without giving myself away.

I was still sliding the salt shaker back and forth between my hands when you grabbed the pepper and began moving it from side to side in quick strokes, as though preparing it for a boxing match with the salt. I smiled at the corniness of the situation, but I played along, pretending to try to corner your pepper. There were no rules to the invented game, but I was grateful for it, because it was the first time we'd had a true interaction in person. We didn't really talk when we were surrounded by all of our other friends at dances, and now, of course, you had Lacey.

"I think I'm winning," you said, your eyebrows raising with the sweet curve of your smile. I felt my heart catch in my throat.

This was utterly ridiculous. I was freaking out over a sentence you'd spoken to me regarding a game that made no logical sense. My *reaction* made no logical sense. But my heart wouldn't stop pounding.

"I think in order to win, you have to have rules," I replied, studying the salt a bit too closely.

"Maybe in order to win, you have to get as close to my shaker as possible without touching it," you said, your voice hinting at concealed laughter.

I played along for a few seconds before summoning the courage to ask, "How's everything going?"

I knew from our IM conversations that you were enamored with Lacey. Your feelings seemed strong, but I could tell you weren't always certain that they were reciprocated. Maybe you had a better idea after the dance.

You were silent for a moment, your hand going through the motions of our salt-and-pepper battle as you considered my question.

"Tonight was fun. I think she enjoyed herself. It's just...I don't know. It feels like she could take me or leave me?" you said, your statement morphing into a question that sought refutation. "When I'm with her sometimes, it seems like her mind is on everything but me. You know?"

You avoided my gaze after your admission, preoccupying yourself by fingering the smooth glass of the pepper shaker. Talking about your feelings made you uncomfortable. Still, you did it with me.

I glanced over at Lacey's end of the table, where she was laughing over something Jenny had said. She was totally oblivious to the fact that we were talking about her—that the boy she had danced with all night was totally infatuated with her, and genuinely cared about whether she liked him, too.

I wanted to ask why you liked her. Everything in me was pushing to ask you this one, very simple question. Still, it was a risky, daring question, and I was still trying to adjust to our hands being in such close proximity on the table.

I ended up telling you,

"Maybe she just needs some time. Maybe...feelings aren't always exactly equal at first? I wouldn't worry about it too much."

That seemed to temporarily reassure you, and I allowed myself to look directly into your eyes as you shot me a half-smile and said,

"Thanks, Morgan."

And when you said my name, I excused myself to the ladies' room to sit quietly in a stall and replay the expression on your face as you said it.

FOUR.

A R O U N D Y O U R B I R T H D A Y in late August, Jenny invited a few of us to go with her to the Grange Fair, which was essentially a fall-themed festival in anticipation of the upcoming season. I'd already made plans that weekend, and Jenny's other friends had bailed at the last minute, so you and Lacey were the only two who'd ended up going that day. When sophomore year started a few days after the festival, Jenny filled me in on how awkward the outing had been.

"All Lacey wanted to do was hang around me the whole time," Jenny said. "She pretty much shunned Wade the whole day. I don't get it."

"Yeah," I mumbled, struggling to neutralize my sardonic expression as I slammed my locker shut.

I hadn't talked to you in weeks—you'd been running on fumes since football practice had started up again—so I didn't know how you felt about the festival, or about Lacey in general. The last time we'd spoken, you'd seemed more reticent than usual, so I hadn't prodded you for details.

"What's wrong? You're a basket of joy this morning," Jenny remarked. The first period bell rang, and we promptly began the walk to class.

Jenny had no idea about you and me—whatever we were at the time. She knew I'd been attracted to you, obviously, that first night at freshman formal, but I'd stifled those feelings when it became clear that you liked Lacey, so Jenny and I didn't talk about it anymore. She had no idea how often the two of us still talked. That was one detail I kept, unspoiled and untouched, to myself.

I shrugged, trying to play it cool despite the heat radiating from my cheeks.

"I just feel like he deserves better. Why is Lacey stringing him along if she's not invested in the relationship?"

"You're right. But that's Lacey for you. In a word: flighty."

It was so aggravating to me that I knew you so well—could give you everything you were looking for in a relationship—and you would still choose the girl who couldn't care less. It was like you had scales over your eyes at the time. You refused to acknowledge me in *that* way, and my patience was wearing thin hearing about Lacey's indecisiveness. I had known I wanted you for nearly a year at that point.

You sent me a message a few days later—as usual, late at night. You went through the motions of a casual conversation, but something wasn't right. You weren't yourself. When I asked what was wrong, you attributed the change I detected to being overly tired from football and harder coursework. But I knew you better than that, so I insisted on the truth.

You finally told me that Lacey had broken things off a day earlier, claiming that "the spark died." When you described her impossibly weak explanation, I could only sit back and stare, outraged, at the words on my screen. I didn't understand how she could have so simply ended things between the two of you with no real reason. *The spark died?* Really? Had she *looked* at you lately?

I noticed, alarmingly, that I was sad as we talked more about it, mostly because you'd taken her rejection so hard. I should have been jumping for joy that the two of you were no longer together, but all I could focus on was the fact that you were hurting. In a desperate attempt to lift your spirits, I offered to do the only thing I could.

Do you want me to talk to her? I typed.

Your response came in seconds: **Would you?**

I was already powerless when it came to my feelings for you—powerless to the point that I would talk to the girl you liked, at my own expense, and try to convince her to get back together with you. Later on, I would become powerless when it came to your influence over my very identity. You took precedence over everything.

For the rest of the week, I sought out Lacey for long, excruciating conversations about her feelings for you, telling her that she would be hard-pressed to find another guy like you. I reminded her that you were sweet, funny, smart, talented, and athletic (gorgeous to boot, but I left that part out), but she wasn't hearing any of it. She insisted that she wanted to focus on school, claiming that you had been "inattentive," and that you hadn't quite "done it" for her, anyway.

That weekend, I let my fingers hover over the keyboard for a few moments before typing a carefully-worded message to you that it was really over with Lacey. I told you that you needed to find a way to move on. You didn't respond, but I had a feeling I would hear from you again soon.

~

A WEEK LATER, JENNY asked if I wanted to go to one of your football games.

"I'm thinking of getting a few of us together—sans Lacey—to go to the game and hang out on Friday night.

It'll be fun to watch Wade play. My mom said she'd have t-shirts made up with his name and football number on them, like jerseys."

"I'm in," I said, already glowing over the thought of seeing you again.

So there I was in the stands that Friday night, my first time ever at a high school football game. Ironically, I couldn't have cared less about the action unfolding on the field. Instead, my eager eyes scanned the endless line of players' backs for your number: 54. And then I spotted you—you were wearing your helmet, so I couldn't see your face—but I got a good look at the rest of you, and I drank in the view. Your shoulders, wide and strong, extended into muscular arms that bulged against the tight short-sleeves of your uniform, which tapered in at your waist and protruded out again over the toned curve of your backside.

Up to that point, I hadn't been attracted to anyone sexually—not *really*. Even the way I'd thought of you over the last year had been purer, more innocent, than the way I thought of you when I saw you in your football gear for the first time. I checked, double-checked, your number to confirm that I'd gotten the right guy. It was you. 54 was your number, and I was wearing it on my own back, cheering you on as you jogged onto the field to assume your position as a defensive end.

All at once, you sprang into action, the entirety of your weight straining against a member of the opposing team as the ball went sailing through the air above you. Around me, the crowd cheered as the running back caught it and began sprinting toward the goalpost, but I couldn't tear my eyes away from you. Every move you made was beautiful, made me swell with pride despite the fact that I had almost no understanding of the game. You played, so I was invested. As long as you were down on the field, I would be up in the stands. And so it went for the next three months, all the way up to your championship game in December, which your team won handily.

It began to snow during the second half of that game, and by the end of it, you and your teammates were a shouting, grinning, out-of-control band of brigands who had just played in the game of their lives and *won*. I called your name from the stands—mostly because I knew there was no possibility that you would hear me—and jumped up and down in the frosty air with Jenny until I was warm with exhilaration and the pumping of my heart.

Until Jenny's mother came to pick us up, I waited there for you to turn your attention to the stands. I yearned for your eyes to scan the crowd, looking for me. We were still close friends, after all. I half-prayed for your acknowledgement, reasoning that if you looked for me in the midst of all this excitement, it would have to mean something. But you never did.

I went home that night, thrilled for you but sorry for myself, vowing to kick my seemingly insurmountable feelings to the curb. At the end of the day, they never amounted to anything.

Then, around 11 p.m., my cell rang. It was your name on my caller ID.

"Morgan?"

I couldn't quite comprehend that this was happening. You had never called me before. Finally, I found it in me to answer,

"Wade?"

"We did it, Morgan—we won the championship game!" Then, "I knew you were there."

"Congratulations! I, um, didn't know you saw me."

"I didn't. But I knew you were there."

I didn't say anything, stunned again into silence, until you continued,

"I want you to come to my formal with me next month. Will you?"

I didn't care when it was, what time it would be, what it even meant that you'd asked me. The point was that you *had.* You wanted to spend a whole evening with me. You knew plenty of girls—you were on a winning football team, practically a legend in your school—but you'd asked me.

"I'll be there."

Over the phone, I could almost feel you smiling. You confirmed later that you had been.

FIVE.

A WEEK AFTER YOU'D ASKED ME to your winter formal, you called me again, and I dove for the phone, willing my voice to come across as neutral and as measured as possible when I picked up.

"Hey, Morgan," you said.

Immediately, I could tell that something was off.

"Hey," I said, pausing to give you a moment.

"I might possibly be the biggest jerk in the world for what I have to tell you," you prefaced, sighing. I held my breath, waiting for you to continue.

"So I'm in Ski Club at school, and I thought our trip to Colorado was scheduled for the weekend after formal. Turns out, it falls on that same weekend. I have to go…my mom already put the deposit down, and it's non-refundable."

I didn't know that a feeling could crash and burn, like a speeding car hitting a cement wall, until you'd finished explaining the whole sad circumstance. I'd already begun dress shopping, and was imagining how that night could open the door to so much more for us. Still, always dependable and understanding, I said,

"Hey, it happens. Don't worry about it. Colorado sounds awesome."

"It will be," you said. "But I wish there were a way I could be in two places at once."

I wasn't quite sure how to respond, so I settled on a succinct,

"Have fun."

And that was pretty much the end of the conversation. We didn't speak for the next two weeks. Then I received a Facebook message from an old classmate of mine from middle school—one of your current classmates, Stephen Lowe—asking if I would accompany him to the formal while you were away. Stephen concluded the message with the assurance that he'd already asked you if it was all right to invite me, because he "didn't want to get beat up by a football player." Honestly, I was surprised that he knew anything about our connection, or whatever it was, when my own friends barely knew. Had you been talking to people about me?

I considered Stephen's invitation for all of five minutes, but in reality, I knew immediately that there was no way I was going to a dance with anyone but you, however irrational it was for me to limit myself to someone who didn't seem to feel the same about me. I told Stephen, completely surprising myself, the honest truth: that you were the only person I wanted to go with, because I liked you. And as I said the words, I realized I didn't care if they got back to you. One way or another, I wanted to move forward.

About a week from the dance, which fell on a Saturday, the forecast showed that a blizzard was projected to hit our area that Friday night—the same Friday you were supposed to fly to Colorado. I wasn't really expecting your plans to change, but miraculously, you were back on the phone with me by Monday, telling me that Ski Club had cancelled the trip in light of the impending storm.

"I know it's totally unfair of me to ask when the plans keep changing, but will you still go to formal with me? I promise I'm not getting on any planes this weekend, and the roads should be mostly clear by Saturday night."

As hope surged through me for the second time, whatever pride I had compelled me to say,

"What if I already said yes to someone else?"

The line was quiet for a few moments, and then you said,

"I know you told Stephen no."

It felt like you were going to say something else, but you stopped yourself, and I didn't push you to finish your thought. Finally, sighing with a bit of sass, I said,

"Well, if you must know, I do have a dress."

"What color?"

"…Red. But not bright red. More of like a burnt, cranberry red."

"I'll try to find a matching tie."

By the time we hung up, there was no controlling the dangerously giddy emotions that had resurfaced all over again.

~

I WAS A BUNDLE OF NERVES, practically coming undone at the seams, all day Saturday as I primped—and "primped" was an understatement. I indulged, totally shamelessly, in six-and-a-half hours worth of facial masks, nail polish, hair conditioning cream, heat-styling hair tools, and wax treatments. When phase one was complete, I proceeded to deliberate over three pairs of heels, two bras with different padding, and hair accessories. Finally, I applied just the right makeup to appear glowy and a little dramatic, but simultaneously natural.

I was exhausted well before the evening even started.

"Want me to throw some pizza in the oven?" my dad asked, innocently, as I clacked down the steps in my open-toe heels around 5 p.m.

My anxious stomach turned at the thought of food.

"Dad, I'll throw up if I eat," I said, matter-of-factly.

He rolled his eyes. "You always work yourself up for no reason. It's just a dance."

Just a dance. If only he knew. I'd only been waiting a year for this moment, but no big deal. No pressure or anything.

My parents and I piled into the car after that, my dad glancing at the old-school directions to your house that he'd printed despite the fact that we had a perfectly functioning GPS. Twenty minutes later, our little clan was on your front stoop, ringing the bell.

Your mother answered the door. She was objectively beautiful with her mane of golden hair big blue eyes, and I realized how much you looked like her for the first time that night. Still, you had your father's smile and square jaw—masculine, through and through.

"Morgan, that dress is stunning," she told me, leading us into the kitchen. "Please, help yourselves!"

Your mother had spread out an entire feast for us on your kitchen table, every plate of hors d'oeuvres impeccably put together, the floors and counters spotless.

"Oh, how lovely everything looks! Are some of Wade's friends meeting here to drive over with you?" my mother asked.

"No—unfortunately, it was very short notice for us that Wade was even going at all, with his trip being cancelled."

While our parents talked, I wandered into the foyer area, waiting for you to come downstairs. I studied each photograph that was tastefully framed and displayed on the antique marble table: you with your little sister, Leigh, in Busch Gardens; you making your Confirmation; Leigh making her First Communion. Then there was that picture of you in your school band—the one where you were playing guitar—and I lingered a little longer on that one, because every time I saw it, I was floored all over again by just how handsome you were.

"I look like a deer in headlights in that one," you said, suddenly walking toward me. I hadn't even heard you come downstairs, but there you were in a tailored black suit, standing closer to me than you ever had before and making me hyperaware of my mouth, my eyes, my hands.

"You're beautiful," you told me. "Do you know that?"

I realized I couldn't swallow. My throat was suddenly, maddeningly, paralyzed. Luckily, our parents walked into the room, saving me from having to respond.

"Time for pictures! Wade, it took you long enough to get ready. I'll bet Morgan primped less than you did, today," your mother joked.

I wanted to burst out laughing, but was still too overcome by your compliment to react to any external stimuli. Never had I thought that mere words could carry so much weight.

After exercising a ridiculous amount of patience for the seemingly endless period of camera flashes, my parents finally left. We stole a few bites of the snacks your mother had provided, and then your father was jingling his car keys, mumbling through a half-full mouth of food,

"Let's go, kiddos."

In the car, you sat in the back with me and talked to your dad about school and band and football as he drove. Then your father asked,

"Do you play any sports, Morgan?"

You smiled at me in the darkness as I replied,

"I've been figure-skating competitively for the past six years."

"Isn't that so cool?" you said, before your father even

had a chance to respond. "And on a side note, she sings, too."

"I did hear something about an album. It's on iTunes, right?" your dad asked.

"Can confirm. Just type in her name," you said, winking at me. And I knew then that you were bragging about me—that maybe you were proud of me, the way I was proud of you when I saw you on the field.

We pulled up to your school half an hour later, and you came around to my side of the car to help me out. As soon as we stepped through the main entrance, you were accosted by every single person standing in the hallway, and I clung to your sleeve for fear of getting lost in the mob.

"Wade, what's the good word, man?"

"What have you been doing with all your extra time since football ended?"

"...still can't get over that championship game..."

You must have stopped to talk to at least fifteen people—including two priests and three teachers—as we inched our way toward the auditorium, but I enjoyed watching you as everyone greeted you. The natural ease you possessed conversing with people was charming, to say the least. You knew how to handle yourself perfectly, and managed to introduce me to each of your friends with minimal discomfiture. I wanted to ask what your secret was, but I didn't want you to think I was an antisocial loner. We weren't *that* close, yet.

When we finally stepped into the auditorium, it was difficult to find a spot to even stand, let alone dance. The room was completely packed with your classmates, and I recognized some of their dates from school, who waved when they saw me.

Then came the sound of yelling over the unrelenting

bass. I turned in time to see one of your football friends towering over another boy and his date, his eyes flashing in anger as the girl stepped between them.

"What's that about?" I asked, and you squeezed my hand and said,

"I'll be right back."

I watched you talk to your friend as the other two walked away, the boy glancing over his shoulder as his date pulled him onto the crowded dance floor.

When you returned a few minutes later, you explained,

"Turns out, the girl Robbie's been seeing came here with someone else. She led him on for a long time."

I couldn't understand how people could be so indecisive, so inconsiderate, when it came to dating. I could never do what Lacey had done to you, or what this girl had done to your friend.

"Well, don't worry," I said. "I don't have a secret boyfriend here."

You shot me a winning smile and squeezed my hand.

"Good, because I'd have to beat him up. You're mine tonight."

And then you pulled me onto the dance floor, my legs quivering in response to your words, over the thought that I was *yours*. I hadn't known it could feel like this to fall for someone—to want their attention, their affection, their reassurance above everything else.

As we finally approached a clearing where we could dance, I wanted to pull you close, to run my fingers through your hair.

So I did.

I thought back to the way your face had looked when you danced with Anna just a year ago at freshman formal, and recalled how you'd looked dancing with Lacey at

Aloha at the end of the school year.

...Neither of those instances compared to the way you were looking at me in that moment, like maybe, the slope of my small hips beneath your hands was everything you'd been waiting for.

We stuck together like glue all night, our bodies moving together in perfect synchrony to the throbbing beat of the music. We were in our own world, you and I, totally unaware of everything around us and completely pulled in by the other's magnetic field. Every time your hands moved on my back, every time you pulled me closer, electricity hummed in my veins and manifested itself in a prick at my underarms. The auditorium was unbearably hot between the blasting heat from the radiator, body heat, and the rapid beat of my heart from being so close to you.

"I don't even sweat this much at football practice," you joked, taking a moment to wipe your face with your tie. Then you grinned sheepishly.

"Sorry. I'm usually not this gross."

I rolled my eyes and smiled in response. The truth was, I couldn't care less.

"Just dance with me."

So we danced until the end of the night, when the DJ blasted "Don't Stop Believin'" as the finale, and everyone began fist-pumping, jumping up and down and singing at the top of their lungs. You spun me around, never letting go of my hand, and then we were both jumping along with the rest of the crowd, animated by the music and exhilarated by the overpowering reality of our own hormones.

Once the song ended and the mass exodus to the hallway began, I stood on my tiptoes and kissed you on the cheek for the first time—your totally sweaty, flushed cheek—and my heart promptly skyrocketed in response to my own fearlessness.

You couldn't stop smiling as we made our way out of the auditorium. You got our coats from the coat check and guided my arms through the sleeves, then called your dad to locate his car before we walked out of the school hand in hand. The icy air was the perfect antidote to my steaming skin.

"Did you have a good time?" your dad asked as you slid into the car beside me.

"It was a great night," you replied. And then, because it wasn't enough for you to hold my hand, you linked your foot with mine the whole ride home.

When we pulled into my driveway, you got out to walk me to the door. Before I could rummage around in my purse for my keys, you grabbed both of my hands and said,

"I know you told Stephen you wouldn't go with him tonight. But I also know *why* you told him you wouldn't go."

My initial reaction was to try to downplay what I'd said to Stephen, but as I opened my mouth to speak, I realized I didn't want to downplay the way I felt about you. Besides, it finally seemed as though my feelings were being reciprocated.

We stood there for a moment, and I briefly wondered whether you would try to kiss me. I didn't know if my nervous system could handle much more—my feelings had practically been on steroids for the last six hours. But you only brushed my cheek with the back of your hand and said,

"I'll call you. Thanks for a great night."

And then you disappeared down my walkway.

I stayed awake practically all night, replaying every shared moment, every touch of your skin against mine, every electrical impulse on an endless reel in my mind. I was afraid to fall asleep and risk forgetting any of it.

Reality was too good to ruin with a distraction like sleep.

SIX.

DESPITE THE EXTRAORDINARY night we'd shared at the dance, which had—for me—been like living in a freaking Judy Blume novel, our relationship developed slowly. You weren't overeager, but we continued to talk nearly every day, giving us both time to adjust to what we were becoming to each other. Our friends caught onto the fact that something was happening between us—Jenny hounded me for a solid week following your formal, begging for any additional details I might've neglected to tell her, like a starving dog begging for scraps. Lacey mostly ignored me, and Anna accused me of "stealing Lacey's man," neither of which particularly bothered me. Lacey had been more than insistent about the fact that you were wrong for her, and Anna only cared because she'd failed to make an impression on you the year before.

In spite of this unavoidable drama, you and I formed a shared and special bond, our feelings remaining in a private sphere that kept us secure from prying friends and probing questions. I could feel your energy toward me in the flirtatious texts we traded, the same way I could hear the smile in your throat every time we talked. Those early stages of our undefined relationship were everything innocent, passionate, loaded, and surging that first love is, and I knew that all of it was leading up to something—knew, probably even before you did, that it was only a matter of time before you officially asked me out, because you and I were inevitable.

It happened while we were on the phone one evening, which was quickly becoming a bedtime ritual for us. You'd been strumming your guitar between sentences, but stopped abruptly to ask,

"You wanna do something Friday night?"

For a moment, my body felt totally frozen, as though your words had paralyzed me. My entire state of being shifted into something resembling a fight-or-flight reaction as I gave myself over to a slamming heart, widened eyes, and shallow breath.

"Uh, yeah," I finally said, barely able to choke out the words.

In the seconds that followed my response, a slow smile spread across my hot face as I folded my knees to my chest, resisting the urge to squeal into my pillow.

"How about we catch a movie? I hear that *Percy Jackson and the Olympians* is supposed to be really good."

"OK," I agreed.

"I mean, does that work for you? We can see something else if you want," you said.

"Wade—it *really* doesn't matter to me what we see," I insisted, giggling nervously.

"OK, then. Friday night it is. I'll text you with the time."

When we hung up, I plopped my phone on my chest and stared up at the ceiling, wondering how this was going to go. My toes were already curled in anticipation.

"I have a date tomorrow night," I told Jenny the next morning, throwing it out there as casually as I pulled the books from my locker. But my hands shook a little as I said the words.

Jenny slammed her locker shut.

"Excuse me?"

And then, before I could get another word out,

"You realize what this all means, right? You're basically his girlfriend. I mean, that's what this is all leading up to, right? What are you going to wear?! How will you do your hair? Morgan, what if he tries to kiss you?"

My cheeks went hot at the mere thought of your lips on mine, and I turned away from Jenny to hide it and began walking down the hall. She followed about two steps ahead of me, if that even makes sense, waiting for answers I didn't have.

"I'll probably just throw on a nice sweater and some skinny jeans. Maybe straighten my hair. Is that OK with you?" I joked.

"Morgan," she warned. "Don't make me pull teeth to get answers from you on Saturday. First thing in the morning, I want a full report. Got it?"

I nodded seriously, trying to suppress a smile.

"Yes, ma'am."

All day long on Friday, I suffered through my classes, my anxiety building to sporadic waves of nausea over the thought that I would be completely alone with you for the first time ever that evening. The bus ride home from school took forever and a day, and as soon as my feet hit the driveway, I was moving at a hundred miles per hour, scouring my closet for something date-worthy that wouldn't seem like I was trying too hard. I finally settled on a cream-colored, V-neck sweater with a navy camisole peeking out from underneath, my favorite pair of skinny jeans, and a pair of boots. I worked out all of the wavy kinks in my hair from the last time I'd haphazardly straightened it, and then I touched up my makeup.

You texted me and asked whether 6:15 p.m. worked for me, as if timing really mattered. I would've made 6:15 in the *morning* work, if necessary.

You got to the theater before I did—one of the few times you would ever show up early to anything throughout our entire relationship—and you were already waiting, tickets in hand, when I walked through the doors at 6:03 p.m.

"Hey," you said, your face lighting up as I walked toward you. You wrapped me in an automatic hug.

"Hi," I said, breathing in the husky scent of you. You were wearing a long-sleeve American Eagle shirt and a pair of faded jeans, and when you pulled me close, you were warm through and through, a welcome contrast to the cold March air.

You slipped your hand into mine easily, our fingers interlocking as we walked to our theater.

"How was your day?" you asked, and I was struck by the sincerity in your voice. It was clear that you actually cared about my answer—you weren't just asking to make conversation, like everyone else.

"It was good," I replied. And then, because you had seemed so genuine, I added, "I was a little nervous."

"Nervous? Did you have a presentation or something?"

You looked into my eyes, and I shook my head, smiling a small smile at you. Then you squeezed my hand, because you understood.

"Me too," you said.

In the darkness, we climbed past rows and rows of seats to a two-seat section near the top, and you helped me out of my jacket just as the previews ended and the opening credits flashed on the screen.

I tried to settle comfortably into my seat, but we were sitting far too close to each other, and every cell in my body was on fire, electrified by the scent of you. A warm, gentle heat radiated from your shoulder as it brushed against mine, causing a series of chain reactions to unfold beneath my skin that I'd never before experienced. Consequently, all I could manage to do in the time that followed was to sit completely still, simultaneously panicking and swooning over the lightning in my veins while trying not to give myself away.

Then—unknowingly adding to my inebriation—you weren't shy about moving your arm around me, your hand causing my skin to smolder beneath my sweater. I stared straight ahead, pretending like I was utterly absorbed in the story unfolding on the screen, but I couldn't have told you a single thing about the storyline. In truth, I was paralyzed by feelings I hadn't known were real until that moment. I was afraid of how strong they were, startled by just how much you were capable of making me feel.

Then your thumb began a slow dance on my shoulder, tracing along the seam of my sweater, and I started to shake—actually shake. I knew at that point that you were looking directly at me, but I couldn't bring myself to turn my own head and meet your gaze.

You ended up doing it for me, placing your large, callused hand on the far side of my face and guiding it to yours until we were inches apart. Then your mouth closed over mine, and there was tongue—so much tongue—inside my mouth. I hadn't expected this kind of a kiss at all, but then again, I wasn't your first kiss.

…But you were mine, and that first kiss was everything.

When we walked out of the theater a few hours later, we were completely at ease with each other in a new type of way. You grabbed my hand and exaggeratedly swung our arms back and forth, making me laugh as you knocked your shoulder against mine playfully.

From the depths of my purse, my phone buzzed.

"Oh," I said, glancing at the screen. "My dad just got here."

"I'll walk you out," you said. "I had an amazing time, Morgan."

I smirked a little as we entered the lobby.

"What?" you asked.

"Amazing is such an understatement," I replied.

And you squeezed my hand a little tighter before dropping it as we walked through the door.

My dad was waiting for me front and center, and you extended your hand to him as you said hello. Again, I marveled at your strong assuredness, and at the ease of your interaction with other people—particularly with my father. You were respectful and conscientious without needing approval. Even *that* was an art you'd mastered without trying.

How can I even begin to convey how in awe I was of you?

"I'll see you soon, Morgan," you said, hugging me goodbye like this, like we, were the simplest thing in the world—a puzzle that had already been assembled to form a clear image.

At that point, a cold drizzle had started, and my dad was already booking it for the car. I started after him on pure adrenaline, my boots clumsily pounding the pavement until, to my horror, I flat-out tripped over a small pothole, taking a nose-dive right there in the parking lot.

Luckily, my hands bore the brunt of my fall, but the smarting of the asphalt on my cut-up skin was nothing compared to the sting of my embarrassment. I was fairly certain you'd seen the entire thing, and my fear was confirmed when I received a text from you moments later in the car, asking if I was all right.

My hands healed within a few weeks, but there was one cut on my knuckle that I compulsively picked every time it scabbed over.

I still have the scar from that scab to this day—a small

memento to ensure I would never forget a moment of that night.

SEVEN.

Y O U   A S K E D   M E   T O   O F F I C I A L L Y be your girlfriend in the least ceremonious way possible a few weeks following our first kiss: over Facebook chat. One minute, we were talking like we always did, and the next thing I knew, you had typed that I was beautiful and funny and smart, and that you would be honored if I let you be my boyfriend.

In true 16-year-old fashion, I stared at the screen for a few seconds, then proceeded to happy-dance around my room, *then* called my mother from downstairs to invite her to join my private celebration.

I probably made you sweat it out for a good 5-10 minutes while all of this occurred, but my answer to you was finally an emphatic "yes" in all-caps, a grinning emoticon following the words. I started listening to the song "Smile" by Uncle Kracker on repeat in the days that followed, as you had asked me out on a Sunday night, reminding me of the lyrics.

Being your girlfriend was thrilling and exhilarating and just the right amount of comfortable, all at once. We slipped easily into routines of ending all of our messages with hearts—even when it made no sense to do so—and texting pretty much all day, every day, even through some of our classes. When I wasn't texting you under my desk, I was doodling your name on all of my notebooks. In some cases, I was even brazen enough to link your last name to my first name. I was on a perpetual high from thinking about you constantly, and when our parents made us hand over our phones at night to prevent us from staying up too late, I fell asleep thinking of you—about the way your lips felt on mine, and about the way every interaction between us felt like a rare and momentous discovery. We may as well have been the first two people to invent a chemical reaction.

On our first date as boyfriend and girlfriend, we went to the movies again—because where else can two teenagers easily go to be "alone" on a date—and beginning with the previews, you were all over me, taking my hand in yours and demanding softly,

"Talk to me about these bracelets. Where did you get them?" Your fingers traced the Tiffany silver chain and the white braided bracelet around my wrist, as though their significance was everything to you.

"Well, the chain, I got from my aunt for my Confirmation, and the other one is just for fun," I replied, smiling as your bear paw enveloped my small hand.

"And what about your necklace?" you asked, leaning in as though you were intently studying it. I knew, in fact, that you were actually just trying to move closer to me.

"My mom," I said, shrugging. "See? You really are my first boyfriend."

"I don't know how that's possible," you breathed, moving my hair behind my ear and kissing me deeply, right there in the third row of the theater in front of a hundred onlookers.

It was May at that point, and our school year was on the brink of ending. The evening air was balmy, the sky dotted with specks of starlight when we stepped out of the theater two hours later.

"Don't call your dad to pick you up," you said. "I'm not ready to say goodbye to you just yet."

I hadn't been ready, either. In fact, I had a small surprise for you to celebrate the fast-approaching beginning of summer, but we needed to find a place to sit first.

"Where to?" you asked, swinging our arms between us as we turned the corner of the theater.

"Let's just walk," I said, hoping there would be a bench somewhere around back.

Behind the building, there was a dimly-lit parking lot and several emergency exits that led down from each theater room. One set of emergency steps was half-concealed by a wall, and I tugged at your hand and pointed.

"Let's sit there."

So you helped me onto the wall, lifting me with ease before hoisting yourself up to join me. I reached into my purse.

"So…I thought we should celebrate the end of our sophomore year of high school properly," I prefaced, digging out a jumbo-sized bag of Take 5 bars. Your eyes lit up at the sight of the orange packaging, and I jokingly held it away from you.

"What's the magic word?"

"I don't need a magic word. I can just do this," you insisted, leaning over and planting another kiss on my chapped lips. In the theater, we'd kissed so much that my mouth was practically raw.

You were always obsessed with chocolate, and Take 5 bars were your favorite, so we sat there on that wall in the abandoned lot like we were handling contraband, killing the bag of candy as we traded stories and wishes.

"What's the deal with this girl who kissed you a few years back?" I teased, playfully punching you on the shoulder as you crumpled another wrapper in your hand.

"It was hardly a kiss. It was a *grandma* kiss," you said exaggeratedly. "What about you and what's-his-face? Ohio kid?"

"Dean? Met him when I was visiting my cousin in Ohio. We talked for a few years. I thought I was in love," I said dismissively, the idea seeming so preposterous to me now.

"Were you?" you asked, your voice taking on a more serious tone.

I smiled at you and reached for your hand.

"No. In fact...he hurt me pretty much every time I talked to him. He knew how I felt about him, and used my feelings to manipulate me and make me jealous. His dad's been really sick with stage four colon cancer for as long as I've known him though, so I guess I always wanted to help him get through it. I liked being there for him. I like helping people," I concluded, feeling like I was in kindergarten with my stupid, final statement.

"Well, I love that about you," you said, squeezing my hand. "But that doesn't give anyone the right to take advantage of your selflessness."

Then, after a few moments of silence, you turned to me and said,

"I would never hurt you, Morgan."

And I believed you more than I'd ever believed anyone. You were always easy to trust—solid, stable, dependable. Trust was never our issue.

"I know," I replied, smiling at you in the darkness.

I'd begun to shiver as the night air turned cooler, and when you noticed, you shrugged off your huge letterman jacket and wrapped it around my shoulders. As you moved, your championship football ring flashed beneath the parking lot lights, the wide blue rock planted snugly on your finger.

"It looks so big," I remarked, pointing.

You pulled that off, too, and handed it to me: *what's mine is yours.* When I slid it around my index finger, it hung like a hula hoop; I tried my thumb next, only to find it was scarcely any better.

"You have baby hands," you chuckled, holding yours in the air as though preparing for a high-five. I placed mine up against it, and the tips of my fingers barely brushed your knuckles.

"I love how petite you are."

"I love how big you are."

"Is that a fat joke?"

"Absolutely," I said, feigning seriousness. Then we both burst out laughing, and I leaned into you, wanting these shared, sacred moments to stretch on forever.

"I just meant that you're so…masculine. It feels like you could take care of me," I explained.

"I'll always take care of you," you said simply.

Never. Always. You were making such definitive statements so early in our relationship. Someone should have told you not to make promises you couldn't keep. At the time, I hung on every word you said.

Our parents dutifully arrived to pick us up sometime around 11 p.m. I'd never had much of a curfew, having always been the classic "good girl." Your parents actually preferred that you were in for the night earlier than mine did, your mother calling the shots even in the later years of our relationship. I noticed she was more lax about your curfew in the summer, though—especially when we weren't out alone together.

A few hours after the conclusion of sophomore year, we kicked off that first summer as a couple with an evening pool party over Jenny's house. I'd gone home with Jenny that afternoon, along with some of our other friends, and we had all jumped into her pool still fully-clothed in our uniforms, kilts included. Then we changed into our bathing suits and caught whatever sun we could before day slipped into night, and you and your friends showed up for the party.

It was a summer evening filled with the first fireflies of the season and the camaraderie of carefree students. Our group didn't consist of the type of teenagers who got drunk or high or had sex—we were unusual in that we had our own unique version of fun, a bunch of Catholic school kids who only needed each other's company and some junk food to have a good time. From the outside, we probably seemed like a bunch of straitlaced, goody two-shoes, but we didn't care what our peers thought of us. We were our own unit.

"Hey, you," you said, closing the space between us on Jenny's patio and scooping me up in your strong arms. You planted a kiss on my forehead as you set me down.

"Hey," I beamed up at you. "I've been missing you all day."

"Just *today*?" you asked incredulously. I giggled in response as you took a step back, realizing for the first time that I was wearing a bikini.

"Wow," you said. "So, you look amazing."

I winked at you as your huge friend, Webb—whom we always called by his last name—came running at you full-force and tried to tackle you into the pool.

"Dude," you said, once you had successfully fought him off. "I'm a defensive end. I can take you."

"Don't think I don't know how much you enjoyed that," Webb replied, totally straight-faced. "Morgan, Wade and I are having a bromance. We're actually in love."

I snorted, dying over the thought of these two large, completely heterosexual guys in love with each other.

"OK, Webb," I said, throwing a thumbs-up in his

direction as I plunged back into the pool.

For a while, you played pool basketball with your friends while I gossiped with mine beneath the diving board, six pairs of manicured fingers gripping the edges as Webb suddenly threw himself on it, launching outward into a cannonball and making us girls scream in surprise.

Your arms found my waist later that night as you swam away from the ongoing game for time alone with me.

"Hi," you said, shaking your wet hair all over my face, like a dog. I pretended to push you away, but your grip around me only tightened in response.

"I don't think so," you said, tugging me away from the action over to the more secluded steps of Jenny's pool. You placed me sideways on your lap once you sat down, your dripping arms still enveloping me like you were rocking a baby.

"How are you tonight?" you asked, kissing my ear and making me shiver.

"I'm perfect. Especially now," I whispered, and you turned and kissed me on the lips.

"HEY," your friend, Shawn, yelled. "Leave room for the Holy Spirit!"

We all burst into laughter, but you only pulled me closer. I could feel the steady beat of your heart as I pressed the side of my face against your chest.

When we'd ceased to be the focus of everyone's attention, I looked up at you as you played with my freshly polished toes and couldn't help telling you,

"I think I kind of love you."

It was such a juvenile way to convey for the first time how I truly felt, but we were so young, and I was still afraid of putting too much out there—afraid I'd somehow scare you away.

You looked at me then like I'd just made you brand new. There was a gladness and a wonder in your eyes as you replied,

"I think I kind of love you, too."

I spent the rest of the night glued to your side or on your back. After drying off, we played manhunt in Jenny's development, and even though it made no sense for dexterity's sake, you'd insisted on giving me piggy-back rides wherever we went. You wanted me as close to you as possible, even if it meant that we were among the first on our team to be found.

And so went our whole summer, whether it was lying next to you on twin floaties in your own pool on lazy afternoons, or chasing you around your house with your little sister, Leigh, armed with squirt guns against the hose you carried, which is still one of my favorite memories of the early years of our relationship. Leigh and I had finally decided—after about half an hour of playing cat-and-mouse with you—to ambush you head on, and we came at you full-force, pumping our squirt guns like semi-automatics on a battlefield. You aimed the hose directly at us, drenching us in a stream of freezing water as we ditched our guns and ended up tackling you, Leigh wrestling the hose from your hands as I tickled you until you fell to the ground.

At night, after Leigh had gone to bed and while your parents watched TV, you and I slipped into the hot tub and kissed in a way that would've made us both flush with embarrassment had anyone walked outside and caught us. You ran your hands over my shoulders, down my back, letting them linger just above my backside. When you kissed my neck, I felt your lips eventually slip further down over my collarbone, dusting it with your stubble and hinting at traveling lower. I had to remind you that we couldn't go there—that second-base territory was technically a sin, according to Catholic morality. You weren't resentful, but I think at the time you'd assumed that I just wasn't ready for more because of our mutual inexperience.

"I have to go," I finally told you, coming up for air after nearly two hours spent completely wrapped up in you. As I stood to get out of the hot tub, you pulled my arm so that I fell back on your lap, splashing you and making a watery mess on the surrounding patio. You machine-gun kissed me all over my face until I was laughing so hard I could barely breathe, and then you stood with me to get out and dry off.

In the darkness, wrapped in our towels and shivering in the light summer breeze, you pulled me against the white picket fence surrounding your backyard, leaning against me and tugging gently at my sopping hair. My mouth opened to greet your tongue just as the sliding screen door opened behind you, and we both jumped several feet away from each other within seconds. I pretended to fiddle with tying the towel around my waist as your dad stepped outside and shot us a knowing look.

"Mom and I are heading to bed soon. Morgan, I assume you're about to drive home?"

I nodded, feeling about two inches high.

"We just got out to dry off."

"All right. Great having you. We'll see you soon," he said, turning back into the family room and switching off the outdoor light as a final message.

"Don't go," you whispered urgently, your arms wrapped around me again.

"I have to," I insisted, slipping on my cut-offs over my bikini bottoms.

So you walked me to the driveway, where we kissed some more up against the side of my car before you hugged me goodbye and wished me sweet dreams. And I drove the twenty minutes home wondering how on God's green Earth we were going to wait to have sex until marriage. We already wanted each other too much, but I was firm in my resolve to wait. I knew that it was important, but I'd simply never thought twice about the difficulty of chastity because I'd never before been confronted with such temptation. Now, every time I saw you, all I wanted was to intertwine myself with you until I forgot where I ended and you began.

More than my Catholic faith, though, we were in *high school*. And I wanted to be fully in high school without worrying about being "late" each month—without worrying about the what-ifs, about the consequences that would follow if anything were to happen as a result of that choice. I wasn't truly ready, and I didn't think you were, either.

By the time I got home, I'd contented myself with the knowledge that we had no choice but to wait. I brushed my hair over the hickeys that had formed on my neck and walked into the house, wondering for the first time what I really believed, and whether it was worth holding onto when I was holding you.

EIGHT.

"B L E S S M E F A T H E R, for I have sinned. It's been two weeks since my last confession, and these are my sins."

I found myself kneeling in a dark confessional for the second time that month, confessing the same sins I'd confessed last time around. Fortunately, I could tell this wasn't the same priest—he seemed smaller, older, from behind the screen, and I took a deep breath and confessed that I'd committed sins against purity, my stomach twinging in discomfort as I uttered the words.

When I finished reciting my list, scanning my memory to ensure I hadn't forgotten anything, I concluded with,

"And for these and all of my sins, I am truly sorry, Father."

Sometimes, I *was* sorry—repentant—over the thought that I'd hurt God, whom I'd always loved so much. Other times, I went to confession as a Catholic duty, knowing I had to get the stain of sin off my soul in order to receive the Eucharist, and in order to live as a true Catholic. What I didn't understand at my young age was that confessing the same sins over and over again, with no true resolve to actually correct my lifestyle, was sacrilegious. It defeated the purpose of confession. All I knew at that point in my life was that, upon confessing my sins, I was ridding myself of the guilt that inevitably followed each time you and I crossed a physical boundary.

"For your penance, say one Our Father and one Hail Mary. Don't worry—Jesus loves you so very much. Go in peace," said the priest, in his thick Polish accent. I smiled through my tears, touched at his simple way of relaying Jesus' mercy.

Since we'd started dating three months earlier, this pattern of kiss-and-confess had become a norm for me, because it was never just simple kissing with us. If we're being honest, from the very beginning it had never been just simple kissing. You and I craved each other in a way that was completely unparalleled, beyond what I could've expected even when I thought of what falling in love would be like. And so we found ourselves in the back of the movie theater, around the side of your house, on the golf course behind your neighborhood once it got dark, and anywhere else we could steal some time to be completely alone.

Still, as much as we were equally consumed by the other, it was a frustrating dynamic with us, with you always prodding, pushing for more while I pumped the breaks. Your hands moved all kinds of places they shouldn't have, and I found myself always reluctantly sliding them back to safe zones. I wanted to kiss you, to relinquish every part of myself to you, with no restraints and no restrictions holding us back. But I knew, even then, that physical love is never devoid of consequence.

"What's the matter, Morgan? Don't you *want* me?" you'd asked one overcast Friday evening. We'd gone to see a movie, which had become our weekend routine, and were kissing afterward on some partially concealed grassy patch we'd found in the same plaza. You'd tried to move your hands under my shirt, and I'd pushed them down again, cringing at the thought of what would probably come next.

I'd been right.

"It's not about whether or not I want you, Wade. Don't you get that?" I asked, standing and dusting the loose grass off my clothes, out of my hair. "I have to wait for marriage for anything more than what we've been doing. It's a pretty serious sin to do anything more," I explained.

At the time, I'd thought this reminder of Church teaching—with which we'd both been raised—would be a perfectly reasonable explanation, but I discovered that evening that it wasn't enough, and that it would never be enough for you to accept.

"Listen," you said, completely ignoring what I'd just said. "I love you. You love me. What's the problem?"

"What's the problem? The problem is that we're sixteen years old, Wade. I could get pregnant. We could destroy our future. We're really young. And it's too soon," I said, trying a different approach to make you understand.

That reasoning finally seemed to make sense to you, and even for a while after that night, but nothing could have indefinitely prevented us from trying to get as close to each other as possible.

In reality, we weren't as bad as other couples we knew, who were completely shameless even when several of us gathered over someone's house. One of your friends from school, Andy Merchant, invited the usual suspects in our group over for pizza and gaming one Saturday night, and two of our friends—Brie and Tim—spent the entire time locked in the basement's guest bedroom doing God-knows-what. Brie was pretty rebellious to begin with, which likely stemmed from the fact that her ultra old-fashioned parents had insisted that she wait until she was eighteen years old to date. When she did get to see Tim at parties, it was pretty much a free-for-all.

Do you remember that night? We played *Dance Dance Revolution* until we were all panting on the floor and laughing hysterically over our pathetic attempts to replicate the dance moves on the screen. You faced off against Webb in a salsa-reminiscent routine, trying to move your thick football hips in time to the rhythm and failing miserably, but still beating Webb because he was even bigger and clumsier than you were. When I made fun of you, you lunged for me, scooping me up before I could escape and lifting me high into the air to spin me in circles.

Someone captured that moment in a photograph. Your lips are pursed from when you made a "whoosh" sound upon lifting me, and I'm already mid-laugh, my face glowing like it's Christmas morning.

I'd just gotten my driver's license a month or two earlier, so I drove us home afterward, despite the fact that you lived out of the way from my house and it was already past 11 p.m., the Pennsylvania state curfew for drivers under seventeen.

"Let's get some Santana up in here," you said, connecting your phone to my USB hook-up and turning the volume up full-blast. I cranked the sunroof open, the chilly night air streaming in as the thump of the bass flowed out. You took my hand and started singing to me,

"Why don't you and I get together, and take on the world and be together forever?"

I looked over at you from the driver's seat, grinning widely as your eyes met mine.

"We're going to live in Nashville, right?" I yelled over the music, in reference to my constant songwriting and recording sessions.

"And adopt an Alaskan Husky named Balto," you shouted back, your foot tapping against the floorboard.

"And have four kids."

"And a house with a pool in the back."

"And a wraparound porch."

"Why don't you and I hold each other, and fly to the moon and straight on to heaven...cuz without you, they're never gonna let me in."

We went speeding down an endless stretch of downward-sloping highway as we sang, the only car on the road, lighting up the night around us.

"Where even *are* we?" you asked, once the song had ended.

My GPS was spazzing out, insisting I "make a legal U-turn," as I had clearly missed an exit at some point amidst the yelling of shared, future wishes and relevant song lyrics.

"I'm just gonna keep going," I said. I would've driven all night if it meant I could sit next to you, blasting more music in the simple pleasure of your company.

"Good plan," you said, selecting the song "Walk" by the Foo Fighters and goofily head-banging to the intro as I laughed at the exaggerated rock-and-roll expression on your face.

At some point, the GPS redirected us, but in getting lost with you on a lonely highway at midnight, I already felt like I was home.

NINE.

T O W A R D   T H E   E N D of that first summer together, our parents signed both of us up for a spiritual retreat hosted by Franciscan University of Steubenville, and we were ambivalent about it, at best. Your parish would be transporting a group of interested teenagers to the university in Ohio, about a six-hour drive from our hometown, for exactly one weekend.

I'd never been to a retreat before, so I didn't really know what to expect, but I wasn't uncomfortable with the idea. I knew it would be a type of faith immersion, and I was so used to Mass, prayer, and discussing Church doctrine and theology with my family that this was hardly anything new for me. For you, on the other hand, it must've been overwhelming, because your family did little more than occasionally go to Mass on Sundays. Your faith wasn't something that was discussed or nurtured at home.

As I climbed onto the bus the morning of our trip, I quickly realized I didn't know any of the people going with us—they were all from your church, and many of them were kids you'd known since grade school. You took a seat in the back with several of your old friends, which meant I was on my own for the majority of the ride. I stared out the window and listened to music, missing you even though you were a mere six rows behind me.

When we finally got to the university after the longest day ever on the road, we went to the dorms and got settled in, then reconvened for the first "welcome" conference that night. Housing was single-sex only, so when we all streamed out onto the sidewalk in front of the dorms, you hung back so that we could walk behind everyone else, taking my hand in yours and swinging our arms between us.

"How are you?" you asked.

"Blech," I said, making a face. "I got my monthly visitor on the bus. I've felt nauseated all day."

"Oh," you said, clearly caught off guard. You were still learning how to react properly to such feminine matters. By the end of our relationship, I'd have you trained in the art of properly filling hot water bottles, and well-versed in the science behind the preferred comfort of Kotex vs. Always.

When all of us spilled into the huge auditorium, there were giant concert screens on either side of the stage that read: ROOTED. Looking at that word, I got chills. In fact, every time I looked at it during the retreat, goosebumps promptly rose on my skin.

"Good evening, and welcome to our annual Steubenville Youth Conference," the speaker began as we took our seats. The lights were dimmed, and suddenly we found ourselves thrust into darkness, the stage the only illuminated section of the room.

"Do you see that word up there? 'Rooted?'" she asked, pointing to the screen—as though we could miss it.

"You will spend your whole life making choices that either confirm you are the person you say you are, or contradicting the person you claim to be with your actions," she continued. "One of the hardest things in life is living up to your own standards, and living by your faith. While we recognize that certain values and virtues are beautiful and desirable, we are human, and therefore never remain stagnant and never achieve total perfection. Still, the choices we make eventually define our character.

"It might not always be easy. It might not always seem

possible to choose to live your faith, day in and day out. But remember this: you are *rooted* in faith, and in your identity in Christ. It is the basis of who you are, for the decisions you'll make, throughout your life.

"We hope that you'll enjoy the next two days of presentations. We have some awesome speakers here who have traveled from all over to be with us this weekend, so really allow yourselves to be absorbed into this atmosphere. Give God your whole heart over these next few days, and He will open doors for you that nobody can close."

Her speech ended with a wild round of applause from our overly-excited audience of youth group leaders, teenagers, and even some clergy. I was already inspired by what I'd just heard, and found myself eager to attend the presentations that weekend. But when I looked over at you, you'd seemed disinterested—bored, already.

The rest of the night was fairly uneventful. We returned to our dorms shortly after the presentation to retire early for the long day ahead of us, and I prayed that night that God would bring us together in our shared faith and love for Him that weekend. I was innocent and unaware back then that things could ever turn out any differently.

When our group reconvened for breakfast the following morning, you came running up to the cafeteria, trailing behind the rest of us because you'd started your morning by pouring pure rubbing alcohol on your contacts rather than contact solution. You'd apparently screamed bloody murder in your dorm's bathroom, and now all of the guys were giving you flack for it.

"I can't even express how much I *don't* want to be here right now," you murmured, sitting beside me with your breakfast tray and burning eyes. Despite the fact that I could understand where you were coming from, already worn out from a lack of sleep myself, you were in a genuinely bad mood. I guessed that the day ahead wouldn't do much to improve it.

After breakfast, boys and girls were separated for individual conferences, where a renowned ex-model, Leah Darrow, spoke with the girls about pure relationships and authentic love, while chastity speaker Chris Stefanick spoke with you boys about chivalry, and protecting a woman's virtue. In my single-sex assembly, I watched shamelessly as the girl in front of me wrote in her notebook:

"I'm scared that if I tell Dylan no more sex, he won't love me anymore. I don't know what his reaction will be. But I want to try to give this to God."

I couldn't tell how old she was, but I remember reading her words and thinking that she was brave. At the time, though, I felt such a disconnect between my circumstance and her situation. I hadn't known that in a few years, I'd be in a similar position.

 As we inhaled a dinner of questionable meatloaf and wilted vegetables that evening, I asked how your presentations had gone.

"That one guy was such a quack," you said, rolling your eyes. "There was so much he said that I didn't agree with at all. If you really love someone, why would you want to hold yourself back from them? Why does sex have to be a sin?"

I didn't know any good arguments at the time—I wasn't yet seasoned in debates over the case for chastity, as you would inadvertently condition me to become in later years—but I remember how disappointed I'd been over your reaction. I'd been hoping all day that you'd experience something that would resonate with you.

Perhaps the highlight of that trip for me was Praise and Worship, and Exposition of the Blessed Sacrament, which followed the first day of conferences. The atmosphere of worship was nothing like the silent, often mind-numbing, Eucharistic Adoration I was accustomed to in my church. Here, a priest brought the monstrance around for individual people in the crowd to adore one-on-one, and I watched as people fell to their knees, tears streaming down their faces as they surrendered themselves to a type of deep spiritual beauty I hadn't ever witnessed before.

I couldn't help but shed a few emotional tears of my own as I stood next to you in that crowd of believers, deeply moved by such strong displays of faith. You squeezed my hand when you noticed, but I knew you didn't understand. It wasn't likely that anything unfolding in front of you was having much of an impact on your faith, though I couldn't fathom why not.

Later, the worship band on stage began to play a song called, "Oh, How He Loves Us," and by the second chorus, you were looking over at me, changing the words to, "*Oh, how I love you*" as we swayed back and forth in the dark.

I was already the center of your universe, Wade. Faith was never going to be one of your priorities. I was all that ever mattered to you, and as we exited the auditorium into the humid night air, we had our first real conversation about it.

"This is the best night of my life," I told you, the two of us sliding onto a bench to talk.

"The *best* night? Really?" you asked in disbelief.

"Well…I mean, definitely one of the best. What, it doesn't make your list?" I joked, elbowing you in the side.

"I don't know, Morgan," you said, shaking your head as you stared out into the night. "I don't get all of this. It's…

overwhelming. It's scary that people are this obsessed with something they can't even see—that they can't even guarantee is *real*."

I stared at you as the reality of the conversation hit me, and I suddenly came to terms with what it meant: you didn't like or understand anything we'd been hearing or witnessing that weekend. Quite possibly, you didn't even believe in any of it.

"I mean, this is...everything, Wade," I said, inspiration still coursing through my veins. "This is the reason why we're here, sitting next to each other right now. God wants us to love Him—He created each of us for a unique purpose. You believe that, don't you?"

"I don't know," you reiterated. "And even if Catholicism is historically accurate, why should we necessarily follow some white guy who lived in the Middle East?"

I was floored by your blasphemous remark, shocked that you were that cynical.

"Come on, Wade," I said, desperation seeping into my tone as I leaned forward to meet your downcast eyes. "Have a little faith."

"I can try," you said. "For you."

"No," I insisted. "Not for me. For God. For the Person who made you."

"How can you be so sure he exists?" you asked.

"Because...He just does. I feel it. I know it, with all my heart. I have to believe there are some things you *know* without knowing for sure. It's something that your intuition tells you. Wade, all of this is true. I know without knowing, is all I can say."

We sat in silence after that, and I surrendered to the fact that I wouldn't be convincing you of anything that night. I'd assumed, though, that we were both still young—you had plenty of time to grow into your faith. The tradition of it, at a minimum, was something you'd known on a personal level throughout your life. It was an institution you'd been born into; it had even been at the center of your education for the last decade. Catholicism was a cultural part of your identity. You wouldn't *really* turn your back on it for good.

I often think back on the naive hope I harbored during that retreat, floored by the fact that your mistrust—your skepticism—only grew in the years that followed. It was simply easier to ignore the core differences between us at the time, even if your reaction had startled me, had set off warning bells in my head.

I was already in too deep with you to consider anything to be a real problem between us, even though from the very first year of our relationship, it was.

It always was.

TEN.

I FOUND IT STARTLING to gradually discover that all of the clichéd sayings to which I'd never paid any credence—"don't burn your bridges,""be true to yourself," "time flies"—all turned out to be spot-on accurate as I grew and matured, though they only began to resonate with time and experience.

Of all the idioms I'd grown up hearing, "time flies" now hits the closest to home. When I was in high school, all I wanted was for it to be over; consequently, the days lagged. Then, before I knew it, I was receiving my diploma on a football field on a warm afternoon in early June, ready to take on the world—but mostly, just ready for college.

You and I had made it through two and a half years of a typical teenage relationship, the golden couple of all of our friends—the "lucky ones." Together, we'd dressed up on Halloween, attended a flurry of Christmas parties and birthday parties, spent our first New Year's Eve together, and weathered four proms. We'd met all of each other's friends, most of our local family members, and had promised each other that we were going to be the high school sweethearts who defied the odds and stayed together. We were always making plans, always wondering what the future would be like. I spent so much time in my head that you actually had to remind me quite frequently to stop getting ahead of myself—that I would miss these days once they were gone. But I paid little attention at the time.

On my graduation day, I scanned the risers searching for my family, but mostly for you. You'd known what time my graduation ceremony began, and I assumed you would have met up with my parents to sit with them. I itched beneath my unflattering yellow robe and lopsided cap, aching for the ceremony to finally end so that we could all go to dinner and celebrate.

You'd graduated two weeks before I had, but my waitressing schedule had made it impossible for me to attend your ceremony. I'd hoped, on the evening of my commencement, that we could finally celebrate our accomplishments together.

But Wade—you didn't show. When I managed to find my family after the ceremony amidst a stampede of new graduates, and my father relayed that you'd never texted him to work out the details, I was nothing short of livid. It was the first time you'd really, truly let me down. I'd blithely assumed you would be there, no push from me needed. I would become all too familiar with the way my stomach dropped and clenched each time you would disappoint me in the years to come.

I fake-smiled through the family pictures following the ceremony, wondering what had kept you away, and comforting myself with the knowledge that there had to have been a good reason. When I'd texted you earlier, it had sounded like you'd planned on coming. In fact, I began to worry that something was seriously wrong by the time I made it back to my car to call you.

You picked up on the third ring.

"Hey, congratulations, Morgan!"

I couldn't believe that you'd answered the phone so lightheartedly, as though nothing could possibly be wrong.

"Morgan?" you repeated, when the line remained silent.

Finally, I said flatly, "You weren't there."

"I know, baby. I'm sorry. My mom wanted me to pack for Senior Week."

Ah, Senior Week. The week I'd been dreading for the

last three months. The week where all hell would break loose in the towns along the Jersey Shore, particularly Ocean City, where you would be staying in a house with several of your football friends. I knew the type of guys they were simply by understanding that you were the exception to the rule when it came to the character of a typical football player. My own Senior Week would be quiet—a true beach vacation. I was staying in a house with Jenny and two of our classmates in Wildwood, sans alcohol or boys. I knew that your house, on the other hand, would probably resemble a cross between "Girls Gone Wild" and a Corona ad, and there was nothing I could do about it.

Was there anything *worse* than the fact that you hadn't made it to my graduation because you'd been packing for the week of depravity? I was so mad, so hurt, that I actually started shaking, my muscles tensing against my own dismay. I didn't know how I was going to sit through dinner, looking calm and composed, when all I wanted was to be left alone to cry.

"Babe...it wasn't my fault. My mom made me stay home. She made it sound like we had too much going on for me to get there. I would've been there if I'd been able to," you said.

"...Can you at least come to dinner?" I asked in a muffled voice, looking upward to keep my mascara from streaking down my cheeks.

"I don't know, Morgan. I have to ask, first."

I was so outraged, I threw a small hissy fit.

"Fine. Whatever. Show up or don't show up."

And I ended the call, hanging up on you without saying a proper goodbye.

I met my family about twenty minutes late at the Italian restaurant where we'd made reservations, blotchy-faced from my phone conversation with you. Everyone knew better than to ask whether you were coming after you'd failed to show up at the ceremony.

You called me from the road when we were already mid-meal, asking about the parking situation and reassuring me that you'd be there soon. I hated you so much that day, but I was temporarily pacified by the fact that you were at least making an effort to show up for dinner. I walked outside so you would be sure to find the place, standing in my cream-colored sundress along the side of the road and feeling stupid, and you made a sharp turn into the lot when you saw me. I followed your car in my teetering wedges until you parked.

"Hey," you said, your arms outstretched for a hug.

I barely returned the embrace, instead leaning dully against you.

"Come on," you urged. "I'm here. I'm sorry. Let's go inside."

"We're practically finished eating," I said. I wanted to hurt you as badly as you'd hurt me, but I don't think you fully grasped just how bad the situation was.

We walked inside and pasted see-through smiles on our faces, my relatives all pretending that you weren't four and a half hours late that day and treating you with the same warmth and friendliness as always. I sat and sullenly pushed around the last of my food, because it was my party and I could freaking cry if I wanted to.

By the time the evening ended, my chest was still involuntarily heaving between breaths—I'd broken into tears so frequently that day that even the act of breathing was a chore. I managed to hug you goodbye before my dad walked you to your car, where I watched him talk to you quietly before you drove away. I later learned that he'd reminded you in his cool, level-headed way that it wasn't fair to just surprise me with ruined plans, especially on such big occasions, and I was so thankful that he'd had that conversation with you—that he'd stood up for me in a way that made sense when I couldn't find the words to defend myself.

You left for Senior Week two days later, and I left with my friends a day afterward, feeling half-relieved, half-anxious. I was so ready to enjoy some time on the beach, and to lie out in the sun with a good book and some music. On the other hand, you'd been texting me since you'd gotten to the house the day before, telling me all about the endless rounds of Jell-O shots your housemates were preparing, and how someone had cracked a glow stick open and sprayed it all over the walls.

The thought of you in that environment made me so unsettled. It wasn't because I didn't trust you exactly, but I knew that so much of the person you would become in college—and even in later years—depended on the choices you were already making. It was clear to me back then that you were still trying to figure out who you were going to be, and at the time, you were *my* Wade: the non-smoking, non-drinking, innocent Wade I'd fallen for two and a half years ago. I was afraid of what would happen if you were really pressured, pushed hard enough, to be someone else. I needed you to remain someone I could respect—truly admire—to keep our relationship strong. I knew I wouldn't be able to look at you the same way if you adopted the habit of smoking and drinking with your friends. I didn't want that, of all things, to destroy us.

As a result, I was moody for most of that week, trading cold texts with you but keeping you up at night because I craved your affirmation that everything was OK. Finally,

Andy Merchant, one of our mutual friends who was staying at your house, drove to Wildwood—mostly to visit his girlfriend who was staying with me, but also to give me a ride to Ocean City, where I'd be able to spend a few days with you.

I arrived at your house a little before dinnertime, and you gave me a tour before introducing me to the guys I hadn't yet met. I sat awkwardly beside you on the living room couch, unsure of where to look or what to say to these people with whom I had nothing in common.

"You ready to part-ay tonight?!" the quarterback of your team, Gary, exclaimed, throwing a small Nerf ball in my direction.

"Uh, sure," I replied, forcing a strained chuckle.

"I don't think anything could top last night, though. You missed a great time. Yo, Wade, wasn't last night awesome?"

"Yeah...if Shawn hadn't sprayed glow stick juice all over the walls," you said, rolling your eyes.

"I can hear you, dude!" came Shawn's voice from the kitchen. I looked back and saw him distributing vodka into small plastic cups of Jell-O. A tall, lanky girl in booty shorts and a tank top was helping, and I remember resenting her—nonsensically—for her seductive tan lines and fake nails.

Many of the guys you were staying with had a certain type of girl accompanying them in the house and in their beds at night, who walked around in their boyfriends' oversized sweatshirts with seemingly nothing underneath. They sat on the guys' laps and made innuendo-loaded jokes that I didn't even understand, contributing to the constant stream of locker-room humor like it was the most natural thing in the world.

I understood that you'd grown up with these guys, and that football was the link holding all of you together. I just hoped that you didn't have more in common with them than I'd thought.

When you and I finally left the house for dinner, I missed the last step leading to the back door, landing with a loud "bang" on my knee. You felt you had to go back upstairs to explain that everything was fine—probably because my fall had really been that obnoxious—but it seemed like you were more annoyed than concerned. You told me that I should be more careful, as though I'd always been a hopeless klutz. I felt like a young girl being chastised at school.

We walked until we found a small Mexican restaurant nearby, where we ordered burritos and ate silently on an outdoor patio, neither of us having much to contribute in the way of conversation. Fortunately, one of your friends, Drew, ran into us at the restaurant, and I immediately warmed to him after he revealed that he didn't view Senior Week as an excuse to get trashed for seven days. He was one of the few guys you knew who wasn't into the drinking culture.

You'd had a few beers the night before—I didn't know how honest you'd been about not getting drunk—but I knew that with me by your side, you'd probably refrain from the party scene that night. I was relieved to have a break from the constant stress of worrying about you, but was also frustrated that I was probably coming across as controlling and motherly. We'd already buried one of your classmates earlier that year, who'd overdosed on Oxycodone, and another from alcohol poisoning, so it wasn't exactly like my anxiety was unwarranted. Ultimately, I was desperate about two things: your safety, and our relationship. I refused to feel guilty for having legitimate concerns about either.

Sometime between twilight and nightfall, the sky grew dense with the kind of air that hovers and presses, and the ocean began tossing its dark waves more wildly near the shore as you and I made our way to the nearest drugstore. We walked hand in hand along the water as we made our way toward the more commercialized part of town, the two of us in search of a rather intimidating commodity that neither of us had any previous experience with: condoms.

Given the current state of affairs in your rental house, not to mention the tension we'd been dealing with over the last few weeks, I would've been perfectly fine with postponing the night's planned activity until a later date. Of course, that week—that house—provided us with the rare opportunity to spend the night together before college, and we'd already talked about capitalizing on the occasion a few weeks earlier. Despite the unusual state of disharmony in our relationship, and the less-than-ideal scenario of previously-used sheets, the part of me that *wanted you* was becoming more and more prevalent, infiltrating the rock-solid walls around my conscience until my values became a tenuous boundary that I frequently flirted with crossing.

With a stomach full of flatulence-inducing ingredients from our Mexican dinner, I wasn't exactly feeling sexy as we slinked down the "Family Planning" aisle, pretending to browse the multiple shelves of different condoms when in reality, we were too overwhelmed to focus on our options.

"Why are there are so many different kinds?" you whispered, clearing your throat in discomfort as a woman rounded the other end of the aisle, likely in search of menstrual pads or diapers. It's funny how the means, prevention, and aftermath products for reproductive health are always clustered together in drugstores, lined up in a row like a cause-and-effect progression: *old enough to get your period? Use birth control! Birth control fails? We've got diapers!*

"I don't know, just grab a box," I said, already pulling on your sleeve as my cheeks burned with embarrassment.

The little plastic bag that contained our purchase billowed in the wind on the way back to the house, the knowledge of its concealed contents drilling a guilty hole in the pit of my stomach while you walked on with a perfectly neutral expression. Then, all at once, the ominous clouds released the full weight of their burden upon us, dousing us in torrential rain as we squealed in surprise.

"How far out are we?!" I yelled, my voice fighting the full force of the heavens.

"I don't know! I can't even tell!" you shouted. And then, maybe simultaneously, we burst into the laughter of surrender, admitting defeat once we were thoroughly soaked to the bone. The two of us were flashes of madness sprinting along the darkness of the ocean, running not from the rain, but rather propelled forward by the energy of the moment. It was OK that I was caught in a storm, that I was drenched, that I could hardly see two inches in front of my face. It was even OK that you were holding a bag of condoms, little latex rings that essentially meant the renunciation of everything I was raised to believe. We were together. If I had you—my partner-in-crime, my best friend, my perpetual sidekick who made me feel more *life* than I ever had—I could at least partially convince myself that nothing else really mattered.

When the worst of the storm passed and the rain began to taper off, we found ourselves just a few blocks from your house. I could already hear the driving beat of a party underway in the distance, and automatically drew nearer to you to be comforted by the tenderness of your arm around my shoulders. When you buried your lips in my hair, your scruff itching the top of my head as we walked through the cool, misty air, all was finally well.

Needless to say, we skipped the party that night, skirting around the mobs of gyrating couples and their attempts to hand us red solo cups. You guided me through the mayhem successfully, leading me by the hand upstairs to the only private bedroom in the house. With its queen-sized bed and en-suite bathroom, it was in high demand, and was in rotation among the guys in the house and their girlfriends. As I sized up the room, which was otherwise quite luxurious, I chose not to think about what had unfolded beneath those blankets on previous nights. Frankly, I was grateful just to have a bed.

After we dried off and changed into our PJs—an ironic action, considering the little white baggie sitting unassumingly on the dresser—we made ourselves comfortable on the bed, flipping on the TV but quickly neglecting it as you closed the space between us.

I vaguely wondered why I wasn't more nervous about something as monumental as my "first time," before realizing that I was sharing this experience with a boy who had loved me for the past two and a half years. You'd waited for me. Granted, you hadn't always been the most patient or understanding about my sexual limitations, but it was enough that you'd proven to me that you believed I was worth waiting for. I could trust you.

But something unexpected happened that night. Though I was seemingly relaxed, claiming that I was ready to try, my body immediately rejected you, tensing and tightening against an indescribably searing pain each time we attempted intimacy.

"Is this normal?" you asked.

"I don't know, but you have to stop," I pleaded, my eyes brimming with tears.

When we finally reconciled ourselves to the fact that the night would *not* go as planned, you didn't seem overly disappointed. You fell asleep watching a movie, but I lay awake for some time, trying to figure out exactly how I felt and what I wanted. I was sad and empty, overtaken by the sudden urge to go home and fall asleep in my own bed.

I felt like an island—surrounded by you on all sides, yet completely alone in the expanse of my conflicting emotions.

I managed to sleep for a few hours, and woke to the sun rising through the glass door that led from our room to the balcony.

"Wade," I said, shaking you gently.

Your soft snores were the only response.

I tried again, "Wade. Come watch the sunrise with me."

"I'm tired," you'd mumbled, rolling over and pulling the blankets over your eyes.

So I stepped out to admire the glow of the first light over the ocean alone, staring at the horizon and idly realizing that it should have been a beautiful, romantic moment, and I was experiencing it by myself. I stood there for about half an hour more, taking in the view, before climbing back into bed beside you and slipping into another two hours of fitful sleep.

We awoke to the aroma of coffee drifting upstairs around 7 a.m., and we threw on some clothes and prepared to make our first appearance of the day. You handed me your sweatshirt when I complained about being cold, and rolling up the sleeves, I couldn't decide whether I felt closer to you or as trashy as all the other girls I'd judged just the day before.

"What's for breakfast?" you asked as we walked into the kitchen.

"Coffee, coffee, and...more coffee," Shawn answered.

"Well, that's BS. We need sustenance," you said. "Let's find a place to eat."

"Are you talking about food?" Gary said, appearing behind us and holding his girlfriend's hand.

"Yes. And we're not waiting for everyone else to wake up, either," you said. "I'm starving."

"Well, let's go, then," Shawn said, downing the last of his coffee as the six of us paraded out the door.

We drove to a diner you'd found online that was top-rated, and the waitress showed us to a table, where you ordered a short stack of pancakes and a plate of eggs with toast, home fries, and bacon. I stuck to a short stack, a coffee, and a lemonade.

As we handed our menus back to the waitress after ordering, I overestimated the amount of room my arm had between my glass and your bulky sweatshirt, and I experienced my second clumsy moment of Senior Week: I knocked over all twelve ounces of lemonade, drenching you and spilling some on Gary's girlfriend across from me.

"I'm so sorry," I said, mortified as I reached for whatever napkins I could find.

You were so pissed, so embarrassed, that it only added to my own humiliation as I tried to clean up the mess. The waitress finally came back with a towel to clean the worst of it.

As Andy drove me back to my friends' house in Wildwood later that morning, I was so glad—relieved—to be heading in the opposite direction of Ocean City, away from you. The dynamic in our relationship felt as unstable as a seesaw, and the initial carefree feelings of passion I'd had for you in the beginning were shifting into something more serious. I found myself frequently anxious, always subconsciously waiting for the other shoe to drop when I was with you. Your moods, however subtle, could be unpredictable. You weren't always emotionally gentle with me, weren't always understanding the way I expected you to be. At times, you could be quite gruff. When you wanted to, you were a master at making me feel small, but I would continue to overlook so much of it because I'd decided long ago that I loved you.

What I didn't see coming was that in the future, we'd have bigger, more insurmountable problems to face as we grew into the people we were always meant to become. We never did figure out how to work through the differences.

They say "time flies" for good reason. When things were good, I eagerly counted the days until we could get married, which seemed endless. But in reality, I was only counting the days to our impending end.

ELEVEN.

DESPITE THE FACT THAT graduation and Senior Week had been low points for our relationship, we slipped into the last, lazy summer days of our youth together, mending what had been a brief era of rifts with long afternoons spent in your pool, and warm twilights playing Chip n' Putt. At night, we'd congregate around the fire pit in your backyard with Leigh, the three of us competing to see who could toast the best marshmallow.

We reconnected with our friends a few times, planning bowling outings at the alley across from your neighborhood and hosting pool parties that lasted till late at night, the soft lights alternating colors from underwater and setting the mood. Still, some of my favorite memories of that summer consist of the more quiet moments—the two of us spread out on your couch in front of the TV in the sunset light, your head resting on a pillow in my lap as I played with your thick hair and stared into your eyes like they were the ocean. We talked about forever. I wouldn't even know how to begin estimating the number of "I love you's" traded, both during that summer and over the preceding two and a half years.

In a way, it felt like that summer would never end, with one day flowing seamlessly into the next; yet I began to worry about what was waiting for us at the end of the season, when we would begin our college years at different schools. I didn't know how often we'd get to see each other, and was already feeling intimidated by the highly-intelligent women you'd undoubtedly meet in your engineering program. I worried that I wouldn't be enough for you anymore—that you'd want something different for yourself. Thus, as the sycamores began to shed their first leaves in late August, I began to feel an even stronger desperation to give myself to you completely after our failed attempt in Ocean City. If I couldn't be your first kiss, I wanted to do one better. I wanted to be certain that if we did break up in college, I'd be the one person you'd never forget.

The idea sprang from a monthly chore you were charged with by a relative. At the time, your favorite aunt paid you to drive to her old house in a wooded neighborhood that had been on the market for years, just to sweep the floor of dust and bugs, to make sure the pipes stayed functional, and to make sure everything looked to be in order. Once, you asked me to come along with you.

We pulled into the winding driveway that led to a large, cabin-like house set back and apart from the other houses nearby, parking in the circular strip in front of the door. In the middle of the day, the scene was cute and homey. At night, it definitely felt more along the lines of "When a Stranger Calls," with large, wall-length windows lining the living room and unrecognizable noises emanating from the surrounding trees and shrubs.

Stepping through the front door, a butterfly staircase ascended from the oak wood foyer into a carpeted hallway upstairs, which overlooked the living room below. There was a contemporary-style kitchen, an unfinished basement which housed a single, Narnia-style wardrobe, and five bedrooms and four full baths. You told me it had been sitting on the market for $1.2 million over the last two years.

"Maybe your aunt will give us a discount," I joked.

As we made the rounds, it dawned on me that here was this perfectly good, unoccupied house, lonely on its four acres of land and abandoned without any particular use or purpose.

"Hey," I said, wrapping my arms around your neck. "Can we come back here…?"

I could hardly believe that I was the instigator for a change, but I was frantic to keep you, to make my mark on you, by whatever means possible. I was insecure about so many things at the time. I'd thought that sex would bind us together, would act as a secret marriage that would solidify all of our unofficial vows.

"Yeah," you breathed, bending down to meet my lips and kissing me hard.

We returned to the house two days before your 18th birthday, and a week before moving to college—both of us "adults," but not really. I brought two pillows and a scratchy blanket from Kmart, and you brought condoms. I wore an aquamarine and white-striped babydoll slip from Victoria's Secret, and you wore only your diver watch. We camped out in what was designed to be the master bedroom and made ourselves at home on the carpeted floor, both of us kneeling in the opposite of a prayer before I leaned into you. All at once, your bare arms enveloped my whole waist, wrapping around my back and pulling me close against your warm skin like everything I'd ever wanted, and—admittedly—everything that scared the hell out of me.

Much like our initial encounter at the beginning of the summer, there was immediate, shooting pain right from the start. I winced, willing myself to relax, but it was like willing myself to cut my own arm open.

"Wade, it really hurts," I finally said, biting my lip in an attempt to control my emotions. I rolled off of you, landing on my back and staring up at the ceiling.

"Are you OK?" you asked, turning to me and wiping

away my tears.

I nodded. "But I want you...I want to..." I said, touching your face.

"We don't have to do this," you said. But I could read your expression, and I could see how much you wanted this after waiting as long as we had. Determined, I pulled you closer, holding on tight to your shoulders and fixing my eyes on your watch, which had begun to glow in the darkened room as clouds shaded the afternoon light. I tensed; I waited.

It was over about a minute later, as the sensation had been overwhelmingly new for you. When you rolled off of me, I turned onto my side and buried my face in the pillow, trying to muffle the sound of my sobs that had erupted automatically in the aftermath. I felt shattered—lost, like I'd been pushed down a dark well. I didn't know whether my feelings were simply the result of heightened emotions, or whether I was just deeply distressed in those moments.

You placed a warm hand on my shoulder in an attempt to turn me toward you. When I wouldn't budge, you asked, slightly panicked,

"Baby? Are you OK?"

I finally faced you, my cheeks tear-streaked and pink, and replied,

"Jesus hates me."

You started laughing and pulled me close.

"No, he doesn't. He loves you. I love you," you said simply.

I wondered how it could be so simple for you when it was so complex, so multifaceted, for me. I was all right, but anything but content. I loved you—that wasn't the issue— but I couldn't reconcile what had just happened with my upbringing, and with the person I was supposed to be. It was hard enough trying to understand and accept my faith as a teenager without the complicated nature of the moments we'd just shared. I'd chosen this, had yearned for this experience with you for years. It was equal parts wonderful and terrifying...and unexpectedly isolating.

When I'd composed myself to your satisfaction, we cleaned ourselves up, and I stashed the blanket and the pillows in a random closet with some other abandoned quilts. Then we climbed into your Ford Explorer and headed for Chipotle, where we ate a late lunch and scrolled through Shiba Inu memes as though we hadn't just experienced a gigantic rite of passage half an hour earlier on an empty bedroom floor.

We ended our outing with mini golf at an indoor/outdoor arcade called Happy Times, where you scrawled our initials in a heart on the entrance sign out front, along with the initials of 200 other people who'd had the same idea. Still, the gesture had made me smile.

When I finally got home, my father was in his garden planting sunflowers—my favorite flower—and my mom wanted to take me for new shoes. I couldn't remember the last time I'd felt so guilty.

That night, I curled up on the floor on the far side of my bed and rested my forehead on my knees, wrapping my arms around myself. I somehow always ended up on the floor when I was in the most pain—never on my bed or a chair. It was like the floor was the only suitable place to hit rock bottom. I wept uselessly into my hands, trying to grasp at any thought, at any emotion, that would help me frame my identity into something neat and tidy, but who I was couldn't fit into a box anymore. The reality, though, was that it had been that way for years.

You'd tried to text me three times since you'd gotten home, but each time, I let my phone light up and buzz without acknowledging it. The truth was, I couldn't really talk to you about the way I felt, because my experience had been so different from yours. I couldn't talk to my parents without breaking their hearts. And for the first time, it felt like I couldn't talk to God, either.

When I think about that house in the woods that would never sell, there really couldn't have been a more appropriate place for what we shared behind those walls. The way we loved each other would remain stagnant for so long—always on the brink of something more, something with so much potential, but ultimately stopping short of the future we'd both anticipated.

But I dove all in, fully committed, regardless.

TWELVE.

T H E T R A I N R I D E I N T O Philadelphia is slow, building like suspense as it nears its final destination, 30th Street Station, in the heart of the city. Between Exton—the closest train station to my university and Philadelphia—the sun spills through the treetops of heavily wooded areas that level out to open fields, and eventually into small surrounding towns that lead into the city like a magnificent crescendo.

You'd been accepted to a renowned engineering school in University City, right in the middle of the City of Brotherly Love, and you were on the five-year plan for a Bachelor of Science degree in Biomedical Engineering. I'd enrolled in a state school about an hour between home and Philadelphia, caught between the two like I was caught between my former identity and who I was becoming in our relationship. I'd started out as a psychology major, but transferred to English within that first year. I'd always felt most comfortable with a pen in my hand and my nose in a book.

We were both surprised by how easily public transportation worked to get us between schools, and we took turns most weekends, alternating our visits to each campus. Somehow, though, the arrangement turned into my traveling to Philadelphia three out of four weeks of each month, simply because I was enamored by the lazy way the Schuylkill River ran along the bike path that led straight to the art museum, its famous Rocky statue greeting tireless joggers, fists poised high in the air. I fell in love with the four-story Anthropologie that sat directly across from Rittenhouse Park, and with our favorite coffee place, La

Colombe. Fell for displays of colorful macarons in Miel Pa-tisserie, and with the Eggs Benedict at The Dandelion. Fell for the way the skyscraper lights illuminated the city at night, pouring through rectangular windowpanes and re-flecting on the river, its driving energy reminding me of the song "We Are Young" by FUN.

...Mostly, though, I just fell deeper in love with you.

It was October of our freshman year, and as I sat on the train watching the world whiz by outside my window, my heart leapt at the thought that I'd be with you in under an hour. I'd always count the minutes, the stops, until I would be in your arms whenever I took the train into Philadelph-ia. No matter how badly the week had gone, or what I'd had to endure when I wasn't with you, it was all remedied the second I saw you waiting for me on the platform at 30th Street. You were always right on time.

When the train stopped at Jefferson Station, I put my iPod away, fluffed my hair, and checked my lip gloss in my compact mirror, because I'd be seeing you in fewer than ten minutes. And then the train gradually rolled into motion again, chugging along and slowly rounding a bend that revealed all of Philadelphia as the tracks evened out, from the art museum and the bike path to the towering Comcast building. The sky was just beginning to turn sil-ver as day gave way to dusk, and I was thoroughly en-tranced all over again by the city, and by the way it could make me feel. I must've known, even then, that some of the best moments of my life would unfold on those streets, far below the small cluster of buildings that made up the city's skyline.

"Next stop…30th Street Station," came blaring over the intercom, and the train rumbled to a stop a few moments later.

I filed out into the still-warm, early autumn air with a hundred other passengers, searching for you on my tiptoes amidst the swarms of people. I couldn't find you, so I shot you a text and took the escalator down into the main station while I waited for your response.

The smell of cinnamon pretzels and Subway sandwiches permeated the air as I stepped into the station and was swallowed by the bustle of commuters. Friday evenings were especially hectic at 30th Street, and that night was no exception.

My phone lit up in my hand.

Keep walking, you texted, followed by a winking emoticon.

I looked up, straining my neck for a better view around the mobs of professionals with their unwieldy briefcases, a small girl in street clothes dressed all wrong for the unseasonably warm, fall evening. I stuck out like a sore thumb.

Do you see me? I texted back, but before I could look up again, I'd made full-body contact with something, startling me half to death before I realized the wall of muscle who'd crashed into me was you. You picked me up and spun me around easily with one arm before setting me down and handing me a bouquet of sunflowers.

"For my princess," you said, grinning at me like I was your favorite thing in the world. And I threw my arms around you in thanks, kissing you right there in our own little bubble as the crowds formed a traffic circle around us.

You grabbed my weekend bag from over my shoulder and slung it effortlessly over your own. I admired, for the thousandth time, your easy masculinity; I could struggle under the weight of a fifteen-pound bag, when for you, it was hardly any weight at all. You grabbed my hand and squeezed it, and I skipped a little in response, making you laugh.

"What's the plan this weekend?" I asked eagerly, as we started across the street to your dorm.

"Well, you remember my friend, BJ? He's in the city tonight with his girlfriend, Stephanie. They're all meeting in Webb's dorm for some gaming. I was thinking maybe we could stop by, just to say hi. And I may have a surprise for you," you finished, smiling at me slyly. "The rest of the weekend is totally open."

The nice thing about college was that so many of our friends followed us, or maybe we followed them, completely by accident. Jenny and I had both ended up at the same school as Brie, and you'd ended up in the engineering program at yours with Webb and Tim. There were a lot of familiar faces, some of which became less friendly over time as we naturally outgrew each other and made new connections. You already seemed at home here in Philadelphia, and I felt like this was unofficially my new home, too.

We dropped my bag off in your traditional dorm, where you were living on a single-sex floor with one of your old football friends, Brendan. The bathroom was communal, which made things inconvenient for me—I was constantly going up to the ladies' floor to use the toilet—but otherwise, I liked the feel of your living quarters. I liked that it gave you the opportunity to make friends with nerdy guys, with tech guys, with guys you weren't used to hanging out with in high school. Then again, this was probably all negated by the fact that you were living with Brendan.

"Hey, Brendan," I said, walking through the door behind you, feeling perpetually awkward.

I won't pretend any differently: I couldn't stand the kid.

93

He'd often talk over me when we were all having a conversation, as if my opinions mattered less because I was a woman. He was also a budding alcoholic, as evidenced by the handles of Smirnoff he kept stashed in your bureau that disappeared at impossible rates. As a final selling point, he was also one of the sleaziest guys you knew, constantly referring to the girls he met in graphic terms. Still, when he'd invited you to dorm with him that year, I guess you'd liked the idea of sharing a room with someone you already knew, because you'd agreed.

"Morgan," Brendan said, nodding in my direction before turning his attention back to his computer screen.

"What are you doing, dude? It's Friday night," you said.

"Yeah, well. If I'm going to be pre-med, I have to study like I'm pre-med," Brendan replied, taking a bite of the Subway sandwich he'd picked up next door.

"Again, though—it's *Friday night*," you emphasized.

"My friend's having a party at his place tonight. I'll go out later on, don't worry—you'll have the room to yourselves," Brendan said, smirking as he put his earpods in, ending the conversation.

You shrugged at me, like, *Yeah, OK, he's got a point— we'll want him gone later,* and then we were off again, walking hand in hand to the closest pizza place, where we spent a solid hour laughing and trading stories from earlier in the week.

It was completely dark when we stepped back outside, and Webb texted you, asking when we were coming over.

"Wanna go now?" you asked. "Sounds like BJ and Stephanie are already there."

So we continued down the street to Webb's dorm—the nicest of the traditional dorms—where he met us in the front lobby.

"So glad you're here, man. My room is set up with candles and a Barry White playlist just waiting for us."

Webb always put on a show about his alleged "affair" with you when I was around, hoping to get under my skin. I punched his arm.

"You're gross, Webb," I said.

"I mean, I do like candles. Are they scented?" you asked, and the two of you burst into hysterics. You were still laughing as we walked out of the elevator onto the top floor.

Webb turned toward the floor's lounge, where it looked like a small cluster of people were congregated, but you tugged on my hand and led me in the opposite direction.

"Where are we going?" I asked playfully.

But you remained silent, a small smile giving away something good on your lips. And then, as we turned the corner, I saw it.

The entire city was spread out beneath me as I peered through the wall-length window. It felt like I could reach down and rearrange the cars on the street below. For every illuminated window, I imagined what the lives of the people behind them could be like, the possibilities unfolding like a montage in my head.

I moved closer to the glass, touching my fingertips to it as I drank in the view.

"I thought you'd like it," you said, wrapping an arm around my waist and pulling me close.

"It's beautiful. The lights—"

"You do love your lights."

I faced you, our arms still encircling each other as I lost myself in the familiar blue of your eyes.

"You know me so well. But I only love this so much because I get to share it with you," I said, and you leaned into me for a long kiss.

"Hey—this isn't lip-lock central. You joining the party any time soon?" came Webb's booming voice.

We broke apart, smiling, neither of us embarrassed in the least. And then we finally made our way to the lounge, where we caught up with BJ, Stephanie, and Webb before competing in a Mario Kart tournament with everyone until midnight.

"It was really good to see them. BJ and Stephanie seem so good together," you said when we finally left.

"They are. I had fun. Although I could've done without Webb sexually harassing you every five minutes," I joked, knocking shoulders with you.

"Listen—that's what you get when you have this body. I'm reduced to a piece of meat, Morgan."

I squeezed your bicep to prove your point.

"See?!"

I rolled my eyes good-naturedly.

"Tired yet?" you asked.

I shrugged. "Not really. I'm kind of energized, actually. I could go for something sweet."

You looked at me with an idea in your eyes.

"I know just the place."

So we found ourselves a few minutes later in front of every student's favorite cookie truck, Insomnia Cookies, which stayed open till 2 a.m. for emergency study revivals. It was my first experience with the hot, freshly-baked, melt-in-your-mouth cookies, and I'd selected a classic sugar cookie in addition to a Caramel Swirl flavor. You, ever the chocolate fanatic, ordered a basic chocolate chip in addition to a Reese's Chocolate Chunk.

You led me to a spot behind your school's gym, which was still open for the one or two gym rats who actually worked out on Friday nights (or, at that point, Saturday mornings). We sat on a padded bench, probably intended for some kind of specific workout, and traded bites of our cookies beneath what we could see of the stars.

"I love you…you know that?" you said suddenly, taking your hand in mine and caressing it with your thumb.

I smiled, my lips still warm and smeared from the stain of chocolate and faded lipstick.

"I know," I said simply.

And when you kissed me in the moments that followed, a million small cocoons broke open, the same butterflies reemerging from our first kiss and invading the space around my heart.

~

WE WOKE UP LATE the next morning after our midnight cookie excursion—close to noon—and rolled out of bed to grab brunch at Sabrina's, one of the best French toast spots in Philly. It was a beautiful day, sunny and breezy and warm, so we decided to spend it exploring as much of the city as we could. You were my perpetual navigator, and I trusted your internalized map of the blocked avenues absolutely, letting you guide me like a little girl to each of our stops.

With full bellies, we made our way to the University of Pennsylvania's campus, where we bought tickets for the Museum of Archaeology & Anthropology and spent a solid two hours studying the exhibits. I've always been passionate about learning, even if the subject matter is something completely foreign to me, so it was fascinating to see and read about ancient artifacts that had been discovered in Rome, Greece, and Egypt.

At one point, we walked through a room that showcased the history and process of natural evolution, where models were displayed of the way the human jaw had developed from the earliest primates, in addition to a representation of the modern human skull. You were all too captivated by this display.

"It's crazy how far we've come since then—how we've grown into an entirely different species," you remarked, and I'd nodded and tried to brush off the comment, thinking, *If we evolved from another species, it was because God intended for it to happen that way.*

Of course, you wouldn't have wanted to hear that, so we walked on in silence.

It was late afternoon when we finally left the museum, and you asked,

"Feel like a walk?"

Because the answer was always yes, we promptly headed for the bike path along the river, walking hand in hand like always, pointing out the cute dogs we spotted on our slow trek up to the art museum.

"I want to show you something," you said, smiling down at me like you always did when you had an idea that was bound to make me happy. You knew I loved surprises.

"Something I haven't seen before?" I asked.

"You'll see," you replied cryptically, and I pretended to scowl, my face softening again as you began to laugh at my reaction.

When we reached the art museum, we crossed the street—our lives barely intact after dodging the unremitting traffic—and began the steep ascent up a meandering path that took us to the west side of the museum. I immediately spotted two gazebos overlooking the river, and all of Boathouse Row.

I squealed a little, already tugging on your hand and winning another smile from you.

We leaned over the railing just as the sun began to set over the city, casting the last rays of its brilliant glitter on the water below us. A strong breeze swept my hair back over my shoulders, and when I looked at you, you'd pulled out your phone to snap a photo of me. You managed to capture the wonder and want in my eyes, the perfect reflection of everything I'd felt in that brief fragment of time.

Then, I went and ruined the moment as I studied the little waterfall flowing over the dam below, musing,

"I didn't know beavers could make such big dams!"

You doubled over laughing, tears in your eyes, as you managed to reply,

"That's a man-made dam, babe."

You never let me live that down, relentlessly teasing me about it through our final year together. From that day on, the Schuylkill became home to the infamous "Beaver Dam," which you'd affectionately nicknamed it.

After I'd swatted you at least five times, trying to get you to calm down, I finally scrambled for a diversion.

"What do you want to do for dinner?"

Suppressing the last of your chuckles, you said,

"Let's go back to the dorms first—get cleaned up. I have an idea of where I want to take you."

We made it back to your dorm about half an hour later, where you zipped me into a blue lace dress and I pulled a white button-down over your head between kisses. We barely made it through the changing process before dinner, but I hadn't wanted to ruin my makeup, so you'd rolled your eyes good-naturedly and warned me that I'd have to make up for it later.

When I was in Philadelphia with you, it was almost like being on my honeymoon. The last thing I really wanted was to exercise any self-control, so if Brendan was out of the room and we both wanted each other (which we usually did), all bets were off. I wasn't about to refuse you when I'd already given my virginity to you, and as a result, we made love all the time. It was only when I was back in West Chester—grounded by a more objective reality—that I yearned for the comfort of a confessional. As a result, I started a pattern of doing whatever I wanted with you, whenever, only to run to confession at the next possible opportunity.

The main problem was that, at my core, I didn't want to *not* be a practicing Catholic. I genuinely loved and appreciated my faith, although I didn't always understand it or want to abide by its doctrines. I loved God as much as I could for that stage in my life—for someone who was living in a perpetual state of mortal sin. I wanted to be Catholic and be with you at the same time. What I hadn't reconciled yet was that I couldn't actually have it both ways.

When we were finished getting ready, we walked the few blocks to Landmark Café, which was connected to the other side of your school's gym.

"I think you'll like this place," you said, placing your hand on the small of my back as you guided me through the door.

As always, you knew me well enough to know what I liked. I enjoyed the ambience of the restaurant, and the food was tasty enough for several return visits with you in the future. But I never liked it more than I did that night, when we sat as close as we could to each other in a sleek, circular high-top booth, swapping long glances in a code that only we could understand, playing footsie beneath the table.

"This has been such a great day," I told you, resting my hand over yours on the table after our plates had been cleared away. You slipped it into yours and brought it to your lips to kiss.

"What if it's not over yet?" you hinted.

"I'd love you forever," I joked.

"I thought that was already a given."

"Eh, sometimes," I said, crinkling my nose. "You do like to make fun of me a lot."

"You mean like Beaver Dam?" you said, already dangerously on the brink of laughter.

When we stepped back out into the crisp evening air, you led me down the street to Penn's campus, where we just happened to stumble upon one of the largest Barnes & Noble stores I'd ever seen.

"This was the plan, wasn't it?" I asked, practically jumping up and down as you pulled open the door for me.

"This was the plan," you confirmed, shaking your head in amusement. "Go crazy."

I left no pocket of that Barnes & Noble unexplored, roaming through the aisles and running my fingers over each book as though they were precious commodities. Some people like the smell, the mustiness, of old bookstores, but I've always reveled in the scent of new books. That night, in that bookstore, there was a type of studious freshness that hung in the air—an altogether magical effect that was produced by the bold, black ink of text, standing out against the ivory backdrop of each crisp, untouched page.

You followed me to the poetry section.

"I didn't know you were into poetry," you said.

"I'm not, generally," I replied. "A bit too flowery for me. But I have to check for my main man, Pablo Neruda."

"Who?"

"Chilean communist. Wrote the best damn verses you'll ever read."

I skimmed the entire shelf of Neruda's work for his small booklet of love sonnets until I finally found it, thin and pink and nearly swallowed by larger anthologies of his work on either side. I'd been putting off buying it because I was usually satisfied just flipping to my favorite poem and reading through it a few times, but one of these days, I would make the splurge.

"Here it is," I said. "*Soneto de la Noche.*"

I proceeded to hold the page out for you to read, which you skimmed briefly before replying, to my chagrin,

"So?"

So, Wade? Really? You'd killed my soul a little when you spoke that one, disinterested syllable, because you'd just read the very poem that had spoken directly to my heart on numerous occasions and failed to understand it.

"So, isn't is beautiful?!" I exclaimed.

"It's OK," you said, shrugging.

I let it go, figuring that you were an engineering major— it wouldn't be fair for me to expect you to appreciate romantic sonnets when we had such different areas of interest. Still, our completely opposite reactions to the same words may have revealed something deeper that spoke to our individual ideas about beauty and love.

When we got back to your dorm around 9 p.m., you had yet another surprise for me: you pulled out your guitar after we'd made ourselves comfy on your bed, and you began to serenade me with three songs that will always make my heart twinge when I hear them. The first selection was

"The Scientist" by Coldplay, followed by "Swing Life Away" by Rise Against and, finally, what would become our unofficial song: "Demons," by Imagine Dragons.

"When the days are cold, and the cards all fold, and the saints we see are all made of gold..."

It was the first time I'd ever heard it, long before all of the mainstream radio stations began playing the power ballad on an endless loop.

"When you feel my heat, look into my eyes, it's where my demons hide, it's where my demons hide. Don't get too close, it's dark inside, it's where my demons hide, it's where my demons hide."

The lyrics, as well as the music, struck me as extraordinarily meaningful. I was your enraptured audience of one, spellbound as you performed for me, looking up every so often to gaze into my eyes as you sang the words.

"They say it's what you make, I say it's up to fate, it's woven in my soul, I need to let you go...your eyes, they shine so bright, I wanna save that light. I can't escape this now, unless you show me how."

And then I started crying, tears slipping down my cheeks for reasons I still have trouble understanding.

When the last chord resounded into silence, I threw my arms around you, hardly waiting for you to put the guitar down, and kissed you all over your face, my eyes still damp, my throat tight from everything I felt for you.

You wrapped your arms around me, attempting to return my kisses despite the fact that I was a moving target who never relented, touching my lips to your forehead, the tip of your nose, your cheeks.

I loved you so much back then, Wade. I loved you more than any song or line or memory could ever express. I still think back to the way you made me feel, sitting there on your bed beside you as you opened your heart to me in such a vulnerable way, memorizing lyrics and singing them to me when it was the furthest thing from natural for you.

Seconds later, your guitar was on the floor and I was on top of you, in your lap where the guitar had been. We were a jumble of flying clothes and frantic arms, moving all over each other like there wasn't enough time, like we had to be everywhere at once. You took me places I never knew existed.

There was so much irony in the fact that you'd chosen that song, "Demons," to sing to me that night, like I was somehow a cherub and you were my fallen angel. You knew you wanted to save the light in my eyes, knew that you couldn't escape our love unless I showed you how.

When the time came, I couldn't show you. I could only let you go.

THIRTEEN.

"T H I S T I E, O R T H I S T I E?" you asked, holding up one maroon, one black with silver stripes.

It was a night chock-full of anticipation, and its energy filled me up and poured out of me as I changed from casual clothes into a red, spandex dress. My makeup had been done for an hour already, and my hair was perfectly curled.

I loved dressing up, but what I hadn't fully learned at the time was that dressing up is usually far more fun than the actual event. That occasion, however, seemed like it could be an exception, because I'd be sharing it with you.

The rugby team was hosting a wine and cheese party that night in honor of Valentine's Day at the team's official house. You'd joined the club in late fall and, like clockwork, had quickly made friends. You were, inevitably and effortlessly, the guy everyone liked—the guy they couldn't *help* but like. You'd been that guy for as long as I'd known you.

Unfortunately, the boys on the team were far from civilized, and that's putting it politely. I'd seen some of the emails you'd received from the other players. One of the guys wrote raunchy stories and sent them around to his teammates, while others were just plain sexist. The rugby guys seemed to treat girls like pieces of meat, reminding me exactly of some of the guys on your old football team. Still, that party gave us a reason to be festive and go out, and I'd reasoned: *A Valentine's day wine and cheese party— how bad could it possibly be?*

"Ready?" you asked. I fussed with my hair one last time in the mirror that hung over the door.

"Ready."

You grabbed your student ID and we were off, heading up the street from your dorm.

The rugby house wasn't terribly far—a few blocks, at most—but in my heels and in the cold, it had felt like an odyssey. You pulled me closer.

"Almost there, baby," you said softly, your arm soothing and secure around my shoulders.

A few minutes later, we were standing in front of an old brick apartment building, and everything looked dark.

"Are you sure this is the right place?" I asked dubiously, peering up at you from under the hood of my coat.

"Yes, this should be it," you said, ringing the doorbell.

Maybe twenty seconds passed before the door opened, and a rush of sound erupted from the stairwell behind the guy in the doorframe.

"Yo, Wade! Come in, come in, man!" he said, gripping your hand in a death shake.

Introductions were made, and I offered a small, "Hi, nice to meet you," before we were ushered upstairs to socialize.

It didn't take me long to figure out that everyone there was drunk, and they were filling their solo cups with boxed wine and eating cheese off of wooden cutting boards like no tomorrow. There was a sign scrawled on the bathroom door that classily read, "IF YOU'RE GOING TO PUKE GTFO," but nobody looked sick—yet.

You and I pushed through mobs of college kids, stopping every now and then for you to pat one of your teammates on the back or shake someone's hand like you were the freaking mayor, until we finally made it to the wine station. Red solo cups were the only available drinking vessels that evening, and you filled two of them to the brim and handed one to me.

"Good?" you shouted over the laughter and music.

I nodded, taking a slow, tentative sip.

I was completely green to the drinking scene, and if you had told me in high school that I would actually be attending parties like this, I wouldn't have been able to picture it. I'd never understood the appeal of alcohol—drunkenness had always seemed like a distasteful gamble to me. Still, this was wine, not hard liquor, and I reasoned that maybe it would help take the edge off of meeting these squalid jocks.

When I took that first sip of wine, I didn't like it. I wasn't used to the taste, save for a few small sips from my dad's glass at Christmas. I peered down at the entirely-full cup in dismay, thinking, *I have to down a whole cup of this stuff?*

We made a few more rounds after that, finally stopping for several minutes to talk to a teammate of yours who claimed to have gotten pushed off a roof. Or maybe he fell on his own. What was he *doing* on the roof? I couldn't remember—at that point, I was sipping that wine like 7-Up, the bitterness vanishing the more I sipped. For once, I wasn't overly concerned about what I was saying, or how I was standing, or what type of an impression I might be making on new acquaintances. I just felt...loose.

"Do you want to go to the basement and dance?" you asked.

I nodded vigorously, draining the last few drops from my solo cup. I felt...amazing. I could stay out with you all night, dance all night. My feet had ceased to exist. I was no longer aware of the fact that I was even wearing heels.

"Here," you said, motioning for my cup. I handed it to you and hiccupped, laughing at the way my throat expanded and contracted. You filled my cup a second time, and I looked at you—surprised, but not averse—before accepting it and following you down the skeevy basement. The stairwell was damp, steep, and narrow, and navigating those steps inebriated and in heels was quite a feat.

Dozens of couples were dancing in the middle of the floor, but the larger image of everything I saw was warm and curved at the edges, like a black-and-white photograph faded with age. I also vaguely noticed that at the very back of the basement, there was a pole. Two female guests were hanging on it, giggling and swinging.

Under normal circumstances, I would've been so offended at the mere sight of that pole that I would have burst up the stairs and out the front door. What did it say about the rugby team that they had a *pole* in their basement?

I was halfway through my second full cup of wine, and I was doing my best to dance with you while holding onto it. Finally, I grew tired of having it glued to my hand, and proceeded to chug the rest of it like juice.

The rest of the night is a bit piecey. What I do remember is attempting to hug the grimy wall after dancing with some strange girl, and then proceeding to try to undo your tie before you stopped me, laughing. We left the party about three hours after we got there, and both of us were sufficiently drunk—although of the two of us, I was by far the walking disaster. I had never felt so sick.

We were right outside your dorm when I started to lose it.

"Morgan? Can you get out your student ID? You need to get past security," you said.

I knew that you were saying something important, but everything moved in slow motion as I tried to reach for my wallet deep in my purse.

"I...don't know if I can get in..." I mumbled, taking a few sideways steps toward the door. You grabbed my arm and steadied me.

"Baby, we just need to get you past security, and then I can take care of you, OK? Can you do that?" you implored.

We walked into the lobby, and I managed to hand my ID to the person at the front desk. She gave me the OK to go through the turnstile, and I tripped as I made my way to you, waiting for me on the other side.

As soon as we got back to your room, I grabbed the first trash can I saw and hung my head over it.

"Wait," you'd said, grabbing it from me and replacing it with the one under your desk. "That one was Brendan's."

It must've been Brendan's name that tipped me over the edge, because it was game over from there. The vomit poured out of me, red and burning with ethanol. The sensation traveled up to the base of my nose, igniting my face on fire. I kept throwing up—seemingly a bottomless pit—but as soon as I got a small reprieve, I began chastising you about how my intoxication had been all your fault. I warned that if you ever let this happen again, I was done with you. I told you I couldn't *believe* you'd handed me that second cup, not quite grasping in my stupor that I'd been far more to blame for not knowing my limits.

I threw up some more, still dizzy from the type of drunkenness I vowed to never experience again.

When I found that I could stand, you made me chug a full bottle of water before replacing my tight dress with PJs, and tucked me into your twin-size bed. You rolled out a sleeping bag on the floor beside me, and we both collapsed into darkness.

Sometime around 5 a.m., I woke with a start to you reaching over my head to turn off the lamp.

"Hey, hey, you're OK, you're OK," you whispered.

I rubbed a hand across my forehead.

"What...was that?" I asked, and patted the bed for you to come under the covers with me.

"You were really drunk," you said, evident concern flashing in your eyes. "How are you feeling now?"

I shook my head.

"I don't know. Not awful."

"I was so worried about you. I'm so sorry. This was all my fault," you said regretfully.

"What are you talking about? How is it your fault?" I asked, already forgetting my accusatory rant.

"You kept telling me when you were sick that I was the reason you got like this. You were right, I should have taken better care of you."

I shook my head. "No. This was my fault. I'm the one who drank too much. I should have known when to stop, and anyway, I'm fine now," I insisted.

I could tell you weren't convinced. It was clear you felt awful, but I was too tired to continue arguing with you.

It wasn't long until we were both fast asleep again, your neglected sleeping bag rumpled on the floor beside the bed.

FOURTEEN.

AFTER THE WINE AND CHEESE disaster, you and I didn't go to any other parties for the rest of the school year. I'd had enough of that atmosphere, and ultimately, the only thing I wanted was to spend all my nights with you. I couldn't care less about the stereotypical "college experience"—I was happy with the experience we were creating on our own.

Another contributing factor to lying low was that, when rugby season had resumed in the spring, you'd gotten your third concussion. The first had been from football, and the second you'd sustained at a retreat, of all places, when you were wrestling for fun with one of your friends.

I'd watched the third concussion happen. I was at the game with your parents, who'd made the drive into Philadelphia to watch you play and take us out to dinner afterward. One minute, I was making small talk with your mother as you scrambled for the ball; the next, you were lying flat on the field with the coach and the trainer bent over you, asking you to follow a small light with your eyes.

Your parents had brought you home that evening, dropping me off at campus on the way.

"Please don't play rugby anymore," I'd begged you, growing steadily more concerned about the number of blows to the head you'd received over the last three years.

"This happens all the time in contact sports, Morgan. Gary was the quarterback of our team in high school, and he's had ten concussions and still made the honor roll every semester. I promise, I'm fine."

I figured there were some things that were simply beyond my control—decisions you had to make for yourse-

If—and this was one of them. So, I watched as you took a month to recover before taking the field again like nothing had ever happened, wondering if you were really completely healed, and whether you'd be OK moving forward.

One wet and chilly Friday evening in April, we were planning on doing more of the same as we had been over the last two months: making dinner, watching Netflix, and maybe taking a walk through Rittenhouse Square for some light shopping or lunch on Saturday. After the first half of the year, you'd moved into a newer apartment building on Chestnut Street, which was fully-equipped with a kitchen, a family room, and—best of all—private bathrooms. You still had to share the suite with three other guys, but they were nice enough in that they were nothing like Brendan. I was just glad you'd finally gotten away from him.

"Crap. No burger buns left," you said, leaning deep into the refrigerator like Alice leaning over the rabbit hole. Your George Foreman grill was already out and ready to go on the counter, the burger meat thawing beside it.

"*Don't* hit your head," I warned, as you backed out and straightened up.

"I'm gonna run out. Old Nelson's should have some. Will you start the broccoli and potatoes?" you asked, already shrugging on your Barbour jacket.

"On it," I said, moving from the couch where I'd been curled up watching *How I Met Your Mother.*

"Are you going to get the garlic to red pepper flake ratio right this time?" you teased, one hand on the doorknob.

"Blah blah blah," I said, moving forward to kiss you. "Be careful."

While you were out, I rummaged in the drawer beneath the oven for a frying pan and coated it in olive oil before dumping in a full bag of frozen broccoli. I let it sit like that on medium heat for a bit, setting to work on peeling some potatoes and laying them in a steamer to cook. Then, once the broccoli had thawed and began to simmer in the oil, I coated it in a dusting of garlic powder and red and black pepper. Your mother always prepared broccoli this way, and since it was your favorite, I'd learned how to make it. I'd assumed it would be a recipe our children would love someday, too.

I was just turning the heat off, the vegetables fully cooked, when you stepped through the door, totally drenched from head to toe. You carried a white plastic bag in your right hand, and held it over your head like a boxing champ.

"I am cold. And wet. And miserable. But I have buns," you said, flinging the bag onto the table.

"Yes, you do," I joked suggestively. "Here, leave your jacket in the kitchen. Don't trail it all wet and dripping into your room."

You handed it to me, and I hung it over the hook on the front door while you went to dry off. You reemerged a few minutes later, towel-drying your hair and running your fingers through it.

"Not a bad look," I said. You rolled your eyes, grinning as you tried to swat me with the towel before I darted out of the way.

I left you in charge of making and grilling the burger patties once the broccoli was done, returning to the couch to watch the rest of my show. Between the two of us, we were good little amateur cooks, although I usually played sous chef to your chef.

Even in the kitchen, we were effortlessly compatible. Nothing ever needed to be a discussion—we pulled our own weight in the relationship, with you usually footing the bill as I oversaw most of the domestic duties, like cleaning and baking, even though we weren't living together. Our routines and rhythms evolved organically, making our relationship that much stronger.

We ate a quiet dinner, as two of your roommates had gone home for the weekend and the third was locked in his room at all hours, playing video games and emerging only for the basic necessities, like food and the toilet.

"You make a good burger," I said.

"Broccoli wasn't bad," you remarked.

It was like we were an old couple eating our thousandth meal together.

"*Not bad?* Come on! How hard can it be to get this recipe right?!"

"...I'm just messing," you finally said, pushing back your chair to bring your plate to the sink.

I dove for you, pretending to tackle you, but you were too quick for me, all but flinging your plate into the sink and wrapping an arm around my waist to immobilize me. You planted several consecutive, machine-gun kisses on my cheek before asking,

"Now what?"

I thought for a moment, then stood on your feet.

"Let's dance."

So we traipsed around your kitchen like that, holding hands like we were dancing but mostly just stomping in circles. I was laughing so hard I could barely catch my breath.

"Wait, wait, wait," I said. "Let me go."

You obliged, and I plopped myself down on your shoe.

"OK, sir. I'm ready for my ride at this time."

You began to walk, dragging me along, my ankles scraping the floor as I kept them wrapped tightly around your leg.

"This is *such* a good time. I haven't done this since I was a kid," I said, leaning my head against your knee.

And then you were somehow level with my face, tucking my hair behind my ear just before kissing me.

We ended up making out, laughing together on your linoleum floor, my hands fastened behind your head to keep you from bumping it.

...I always had the time of my life with you, whether we were on one of our Center City adventures or rolling around on your kitchen floor for no good reason.

We eventually got up and washed the dishes together, you flicking suds in my direction as I dried. Then we continued binge-watching *How I Met Your Mother* before deciding that it was officially time to select our Friday night movie—never mind the fact that we'd just been staring at the same screen for the last two hours.

You had a tub of cookie dough in the fridge, so I helped you form the dough into little balls and place them on a baking tray, slapping your hand when I caught you sneaking wads of it to eat. Nevertheless, we ended up on your couch with the bucket between us even after eating the baked cookies, scooping up the raw dough with spoons like it was ice cream.

"Doesn't get better than this," you said, your voice muffled with the thick stickiness of raw dough.

"I can't imagine it does," I agreed.

"Do this with me the rest of our lives?"

I snorted, spooning up another bite.

"We're going to make one fat, unattractive couple if we make this a regular thing."

"I don't care," you said. "We're only nineteen. Stay with me. And we'll still be doing this when we're 90."

It was surprisingly touching. I was usually the one who brought up the topic of marriage, and most of our conversations about the future. I wasn't used to you mentioning it so openly.

"Tempting," I said, crossing my legs and turning to face you on the couch. "Who doesn't want to be proposed to over cookie dough?"

"Seriously, though," you said, smiling at me over the tub.

When the movie had ended and we were both sufficiently nauseated, you snapped the lid back onto the tub and stuck it back in the fridge.

As we got ready for bed, you tossed my favorite t-shirt of yours at me—your rugby t-shirt, which was oversized and soft—and we brushed our teeth together, you standing behind me with your free arm laced around my waist. I looked up at you in the mirror, grinning behind my already-exposed teeth. You returned the smile, white foam coating your lips.

I always slept on the inside of your bed—closest to the wall, where I felt the most protected and secure. You slid in after me on the outside, and seconds later, our bodies collided with all the force of extraterrestrial matter. Suddenly, I was spiraling out of myself, following you into a reckless and radiant universe of our own making—two supernovas that burned through ourselves, adding to the other's brilliance until such activity resulted in an inevitable explosion. Afterward, there was only the intimacy of your hand in my hair, my bare chest rising and falling against yours as we drifted into sleep.

"Goodnight, Morgan. I love you," you whispered.

"I love you always," I returned, my mouth forming the words clumsily against the pull of sleep.

When I finally rolled off of you, I locked my ankle around yours so I'd know you were beside me, even in my dreams.

FIFTEEN.

IT WAS THE FIRST SUMMER in years that didn't really feel like summer because you remained in Philly, stuck in the brutally hot city through August to take classes as was required by your program. I took day trips to visit you on the weekends, but those days never seemed to stretch the way full weekends did when I was visiting you from West Chester. Still, they were the best I could do while living at home for the summer with my parents. We spent our time picnicking in the park, walking along the river, and eating cheesesteaks in the sweltering, over-whelmingly-crowded Reading Terminal Market.

Fall couldn't come fast enough, and as soon as I started my sophomore year, I was back in Philadelphia with you nearly every weekend, lugging my bulging weekend bag onto the train and counting the stops between Exton and the city.

As Halloween approached, you were invited to a cos-tume party, and we talked briefly about dressing up as a couple.

"What if we go as Superman and Wonder Woman?" you proposed, flashing a photo of the costume duo on Reddit to me.

I crinkled my nose.

"I don't know anything about Wonder Woman—I'm not one for comics. You do you," I insisted. "I want to go as Lit-tle Red Riding Hood. You can be the wolf to my Red, if you want."

It was your turn to crinkle your nose in distaste.

"All right, fine. We'll both do our own thing. We'll see who has the better costume," you said, the idea of the chal-lenge already glistening in your eyes.

Wintery weather had come early that year—a scorching summer followed by a frosty autumn—and classes had been cancelled for the latter half of October as fresh blankets of snow continued to accumulate outside. One frosty afternoon, my roommate, Bailey, and I were holed up in our dorm binge-watching *Gossip Girl* when I received an email that a package had arrived downstairs for me.

When I returned with what I was certain was my Halloween costume, I wrestled it from the box without bothering to cut the package open properly, already eager to beat you in your proposed contest. After freeing my prize from a mass of Styrofoam peanuts, I held the peasant-style, velvet dress against myself in the full-length mirror. Dissatisfied, I decided that a test-run was necessary, and proceeded to pull my sweats down over my ankles, yank my t-shirt over my head, and slip on the little red dress. Immediately, I noticed how short the skirt was.

"Hot," Bailey said from beneath her duvet.

"I look like a hooker," I said matter-of-factly, turning in all directions to examine myself from every angle.

Bailey rolled her eyes.

"You do not. I've seen so much worse on Halloween. You look cute. Go get your black boots," she ordered.

I pulled on my high-heeled boots to get the full effect, and I had to admit, it was a good look. At least I wouldn't be wearing lingerie disguised as a costume, as I'd seen several girls do the year before.

"Think it'll beat Wade's costume?" I asked.

"Without a doubt," Bailey confirmed.

I didn't know what your costume would be yet, but you'd hinted that you were going the cartoon route. I couldn't picture you dressed in a full-body cartoon suit, like Mickey Mouse or SpongeBob, but I was curious to see what you'd come up with.

Halloween fell on a Friday that year, which couldn't have been more perfect. When you picked me up at the train station that evening, you asked,

"Got your costume?"

I nodded, trying to maintain a poker face.

"That's good. We'll see how good it is, though, compared to mine," you boasted.

"Hey, don't get cocky. We'll see," I said, swatting you playfully.

"That's right. We'll see."

We ate a pointlessly early dinner, both of us impatiently anticipating the festivities of the evening, which wouldn't begin for several hours. It was still light out as we put the last of our dirty dishes in your washer.

"What now?" I whined, anxious to slip into costume.

"Chill out," you said, tickling my sides and making me jump. "Let's go do something."

"Like what?" I said petulantly.

"Babe…I can't make the sun set any faster. Come on," you said, reaching out your hand.

We set out on a post-dinner, pre-costume Center City escapade, subconsciously making a beeline for our go-to coffee spot, La Colombe, before coming to a surprised stop in front of the dark café about twenty minutes later.

"It's *closed*?" I pouted.

"What a shame. It was the only coffee shop in the city, too," you said, before winking at me and giving my arm a little tug.

We continued on for a few blocks until we spotted a Saxby's on the corner of Walnut Street, which seemed to me like settling for McDonald's in lieu of a steakhouse. Still, I was starting to get cold, and I decided I really just wanted a cup of coffee, regardless of where it came from.

We pushed open the door, which was lined with orange lights, and it became immediately apparent that this shop was about to close, too. The overhead lights were dimmed, and some of the chairs were already overturned on the tabletops.

"Excuse me—are you about to close?" you asked the barista.

"You have half an hour," she said. "What can I get for you?"

You, ever the manly-man, proceeded to order a plain coffee—no sugar, no cream—while I indulged in some latte of the pumpkin variety. You made a face.

"Oh, please," I teased as we grabbed a table. "Don't pretend you don't have an even bigger sweet tooth than I do."

"Not when it comes to coffee," you insisted. I raised my eyebrows at you, knowing full well you would have much preferred my latte to the bitter drink you'd ordered just to make a point. I ended up changing the subject.

"So my costume's gonna kick your costume's butt tonight."

"Those are some pretty strong words, Little Red. You sure about that?"

"I may not be Little Red," I said, attempting to throw you off. "I could be something you never see coming."

"I could say the same," you grinned.

"I'm going to win," I maintained, taking a short slurp of my coffee and setting it down with an assertive plop on the table.

"I don't think so, love."

"I will. And when I do, I'll get to say 'I told you so,' because I will have been right. Like I usually am."

"Like you usually are."

And then we were staring at each other with stupid expressions on our faces, the two of us lost in a shared and secret glance that read, *Hey, you. I know everything about you. You drive me crazy sometimes, but God, do I love you.* Outside, 1.6 million lives went about their business in this enchanting city built on the concept of "philia"—the Greek term for "affection" or "young lovers," according to Aristotle—but in an empty coffee shop on Walnut Street, it was just you and me in a world that revolved around the other.

About twenty minutes later, we were still the only guests in the café, and I could tell that the barista was getting antsy. I finally said,

"I'm just going to run to the bathroom, and then we should head back. I'm ready to win this, once and for all."

"Again—we'll see."

I left my purse and my phone with you at the table, and when I came back, I noticed my phone was turned in a different position than the one in which I'd left it.

"What did you do?" I asked suspiciously, unlocking my phone screen and checking my texts. You hadn't sent any embarrassing messages to any of my friends, so I headed to the next likely source—social media—to check for damage.

Sure enough, the most recently-posted photo on my Instagram was a goofy selfie you'd snapped on my phone, your lips downturned in an exaggerated frown, the caption reading the classic symbol for a frowning emoticon: :(

I couldn't help but laugh, because this was so classically you. I left the photo on my Instagram for years afterward, because the memory of that night—sitting in a vacant Saxby's with you—was one I would always treasure.

It was officially dark and growing colder as we began the trek back to University City. I was already shivering about five minutes into our walk, gripping your hand a little tighter to distract myself from the chill.

"Want a piggy-back ride?" you asked, stopping right there on the sidewalk of the bridge as we followed 19th Street across the river. A forceful wind swept over us from off the water, and the city lights flickered in response like flames threatening extinguishment.

"There's no way you could carry me on your back all the way back to Chestnut," I said, my words forming a small cloud as they landed beyond my nose. But it was like a dare to you, so you crouched down, your back level to me, and I climbed on, clasping my arms around your neck and locking my legs as tightly as I could around your waist.

Somehow, you carried me the full distance—twenty ounces of coffee sloshing around in your stomach the entire time—but you never once complained. You weren't the complaining type.

Back inside your apartment, I changed into my costume in the bathroom, emerging after ten minutes of sliding and tugging and tying to give you the full effect. I stepped out into the kitchen, spreading my feet in a strong stance, placing my hands on my hips.

"Wow," you said from the couch. You were wearing a simple, tight black t-shirt and a pair of shaded sunglasses. Your hair was spiked on top.

It didn't dawn on me that you were already in full-costume as I did a little twirl for you, letting you admire my get-up from all angles. It was only when I was done parading around that I stopped, gave your outfit a good, long look, and asked,

"Who the hell are you supposed to be?"

"I'm...JOHNNY BRAVO," you said, flicking your index fingers in my direction, your hands curled in the shape of fake guns.

"Interesting," I said, forcing you to stand so I could circle you. "That's it, then? The shirt and the glasses?"

"You betcha, little lady," you replied, already getting into character.

I rolled my eyes.

"I'm already sick of Johnny."

"Get used to him," you teased, wrapping me in a hug from behind and planting a kiss on my cheek. You gave me a little spank as you released me, and I squealed and darted away.

"I am SO going to win," I yelled from the bathroom, swiping on another coat of red lipstick.

An hour later, we traipsed outside hand in hand. I'd refused to wear a jacket, unwilling to take the chance of ruining the effect of my costume, but it turned out that a jacket wouldn't have actually impeded my odds of winning our little contest.

We ran into some friends of yours just outside of your apartment complex, who stopped to do that weird boy-handshake thing with you that I could never quite master, despite the fact that you had once conceded and shown me how. Their reactions to your costume were immediate.

"Wade, sick idea, man! Johnny Bravo—so original!"

I was taken aback. They *knew* you were Johnny Bravo?

"Who are you supposed to be?" one of them asked me, gesturing to my cloak like I was dressed in a sack.

"I'm...Little Red," I said in disbelief.

As they walked away and we continued on, I peered at you suspiciously from beneath the brim of my hood.

"Did you stage that?"

You began chuckling.

"I did not."

"You *did!*"

"Babe," you said, glancing sideways at me with a telling expression in your eyes. "You look hot."

I blushed a little—a compliment like that coming from you could shut me up at any given moment, even in the midst of a full-out costume war.

The entire night consisted of painful conversations with other people in crafty costumes like yours, who all acknowledged your unique idea of Johnny Bravo while asking me, with the same puzzled expression on their faces,

"Who are *you*?"

As we walked back to your apartment later, I couldn't help but feel the slightest bit dejected. Not one person had known who I was, even though it should've been obvious. I had to admit defeat.

"You win," I mumbled, the two of us taking a shortcut through the park across from your building.

"What was that?" you said, leaning down and cupping your hand around your ear.

"Careful," I said. "I could yell right into your ear."

"Well," you replied, "I must say, I never expected to hear the words from your lips. Although, I think I know why everyone was so confused."

"Really? Did I wear it wrong? You knew the whole time and didn't tell me?" I accused.

"No," you said. "I think they were confused about whether you were Red, or Miranda Kerr on the Victoria's Secret runway. You look *that* good," you said.

I smiled shyly at you from the side.

"What?" you asked.

"You win. So you get a prize."

"Do I?" you probed, playing along. "When do I collect?"

"As soon as I'm out of this itchy, freezing dress that is currently cutting off my air supply. You can even take it off—if you want," I said casually.

"It's never been a better day to be Johnny Bravo," you teased, squeezing my hand as we walked into the lobby of your building.

"Wrong. I don't want Johnny. I want Wade," I said.

Both of us were bursting with giddiness, two kids kissing in an elevator until it came to a stop with a "ding" on your floor. You carried me inside, and I locked my hands around your head to prevent you from bumping it—just in case you got too close to any doorframes.

"I love you," I told you between kisses. "I love you, I love you."

"And I love you," you said, sealing the words over my lips with a promise. "Always."

SIXTEEN.

T H E   S N O W   I N   O C T O B E R had been a harbinger of the unusually cold winter days to come. That winter, the university closed a grand total of fourteen times with each storm that hit the Philadelphia area, resulting in roughly three weeks of class cancellations and three weeks' worth of binge-watching Netflix for Bailey and me, snuggled up under our covers and venturing out only to the dining hall for our fix of greasy food.

How I miss those days of not having a care in the world. When it snowed, the world stopped. The little work I had was already done, so I spent all of my time talking to you, watching TV, and saving ideas to my Pinterest boards online. College was nothing like I've found the real world to be, where snow doesn't count as an excuse to burrow inside all day.

The only issue with the snow was that one of those fourteen storms hit the same weekend as Valentine's Day that year, making public transportation much trickier and more unpredictable than usual. I was, as always, prepared to come to you, because what good was West Chester when we could be in the city together? So, with the shuttle bus to the train station no longer running due to the cancellation of classes, I took the SEPTA bus to 69th Street Station that Friday afternoon.

69th Street was nothing like 30th Street Station. It was not nearly as clean or convenient or safe as 30th Street, and it serviced buses and subways only, which dropped their passengers in the middle of the extremely sketchy Upper Darby neighborhood. Very few commuters took these buses into and out of the city. They were more commonly used by inner-city residents to ride short distances from point A to point B.

When my bus came to a stop at the 69th Street platform an hour and a half after I'd boarded, I all but flung myself at you in sheer relief. It had been cramped, smelly, and foul on that bus, but it was worth it to be in your arms again.

"Let's get you home," you said, kissing the top of my head as you took my bag.

We descended the steps into the subway area beneath the bus station, and in no time we were flying through the black tunnels, the street numbers going down with each stop. You squeezed my hand at 34th Street, and together we made our way through the sliding doors and out into the relentless snow.

Neither of us could get to your apartment fast enough, the cold already setting in deep beneath our skin. It was projected to drop to -8 degrees that weekend, the intolerably cold air already hinting at the sub-zero chill to come.

When we finally pushed through the doors of your building into the warm lobby, we exhaled in relief as though we'd been stranded on the plains of the tundra for days.

"I have a surprise for you that will help make up for the miserable trek here," you promised in the elevator.

"I highly doubt that," I mumbled, my lips still thawing from the bite of the wind.

"You'll see. There are a few surprises, actually," you clarified, rubbing my small, frozen hands in yours in an attempt to warm them.

When you opened your apartment door, the most wonderful smell was wafting through the air. You were cooking, and the best part was that the kitchen was even warmer than the lobby had been.

"I'm going to put your stuff down," you said, "but you should check out the bathtub in the meantime."

The bathtub? I thought dubiously.

So I peeked into your bathroom, which smelled like lemon instead of piss and sweat for the first time ever. I took a cautious step inside and noticed all at once that everything was uncharacteristically clean—there were fresh towels, a clean toilet, and a sparkling clean bathtub. You'd placed a bouquet of roses on the countertop, and had balanced a LUSH Cosmetics paper bag containing one lavender bath bomb on the wall of the tub.

I stared in shock for a moment, drinking it all in. When I looked back, you were at the stove, smiling down at the pan as you stirred our favorite broccoli dish.

"You should take a bath—get warmed up. I'll handle dinner. Did you bring a dress?"

I nodded, still unsure of whether I could speak.

"Change into it when you're done," you said.

It was unlike you to do anything quite this thoughtful. On most special occasions, I had to remind you just to get me a card, yet somehow, you'd managed to pinpoint exactly what I'd love the most: a warm bath in a clean tub—complete with a bath bomb—and dinner waiting for me, afterward.

I tied my hair up and slipped into the tub with the book I'd brought, bubbles fizzling all around me as I let the residual chill from outside melt away. I proceeded to spend a solid twenty minutes in your bathroom, appreciating hot water like never before, when you knocked on the door and opened it a crack to tell me that dinner was ready.

"This is so improper," I joked, slipping deeper beneath the bubbles. "We haven't even had dinner together, yet."

"Don't you worry about that," you replied, winking

at me as you closed the door softly behind you.

I dried off and changed into a black Juicy Couture dress, letting my hair cascade around my shoulders before I stepped out into the kitchen, where I was promptly floored all over again.

You'd set the table with candles, a bottle of sparkling cider, a bottle of wine, and two plates full of steak, mashed potatoes, broccoli, and perfectly-sliced bread. In the background, you'd found a YouTube video of a crackling fire to play on the TV, and you had your phone set to a Pandora station that played jazzy, romantic music.

"This is too much," I half-laughed, blown away at the sight of everything, and at the sight of you, especially. You'd changed into a white button-down shirt—sleeves rolled to the elbows, just the way I liked—and a pair of black slacks with dress shoes.

"Wait," you said suddenly, as though you'd forgotten something. And you went barreling toward the bathroom, reemerging with the bouquet of roses, which you placed in the middle of the table.

"Ta-da!" you exclaimed, grabbing a single rose and pinching it between your lips.

I laughed for a few seconds before I threw myself at you, hugging you with all of my strength and still feeling like it wasn't enough. You held me tight in response as you whispered, "Happy Valentine's Day, love," in my ear. I shuddered a little the way I always did, the effect of your breath on my skin never failing to make me react, and stood on my tiptoes to kiss you. I would've turned that kiss into a full-on make out session had you not started chuckling and closed your lips.

"Let's eat before it gets cold," you said.

I let you help me into my chair, and the two of us sat

down to the most romantic meal we ever shared. We would experience some of the best restaurants in the city over the course of our college years for several of our anniversaries, but in my opinion, that Valentine's Day dinner topped them all.

"I have something for you," you told me, once we'd cleared our plates.

I took a sip of wine and laughed some more over how damn perfect everything was.

"I have something for you, too—but honestly, after all of this, you didn't need to get me anything," I said.

"Maybe I wanted to," you replied. And then you pulled a little white box from your pocket.

When I opened it, a 14-karat gold Pandora charm popped out at me—a little lock in the shape of a heart with a key attached.

"This is…beautiful," I said. "I am literally the luckiest girl in the world."

You pretended to think about it, and then agreed,

"Yes. Today, you are. Today, you get the princess treatment. And possibly every other day for the rest of your life."

I rolled my eyes.

"A bouquet of roses and a bath bomb waiting for me every night? *That* kind of princess treatment?"

You reconsidered.

"Well…every Valentine's Day," you finally said, smirking.

My gift seemed like nothing compared to yours, but it had taken a lot of time to put together. I handed you a CD with the words, "To Wade, Love Morgan—V Day" written on it, and you played it through your DVD player.

My own rendition of "Can't Help Falling in Love" came

pouring through your speakers, and you sat back and closed your eyes, letting my voice wash over you. You loved it when I sang. I'd known this would be a gift you'd appreciate.

"That was amazing," you said when it was over.

I shrugged. "It's not as amazing as everything you did for me tonight, but it has a lot of sentimental value. I fall in love with you every time I see you. I'll fall in love with you every day for the rest of my life."

You enfolded my hand in yours and leaned across the table to kiss me again.

~

THE NEXT MORNING, a full-blown blizzard swept through the city, making Friday's flurries seem tame by comparison. You rolled over in bed and planted a sleepy kiss on my lips before reaching for the blinds to peer through the window.

"It's coming down," you said. So I snuggled closer to you, burrowing into the side of your arm like it was the only thing to do, given the snow-pocalypse occurring outside. You smelled pleasantly of morning—different from your usual scent. In reality, it was probably just the smell of your skin mixed with the slightly sour smell of sweat, but I would've bottled it if I could've. I still miss the way your solid white t-shirts smelled on you first thing in the morning—miss the way your sandy hair stuck out in all directions, and how you walked around in glasses and your UGG slippers for hours before we finally thought about doing something with our day.

We ended up making pancakes from scratch and watching SpongeBob reruns until noon. Then you switched the station to play Call of Duty while I sat next to you on the couch, curled up with *Great Expectations* like the typical English major that I was.

I looked up every so often to catch bits and pieces of your progress, watching as your fingers jumped and twitched over the buttons of the controller with each kill you scored. Finally, I insisted,

"Let me try."

You raised your eyebrows.

"Oh-kay," you sing-songed, smirking already as you handed me the controller.

When my round started, I took a few tentative steps forward, whirling the barrel of my gun every which way as I struggled to get my bearings. The next thing I knew, I was dead.

"What?" I said, my voice rising. "Are you kidding me? I didn't even see anyone! How is that possible? Re-start it!" I demanded. And you did, laughing hysterically at the way I jumped each time someone shot me and the game re-started.

I eventually handed the controller back to you.

"This is a sick, sick game," I muttered, heading for your room.

"Where are you going?" you asked, but I waved your question away. I was going to do what I always did when I was staying at your place: clean.

I spent the next two hours making your bed, organizing your desk, vacuuming your carpets, scrubbing the stains off of your stove and microwave, putting away the last of the dirty dishes from breakfast, and wiping down the countertops and kitchen table. Thankfully, you'd tackled the bathroom for my visit, or I would've had to go in with elbow-length gloves to take on the horrors that would've awaited me there.

You'd eventually begun doing homework as I cleaned, and I couldn't help but feel that the whole situation was pleasantly domestic. I liked being your little housewife. God knows, I wasn't the submissive type, but I didn't mind when it came to you—you were the type of man who made me *want* to be submissive. I liked taking care of you in such a genuinely feminine way. I always would.

I helped you do your laundry later that night, and when you brought your warm clothes back upstairs from the wash room, fresh out of the dryer, you dumped them on your bed and I dove beneath them, basking in the warmth like a cat on a windowsill. You'd snapped a photo of me in that pile of clean laundry, cracking up as I covered myself in your fresh-smelling socks, your sweats, your shirts, because I was thrilled with the pleasant warmth and because I knew I looked crazy.

Then Sunday came—the day that was projected to be -8 degrees—and I procrastinated going to Mass for as long as possible. We'd woken up too late to catch the 11 a.m., but there was a 5 p.m. Mass at the Newman Center up the street from your apartment, about six blocks away.

I went to Mass every single Sunday without fail, and sometimes, you came with me, but only because you knew it was generally my expectation. You usually followed me into a pew without genuflecting and sat with me for the hour without reciting any of the responses or following along in the hymnals. You wouldn't even say the Our Father when the time came for the congregation to recite it. I tried not to let this bother me—I told myself it only mattered that you were there. At least I had successfully persuaded you not to receive Communion—which was a sacrilege—without first going to confession if you were in a state of mortal sin.

Because your university's Newman Center generally didn't offer convenient confession times, I was usually in the same boat as you, refraining from receiving the Eucharist as my heart broke a little more each time. Sometimes, I'd cry during the Mass—my split life affected me so deeply—but if I felt the tears begin to form when you were sitting beside me in the pew, I quickly blinked them back. I knew you wouldn't understand, and I didn't know how I could possibly take any action to resolve the situation. I didn't want to think about, nor could I fathom, what it would be like to stop sleeping with you. I loved that part of our relationship—treasured it, because it was so good with you. And, in the back of my mind, I wondered how much we'd have left—how much we'd struggle—without that aspect of our relationship to bind us together.

During my short time as a psychology major, I'd studied a term called cognitive dissonance, which is the state of having inconsistent thoughts, beliefs, or attitudes. I became all too familiar with the definition of this term as it applied to my life, because I was never just *at peace* with myself, and with what I believed. If I felt too strongly pulled in the direction of my faith, that left me at odds with our relationship, and the person I was with you. When I was sucked completely into your orbit, which was always, living my faith was the furthest thing from easy.

I was a master of justifying, of conveniently forgetting. I told myself constantly that I wouldn't be in this predicament once we were married. I reasoned that making love with you would no longer be a sin in three years, in two years. What I didn't realize at the time was that marriage wouldn't fix the big issues—it would likely just dredge up a whole new set of them.

…But at least, if I could get you to come to Mass with me, it spoke to the fact that you cared even minimally about something so important to me.

That evening, I began preparing myself to walk through the bone-chilling weather to Mass. I pulled on three layers of shirts and sweaters before shrugging on my coat, and I wore my Sorel boots that you had gifted me at Christmas to combat the snow.

"You don't have to come," I'd said halfheartedly, hoping against hope that you would insist on accompanying me anyway, if only to help block the force of the freezing wind.

But you didn't. And while I didn't hold it against you, it was something I filed away for the future when I began to seriously consider what our relationship was made of. You let me walk through the darkness on my own, making my way up the hilly streets to the church as the icy air penetrated my jeans and pricked my legs, stinging the way I hadn't known the cold could.

When I finally reached the church after what had felt like a small pilgrimage, I selected a pew in the back, as I usually did, and knelt in prayer, doing the best I could to have a sincere conversation with God. I felt guilty when I prayed most of the time, knowing full well that I was in love with the very sins I confessed—with the very sins that left me so far removed from the God I still loved.

Please be patient with me, I prayed. It was my go-to when I couldn't find the words for anything else. *Be patient with me. Someday, I'll get it right.* This was closely followed by: *Change Wade's heart. Please bring him home to you, in your mercy. Amen.*

I sat through the Mass half-hoping that you'd surprise me and show up, but deep down, I knew better. Afterward, when I began the trek back to your apartment, I was surprised to meet you a few blocks down from the church. You'd been walking your bike up the remainder of the hill until you spotted me, apparently concerned enough to escort me back.

"You're crazy," you said, the cold darkness of the night biting our cheeks as we made our way back.

I remember thinking that even if I seemed crazy, I had done the right thing. I would go to Mass every single Sunday, no matter what life threw at me. At the very least, I could stop into God's house for an hour on a Sunday and show Him in the smallest way possible that I still loved Him.

...Even though, when it came down to it, I kept choosing you.

SEVENTEEN.

T H E   W E A T H E R   R E M A I N E D bitterly cold for southern Pennsylvania in the weeks that followed, but when we wanted to explore Philly together, frostbite warnings generally weren't enough to keep us inside.

The last weekend in February was accompanied by more of the same glacial temperatures, but we'd already decided that we would brave the walk to Rittenhouse Square to do some shopping. The skyscrapers made the city a wind tunnel, and when we stepped outside, it was a struggle for you to even hold the door open for me.

"Whoooo!" you howled, the wind already whipping at your cheeks. "Sure you want to go out in this?"

"Well, I don't want to stay cooped up inside all day," I said.

"I could make it worth your while," you replied, smiling slyly.

I rolled my eyes, smirking as I pushed past you onto the sidewalk.

The whole point was to be outside—away from your room, where you and I could have easily stayed for days in your bed, tangled up in each other. I was trying to behave myself that weekend. I'd just gone to confession the Sunday before.

...But I didn't tell you that, because I knew you'd take it the wrong way.

You grabbed my hand as we continued down Chestnut Street, making a beeline for Rittenhouse.

"So where to, first?" you asked. "It'd be nice to be able to feel my face again."

"You're so dramatic," I teased, but my own nose felt

pricked by a thousand tiny needles as it protruded into the harsh air. "Why don't we start with Barbour? I want to see if I can find a woman's jacket as stylin' as yours is."

"Nothing tops my Barbour jacket," you boasted, rolling your shoulders back so I could appreciate the way you filled it out.

"I mean…it is flattering on you," I admitted.

"Mm, yeah?" you asked. You always basked in whatever compliments I tossed your way, even though you should've been used to my singing your praises at that point.

"Oh, come on," I said. "You know how I feel about you in that jacket."

"Maybe I just like hearing it," you said.

And you really did look *that* good, Wade. Whenever I saw you, I saw fireworks, but I was especially enthralled by the sight of you in that jacket, your thick, blond hair combed to the side, your Red Wing boots peeking out from under the hems of your raw denim jeans. You were suave without trying, but too genuinely good and kind to take yourself too seriously. No matter how frequently I complimented you, you never really saw what I saw in you. It was one of the many reasons why I loved you.

As we approached Rittenhouse, we all but sprinted the rest of the way to the Barbour store, rushing inside and exhaling in relief as a blast of warm air greeted us.

"Women's jackets are over here," you said, leading me toward the back of the store by the hand.

"I see you spend a lot of time in here," I observed, my tone infused with levity.

"Don't judge," you said.

I studied the rows of different styles of waxed cotton jackets before sliding one in particular off of a hanger and over my shoulders. I pulled up the furry hood around my head for experimental purposes.

"Wow, Morgan," you said, before I'd even found a mirror.

When I stepped into the dressing room and posed before the floor-length, I saw what you'd meant. The jacket nipped in at my waist, and was perfectly cut for my petite proportions. I immediately checked the price tag.

$475.

"You need that jacket," you insisted. But I shook my head.

"With what money am I going to buy this?" I whispered, the salesman already beginning to eye us from the front counter. Your own jacket had been a Christmas gift from your parents.

You fell silent, then checked the tags.

"It's the Kelsall style. Just remember that," you told me, pulling out your phone to snap a photo of me in it.

I'd thought, *yeah, right. OK.*

But later on, you'd texted my mother the picture and the style name, and she bought it for me for Christmas that year. After that, we'd walk around in the cooler weather perpetually matching, equally stylish in our fancy English jackets. We both got a kick out of it.

When we finally left Barbour, we ventured into totally different territory: the Army Navy Surplus Store, which you'd been talking about exploring for the last several months. Every time you mentioned it, I found a way to distract you or change the subject, as I didn't want you getting too attached to the idea of camouflage or combat boots. That day, though, I finally acquiesced, letting you pull me through the front door and into a museum of sorts, each rack invaded by an overwhelming number of musty uniforms.

I followed you around a rack of Navy gear and watched as you pulled a Captain's hat off one of the shelves, fitting it over your straw-colored hair. You smoothed the sides with your palms before stepping in front of the nearest mirror to see whether the cap suited you.

My reaction was immediate and uncontrollable, almost an impulse.

"Hi. Come here," I said, taking a few steps to close the gap between us.

You grinned goofily, sliding your hands onto my hips and planting a quick kiss on my eager lips.

"Nope," I said, pulling you in closer again after you'd ended the kiss.

"Morgan," you protested, chuckling and grabbing my hands. "We're in public."

"Uh-huh," I said. "OK. Noted. Come back, though."

You rounded one of the racks, attempting to keep some distance between us as you hid behind a row of bomber jackets.

"Help, I'm being stalked," you joked.

I finally caught you by surprise as I took an unexpected turn and came face to face with you, placing my small hands firmly on your cheeks and standing on my tiptoes to kiss you like I meant it.

When you finally took the hat off, I realized that it made no difference to me. All I wanted to do for the rest of the day was kiss you inappropriately, onlookers be damned. Still, we managed to control ourselves for a while longer as we finished our shopping, stopping into LUSH so I could pick up a bath bomb for later that night, followed by Miel Patisserie to stock up on French macarons. You were allergic to the almond meal they were made with, but you were always considerate about the fact that I had to have them whenever I came to Philly. Sometimes, you would surprise me with a box waiting at your apartment when you picked me up from the train station.

"What are you in the mood to eat for dinner, babe?" you asked, after we'd shopped for the better part of the afternoon. "Maybe we can grab something down here since we're already out."

"Any recommendations?" I asked, already excited over the prospect of dinner in the city. Despite the fact that we ate out fairly frequently, each experience was a real treat. The food was always top-notch wherever we went, not to mention that each dinner felt like a true, romantic date with you, making me giddy like we were both sixteen again.

"I've heard about this place called The Village Whiskey. They supposedly have the best burgers in Rittenhouse. And, you know…whiskey. We could try it out."

I was not a fan of whiskey by any means, but you'd sold me on the burger part, so we called an Uber and rode the remaining few blocks to the restaurant. The wind, at that point, had become absolutely unbearable as the last rays of sun succumbed to the horizon.

The restaurant was cozy and romantic with its dimly-lit ambience, and the cherrywood bar at the center of the dining room was clearly the focal point. It was a small place, but perfectly intimate for date night.

"Table for two," you announced to the hostess when we walked inside, moving slightly ahead of me to handle the arrangements.

"Follow me right this way," she said, leading us to a round, wooden high-top in a private corner. We pretended to study our menus for a while, but we both knew we were going to get a trademark burger. We each ordered *Mad Men*-reminiscent drinks—you'd selected an Old Fashioned, and I'd opted for a $14 Whiskey Sour, expecting that the overpowering taste of liquor would be diluted with the sweetness of other ingredients. The presentation looked nice enough, with a bright maraschino cherry poised on top, so I'd assumed that it would at least be somewhat palatable; however, when our drinks came out and I took a tentative sip, I immediately fought the urge to gag. You laughed at the face I made.

"Hate it that much, huh?" you asked.

I crinkled my nose. "Let me try again."

I took another sip, but it didn't go down any smoother the second time.

When our food came out, you'd nearly finished your own drink, so I slid my still-full glass in your direction.

"Have at it," I said.

"You don't want it? Seriously?" you asked, raising it to your lips. Then, "Oh my gosh. You don't like this? How is that possible? It's so good!"

"Clearly I overestimated my taste for dark liquor."

As we ate, you took sips of my drink, finishing a little more than half of it before the waitress cleared our empty plates from the table.

"Morgan," you said, leaning into me and lowering your voice like you were confessing to murder, "I have to go to the grocery store."

I raised my eyebrows.

"Why's that?"

"Because," you said, "I need to get food for this week. Also, we're out of cookie dough."

"Oh no! Not *cookie dough*!" I reacted, playing along. It's safe to say that you were a little drunk at that point, and it was actually kind of endearing, not to mention entertaining.

"I KNOW!" you exclaimed. "Waitress!"

I slid my hand over my forehead in an attempt to cover my face as our poor waitress came rushing back to the table.

"Check, please."

And before we knew it, we were back on the streets of Philly, making our way as quickly as we could to Trader Joe's. The wind was absolutely brutal, especially since we were walking against it this time. You tried to walk in front of me to shield me, laughing every now and then over nothing, as I silently resented you for your beer coat and for having a good time.

When we finally arrived at Trader Joe's, you grabbed a basket, and the two of us set off down the aisles in search of tortillas, burger meat, broccoli, and the cookie dough that you couldn't live without. *Everything* was causing you to burst into hysterics, and I began to grow irritated over the fact that I wasn't in on the private joke.

"Wade," I said, my voice taking on a tone (which you promptly laughed at).

"What?" you chuckled, nearly tripping again over the perfectly-flat floor.

"You're drunk," I whispered, grabbing onto your arm.

"And whose fault is that?" you teased, poking me in the ribs. I jumped and attempted to poke you back, but you darted out of reach, taking off around the next aisle.

"All right. I see how it is," I muttered, starting after you.

I chased you around that grocery store for what must have been a solid ten minutes, which sounds like nothing but is actually an infuriating amount of time to engage in such silly activity. By the time you allowed me to catch up with you, I didn't know whether I was still annoyed or whether I was actually having fun. You caught me by my elbows as I came hurtling toward you, laughing and kissing my cheeks until my face folded into an unstoppable smile. A few shoppers stopped and stared, confused over our strange game, but neither of us cared.

We got in line to check out, and after the cashier rang up our purchases, you put your free arm around my shoulders, kissed the top of my head, and—suddenly sober— said,

"Let's go home."

Home. Home was anywhere I was with you.

EIGHTEEN.

YOUR RUGBY SEASON STARTED again in March, and I'd been dreading it since your last concussion. I'd still hoped you would decide to quit—that you wouldn't want to chance getting hurt again—but I suppose you wouldn't have been the all-American, red-blooded man I knew and loved if you'd quit because you'd gotten hurt. I never did understand the obnoxious male bravado that seems to dismiss any potential for danger when it comes to taking risks.

It was a surprisingly balmy day for your first game of the spring season; I felt the tickle of sweat beneath my sweater as I tried to keep up with your fast pace. You were a man on a mission when you wanted to be. You slid your bulky athletic bag further over your right shoulder and gripped my hand tightly, chattering to me about the importance of good nutrition, proper hydration, and ample stretching before a game, as though I were about to take the field with you. I was mostly silent as you spoke, nodding absentmindedly in response because I was only half-listening. I was too busy worrying about whether you'd be safe.

"I feel great right now," you assured me as we headed into the gated field area. You must've seen the anxiety written all over my face, the concern shining in my eyes, and I could tell that you felt bad. It was simply that rugby was too important to you to care much about something as trivial as a potential injury. Rugby was your football replacement, your home away from home, and I couldn't pretend I didn't understand that. In reality, I think I understood your motivations better than you did, sometimes.

I walked over with you to where the team was preparing for the game, grimacing as I caught glimpses of foreign paraphernalia like athletic cups and slimy, smelly mouthpieces that had clearly never seen disinfectant.

I stood awkwardly against the outer wall of the locker room as you were greeted with slaps on the back and variations of weird manshakes. Nobody spoke to me, but I was just fine with that. I was already feeling a bit awkward, as though I were an outsider spying on the rituals of a secret club.

"Babe," I called, and you jogged over to me. "I'm going to go grab a spot on the grass. Good luck, OK?"

You planted a kiss on my lips before rejoining your teammates in front of the locker room.

You took the field about fifteen minutes later, and you and your team did that weird thing where two guys were lifted into the air by their teammates to either catch or throw the ball—I never understood the nuances of such a perplexing game.

I finally reached a point where I was tired of trying to keep up—I was about 90% sure your team was winning, and I couldn't take the anxiety of worrying every time I watched you dive for the ball. I cracked open the book I'd brought with me and rested my back against the gate, settling into the ivory pages of *Drown* by Junot Diaz. I had learned long ago never to go anywhere without a book...just in case. You never knew when you might need it.

The game continued on for over an hour, and I felt like shooting myself. You'd always made a point of reminding me that rugby games were "eighty minutes—much shorter than football games!" in a futile attempt to soften my heart to the sport, but I had yet to experience a simple, eighty-minute game. All I really knew was that you played A side, which was sort of like first string in football, and that game lasted for an hour and twenty minutes before B side played its own game. Sneaky bastard—you lied, because even though technically, games *were* eighty minutes each, you stayed for both games. Which meant that *I* stayed for both games, or 160 minutes—about the length of the average football game.

I sighed and leaned hard into the gate behind me, but was quickly startled by the crackling of dead foliage. I turned to find an older man watching the game from the outside, fingers hooked around the metal rings of the gate.

"Say, what is this game?" he asked me, his eyes following the boys across the field.

"It's rugby," I answered, proud that I was able to give him this much information.

"Rugby, huh? I've never seen it before," he said.

Just then, the team gathered in a large circle which I called "the group hug" (but I never told you that), and it was a tremendous struggle of arms pushing against bodies, weight shifting back and forth as though you were all singing "Kumbaya" around a campfire.

"What are they doing?" the man asked in confusion.

I shrugged. "Beats the hell out of me. I think they do this to determine who gets the ball next."

When I turned around again, the man was gone. I didn't blame him—in fact, I was jealous. I wished I could've followed him.

I checked the scoreboard and saw that there were seconds left in the game, and your team was ahead. Another win—probably resulting in an excuse to throw another skeevy party. Nevertheless, I was happy for you. I knew you must've been thrilled. Better yet, you'd made it through the game without getting hurt.

But of course, because Murphy's Law dominated each time you were on an athletic field, you were hit right in the back of your head during the last ten seconds of the game, and it looked like a hard hit. The next thing I knew, you were on the ground. And you weren't getting up.

Every cell in my body froze, and my eyes glazed over with frustrated tears.

He has another concussion. Another freaking concussion. I knew it as surely and as strongly as I'd known you'd be important to me when I saw you for the first time in high school.

I realized vaguely that I had, at some point, risen from my spot on the grass and was running along the edge of the field frantically, never taking my eyes off of you. Your coach and the athletic trainer were crouched over you, much like the last time, making you follow the small beam of light with your eyes.

I came to a stop near the sidelines and waited for what felt like an eternity. It was only after a considerable amount of time that you finally sat up and were helped to your feet, walking slowly back to the sidelines. People applauded because you were standing again, but not one of them had any idea of the ever-growing terror I'd experienced in those last five minutes. It didn't mean a damn thing that you were standing, that you were walking now. Sure as day, you had another concussion, and I didn't need it confirmed by a doctor or trainer to know it intuitively.

I hurried over to where you were seated on the sidelines. You were talking to your coach, but I didn't care. I interrupted,

"How do you feel? What happened?"

You smiled over your shoulder at me and squeezed my

hand.

"I'm OK," you replied.

But you're not, I thought. And then I heard your coach tell you,

"You should take it easy for a while. Maybe sit out next week's game, see how you feel. You don't want a bad concussion."

Everything inside of me snapped, and I stormed off the field. Next thing I knew, I was power-walking through the parking lot and launching myself onto the streets of West Philly, not caring that my purse was flopping against my thigh or that I would probably scuff my boots running this way. Finally, the tears could flow freely.

I was so angry that I didn't even care that I was running through a low-income neighborhood, the residents of those dilapidated homes staring at me because I stuck out like a sore thumb with my designer jeans and petite frame. Still, I would've willingly punched anyone who tried to approach me directly in the nose without hesitation.

It took me a few minutes to realize that I didn't know what I'd do once I reached your apartment, but I'd known that I couldn't just sit there—that I couldn't talk to you or even look at you after you'd allowed this to happen to yourself again.

I felt my phone buzzing in my purse. I took it out, saw your name on the display screen, and promptly hit "ignore." I continued to walk, finally rounding the corner onto your campus.

My phone buzzed again.

Sighing, I realized I couldn't even get into your building unless you were with me, so I hit "accept" and pressed the phone to my ear.

"Morgan? Where are you?"

"I left," I said coldly, stopping in the middle of the side-walk.

"Come back," you implored.

"I will not."

"Please?"

"No," I replied, thin-lipped and choking on phlegm after having cried so much.

"I'll tell you what...I don't know where you are, but at least turn back in the direction of the field? I'll meet up with you."

I hung up, already turning around despite the fact that my feet would've loved to continue walking all the way back to West Chester. I was too furious to deal with you.

He's never going to be the same, my intuition whispered.

I finally caught up with you close to the field, though I refused to meet your eyes.

"Hey," you murmured, trying to lift my chin with your fingers. I obstinately turned away.

"You have a concussion."

"We don't know that," you said. "The coach said I could be fine. So did the trainer. I just have to watch for the symptoms, but honestly, I feel OK. The hit wasn't even that bad."

"Then why did you stay on the ground for so long?" I demanded.

After some time, you finally replied, "I felt fine, but I didn't want to move in case anything was wrong."

That was a lie, and we both knew it. I turned away from you, beginning my second flight down the same godfor-saken street.

"Wait!" you said, struggling to catch up with me.

"Why should I? You're hurt again, and you're lying to me on top of it?!" I yelled.

You didn't refute that you'd twisted the truth, but I let you take my hand, and together we walked dejectedly to your apartment.

"We'll go back, you'll ice the back of your head, and I'll make you dinner," I said. At least I was there to take care of you.

"To be honest, I feel fine right now. We could go out to dinner. We could walk by the river. It's a really nice night," you said. But then I looked at you like, *what are you thinking?* And we walked the rest of the way in silence, defeated.

I spent the rest of the night counting the minutes you spent with the ice pack on and off, preparing your dinner, asking how you felt. When we went to sleep, I didn't *actually* sleep—I continually awoke to place my hand over your chest and make sure you were breathing, as though a side effect of concussions was the sudden onset of sleep apnea.

Sometime around 1 a.m., you stirred, looking blearily at me through narrow eyes.

"Wade," I said, having been wide awake for the last two hours. "Wade, you have to promise me you'll stop playing rugby."

You didn't respond, so I placed my hand on your shoulder and repeated myself.

"Can we talk about this in the morning?" you asked, already rolling over in an attempt to get away from me. I followed close behind you.

"Wade, unless you promise me right now that you'll stop playing, I'm going to have to break up with you. For my own sanity. Please. Promise me. Mean it."

"...I promise," you said groggily, but I knew you'd heard me. Surprisingly, that was the last of the conversation, because even you'd known you were getting hurt too much to continue playing as though you hadn't already experienced four blows to the head over the last four years.

The next day was Sunday, and you'd woken up feeling better than the night before, so we made breakfast together, and then I changed for Mass. I told you that you should stay in and rest while I went alone, but this time around— probably out of sheer intransigence—you wouldn't hear of it.

"I'm fine. I can go," you said.

You took a shower and changed, and we walked the six blocks to the church in silence. It was another warm day, and by the time we got to Mass, I could tell you weren't feeling well at all. Your eyes were glazed over, and you were repeatedly rubbing the base of your head and the top of your neck. Finally, after the Gospel reading, I whispered,

"We should leave."

You shrugged. "I can stay. I'm OK."

Nevertheless, I proceeded to pull you into the aisle and out into the afternoon sunshine.

"I think you should call your parents," I said softly.

"I kind of think I should, too."

I knew that if you called your parents, it would mean I'd have to go back to West Chester, but I didn't care—I just wanted you to do whatever was necessary to heal.

When you reached your mother on the phone and explained what had happened, I listened to her promptly freak out on the other end of the line.

"Why didn't you call yesterday?" she asked, her agitation reverberating through the speaker.

I shot you a guilty look. You hadn't called your parents because you hadn't wanted them to pick you up—you'd wanted to stay with me, and I was equally to blame. I hadn't wanted to leave. *I'd* wanted to be the one to take care of you, to give you ice packs and Advil and make all of your meals while you recovered. I wanted to be able to do for you what your parents could. I wanted you to be able to depend on me always, for everything.

"I don't know. I was waiting for it to get better, and it's only gotten worse."

"OK. Just hang tight; Dad will come pick you up."

You ended the call, and we walked back to your apartment, where I made you lie down on your bed with the blinds closed as I took the ice pack from the freezer again.

"I should go now. He'll be here soon," I told you, stroking your hand. But then I started to cry—you always made me cry, even if it was completely unintentional—and I turned away to pack up my stuff.

You said my name anxiously and patted the space next to you on your bed, but I kept packing, determined not to let you see me this way.

I heard sniffling after a few moments and turned around. You were crying, too.

It was stupid, but the whole situation felt like the end of the world. I didn't know how much worse you'd be the next time I saw you. I wanted you to be all right so badly—would've given my own health for you to recover from that concussion the way you'd recovered from all the others.

But I'd known you wouldn't, and on some level, I'd been right.

When I finished packing, I cried into your armpit for a little while, and you smoothed my hair and tried to comfort me.

My bus was arriving in forty-five minutes, so I needed to leave sooner rather than later to arrive at 69th Street Station on time. I lifted my head from under your arm and gave you a soft kiss on your forehead, tears still spilling down my cheeks. I'd secreted more salt in the last twenty-four hours than I had in the past year.

"Please feel better," I told you, throwing my bag over my shoulder.

"I'm worried about your safety...you've never gone to 69th by yourself before," you said.

"I'll be fine. I can take care of myself," I said, but I don't think I totally convinced either of us. We were both used to you taking care of me.

"I love you."

"I love you more," you replied.

But as I walked out the door, I smiled a little to myself at the knowledge that you would never, could never, love me more than I loved you.

NINETEEN.

AS I'D PREDICTED, YOU NEVER did fully recover from that final concussion. You complained of symptoms for months following your injury, and I'd begged you to make an appointment with a neurologist, but you never did. You paid a few visits to your old trainer a few times to have him check you over, and you also got a CAT scan, which showed no unusual swelling or signs of damage to your brain. You were content with those results, despite the fact that your head continued to ache, but I'd always wished you'd sought further treatment. Even up until the time we broke up two years later, you would continue to complain of bad headaches, nausea, and neck stiffness.

The summer following your concussion, we were apart for a month or so while I studied abroad in Paris. A week before I was due to leave, I'd caught a bad cold, which had turned into a sinus infection. I was still recuperating when it came time to pack and prepare to leave, and my parents had given me the option to stay home if I wasn't feeling up to traveling, despite the fact that every aspect of the trip had been non-refundable. I remember how close I'd come to simply chickening out and cancelling—I was terrified to board a plane to a foreign country entirely on my own, not knowing who or what would be waiting for me once I landed at Charles de Gaulle. But something in me had always longed for adventure, so I'd insisted I was well enough for travel and left for Paris a few days later. To this day, it remains one of the best experiences of my life.

Paris wasn't anything like I'd imagined it would be. It is

a city that is generally romanticized and glamorized, but I'd stayed in a little apartment just a few blocks away from the Gambetta metro station on Line 3—a decidedly artsy neighborhood in northeastern Paris—away from the bustle of the touristy areas surrounding the Champs Elysees and the Eiffel Tower. In fact, the population dominating the area is described online as "straddling a line between bourgeois and bohemian."

I had always enjoyed the concept of being bohemian, despite the fact that I generally had a very classic, streamlined sense of style and preferred the comfort of 4-star hotels to stark hostel rooms. I liked being able to tell people that I'd stayed in a little-known, non-touristy area of Paris, and had gotten to know the city for what it *actually* was rather than for what most people imagine it to be when they hear the word "Paris." My apartment complex was a dated building facing a restaurant along one side of the street, with several small boutiques, restaurants, cafes, and boulangerie shops lining the adjacent street leading uphill to the metro station.

That entire month was a whirlwind of conversational French, art history classes in the Louvre, giant macarons the size of my face, and hopping trains from one city to the next each weekend with a friend I'd made in class—from Brussels to Amsterdam to Milan. I walked everywhere, save for the train and metro rides I took to travel longer distances, and drank a glass of Rosé with most dinners I prepared on my tiny stove. I was only ever able to buy enough food for one evening, because my mini-fridge didn't work, and my bed was essentially a mattress on the floor—it hovered only inches from the ground. Moreover, the air conditioning was essentially nonexistent, and there was no shower curtain in the bathroom, so I'd purchased a cheap, oversized one from a nearby shop that nearly clogged the drain each time I took a shower.

I'd loved every moment of it.

Before I'd left, you'd made a little schedule in an Excel spreadsheet that factored in the time difference between Philadelphia and Paris, highlighting the days and times that would be best for us to Skype. You'd typed a little note below the schedule: *Call me any time, day or night, and know that I love you so much.* I'd taped it to the wall above my desk, and every time I looked at it, I felt like I was reading a love note.

When I flew home at the very end of July, you were the first person to greet me at the Philadelphia airport. As I made my way through Customs after being grilled by a disgruntled Homeland Security officer, I spotted you almost immediately. You were standing in the greeting line for International Arrivals with a big bouquet of roses in your hand, and I flung my suitcase aside as soon as I saw you, sprinting to you with absolutely no intention of stopping. You caught me with all the force of reciprocated passion, sweeping me up in your arms and spinning me in circles as a stream of rose petals fell around us. I didn't care that everyone was watching—that we were the center of attention, and that we were destroying the flowers. I felt so safe, so cherished, with your hand back in mine where it belonged.

My dad arrived a few minutes after you, greeting me with the enthusiasm of a relieved father, and we drove back to my house where the rest of my family was waiting. We had a pizza party that night, and I dug out my mom's comprehensive art history textbook to show everyone the works of art I'd seen every day in the Louvre, and the Musee d'Orsay. But you seemed distracted, disinterested.

You weren't one for art *or* history, so you played for a bit on your phone as I leafed through the pages of the book. Honestly, I was a little upset by the fact that you didn't seem to care about my experiences, but when I walked you to your car later that evening, you made up for it by surprising me with something totally unexpected.

"You remember my friend, Manuel?" you asked.

I nodded. Manuel was one of your closest friends in the engineering program.

"Well...his uncle works backstage for Luke Bryan. And he happens to have two extra tickets to his concert next weekend."

I gaped at you for a few seconds before throwing my arms around you, and you shook with laughter as you returned my hug. Luke Bryan was only my favorite male country singer, and I had yet to see him live in concert.

"But...you don't like country music," I said, and you shrugged.

"I think it'll be fun. And we get to have dinner backstage with the crew before the show. Maybe even meet Luke himself."

This time, you received a big, playful smack on the lips, but then you grabbed me by the waist and deepened the kiss, pushing me up against your car just hard enough to make me lose my breath. When we resurfaced, you brushed my hair behind my ear.

"I love you. I missed you," you said, your breath dancing on my neck and making my nerve endings spark in response, like short-circuited wires.

"I missed you more," I insisted, but you silenced me again by closing your lips over mine, ending the competition as I submitted willingly to a loss.

Exactly one week later, I met you at 30th Street Station

in cowboy boots and a tank-top that read *Crash My Party*, and you were already wearing the type of black cowboy hat that's clearly made just for country concerts rather than for utility. There was no denying, though, that you looked *hot*—your dark gray t-shirt was just the right amount of tight against your muscular build, and you wore jeans and boots despite the heat. I couldn't help sliding my hand into your back pocket as we cut diagonally across the familiar parking lot that led to your apartment building.

"I might want you a little," I said, and you shot me the sideways glance I'd learned to decipher long ago that assured me you wanted me every bit as badly.

Pressed for time, we only briefly swung by your apartment to drop off my overnight bag before heading back out, catching the train to Lincoln Financial Field where we met up with Manuel and his family.

"So glad you could make it, guys!" Manuel said, greeting you with a handshake and leaning in for a hug from me.

"Thanks so much for having us, dude. We're pumped," you said.

"Well, wait till you see the show. My uncle's told me great things. Speak of the devil," he said, gesturing to a tall, broad-shouldered man who was carrying equipment through the back door.

"Hey, you must be Manuel's friends. Come on back," he said. We all too happily obliged, skipping the lines of giddy teenage girls (and a few fully-grown women) to follow the crew backstage, where Manuel's uncle gave us a tour and even showed us the set. We stood looking out at a nearly-full stadium, which I thought was the coolest thing ever, until Luke Bryan's fiddle player walked by and agreed to take a photo with me. When I posted it on Instagram, you joked that I should caption it "fiddler on the roof," which of course I hadn't been able to resist.

We were down in the pit during the concert, and it was uncomfortable to say the least, being pressing against so many people in the sweltering heat when we were both wearing heavy jeans and boots. Still, from the second Luke ran onto the stage, I forgot about the dense evening air and the moisture beneath my bra. I screamed and sang every familiar song at the top of my lungs for the rest of the night, oblivious to the crowds pushing against us because I was in your arms, where nothing could truly bother me. At times, I turned and sang the lyrics against your lips, kissing you when they were especially relevant and enjoying the feel of your hands squeezing my hips, stroking my waist.

Then Luke brought Lee Bryce onto the stage, who had apparently collaborated on the famous Eli Young Band song, "Crazy Girl," and he performed it for us. I gave your arm a little squeeze as the opening chords resounded through the hazy night air, because it was a song I'd shared with you after we'd had our first fight so many years ago. You sang it to me sometimes when you could remember the lyrics, and you murmured them into my ear that night as Lee crooned:

"We're we're gonna do what lovers do...we're gonna have a fight or two...but I ain't ever changing my mind. Crazy girl, don't you know that I love you?"

You looked directly into my eyes then like we were the only two people in that stadium, and I believed it for as long as I held your gaze. Then your breath was hot on my ear again, making my inner world fall silent as snow while my heart pounded on with each strum of the guitar.

"Silly woman, come here, let me hold you. Have I told you lately, I love you like crazy, girl?"

Wade—our soundtrack was endless, comprised of equal

parts you and me to form a strange yet harmonious compilation of *us*. I can listen to many of those songs now without much of a reaction, but this is one that I still struggle to listen to, even though there has long ceased to be an "us."

The night ended with Luke Bryan shaking a can of beer, cracking it open and spraying it on all of us in the pit. We girls screamed, and you men all hooted in appreciation, clapping as he made his way off the stage. Afterward, Manuel's parents gave us a ride back to your apartment, and I watched the perpetually-illuminated Philadelphia skyline whiz beside me through the window, thinking that there was no better city in the world in which to grow up and fall in love. I leaned against you the whole way back, your arm securely around my shoulders as you stroked my hair and talked to Manuel about the concert, and about school.

I remember thinking simply how glad I was to belong to you.

When we got back to your apartment, we barely made it through your bedroom door before we were pulling off each other's sweaty clothes with an equally matched urgency, falling onto your bed the way we'd wanted to hours before. Your lips were everywhere I wanted them to be, covering every inch of me as I writhed under the tickle of your breath.

"God, I love you," you gasped, your strong arms tightening around me as you shook, hungry and high on your desire for me.

...We fell asleep shortly after, the curve of my body a perfect fit against yours, as though we'd been tailor-made for each other.

~

162

AUGUST FLEW BY, and before long, our junior year began. I'd moved into a small, off-campus apartment with some girls I'd thought were my friends, but quickly discovered I had very little in common with them. They frequently demonstrated alcoholic tendencies, going a step beyond the average college student's fascination with booze and taking shots of Nyquil for the sole purpose of getting tipsy when there was no liquor in the house. They also habitually whispered about me when I was upstairs, exhibited passive-aggressive behavior when I returned after weekends spent with you, and generally just made my anxiety skyrocket every time I walked through the door. I didn't understand when or why they'd collectively decided to hate me, but it probably had to do with the fact that I refused to get drunk with them. In fact, when I was on campus, I was usually the one holding their heads above the toilet every Friday at 2 a.m., like clockwork.

The fact that I was so unhappy in my own apartment meant that I spent that many more weekends with you in Philly than I had the year before. I unofficially became your fourth suitemate, stowing a small pink bag of toiletries in your cabinet beneath the sink, and a set of PJs and sweats in your sock drawer.

"Don't let them intimidate you," you'd told me, after I'd proceeded to bitch to you for a solid fifteen minutes when I arrived at your place one Friday night. It was a few weeks before Christmas, and despite the fact that I'd helped my roommates decorate our apartment and make it look festive for the holidays, I wanted nothing to do with it when I had the opportunity to get away.

"But I don't know how to handle passive-aggressiveness. I don't know what I've done to warrant it," I whined.

"Let's see—you're beautiful, intelligent, kind, and don't

need alcohol to have a good time. You also have a boy-friend who loves you. I wonder what it could be?" you mused, your voice dripping with sarcasm as you reached for my hand to soothe me.

"I don't think it's jealousy," I said, shaking my head. "Wouldn't that be juvenile as hell?"

"Morgan—have you met your roommates? *They're* juvenile as hell."

You'd probably been right. Regardless, you got me through my junior year, Wade. *You* kept me sane. You'd been my best friend always, but especially that year, when I'd so often felt friendless and alone. Philadelphia was my escape, and you were always, always my home. I'd walk into your arms like I was walking through the front door of my childhood house, exhaling with the sweet relief of being able to let my guard down.

Despite our comfort with each other, the time I spent with you consisted of highs *and* lows as I continued to try to make my faith a priority in my life. If it had been up to you, you wouldn't have had anything to do with it. This remained our biggest incongruity.

One Sunday in early April, you were plowing through a mountain of homework as I prepared for Mass. As I'd predicted—as I'd been waiting for—you said,

"I think I'm gonna stick around here, if that's OK. Finish this work, clean up a bit."

"OK," I said, already struggling to accept your decision with minimal upset. It wasn't as though I didn't understand your reasoning, and you did accompany me sometimes. It wasn't the end of the world if you couldn't come with me that particular Sunday.

Still, about halfway through the Mass—sharing a pew with no one, as I so often did—I found myself seething, my sangfroid evaporating unexpectedly as I swallowed back tears. Your absence was overwhelmingly painful; it *hurt*, deeply, that you didn't want to share this central aspect of my identity with me. Even more, it hurt that you undoubtedly knew you could upset me this way, yet frequently overlooked my feelings in favor of your own selfishness.

What else could I have done—could I have said—to make you understand that my faith was important? That it was *the* most important thing in my life, apart from our relationship? It was more important to me than football had been to you, than rugby had been. Those elements of your life had been so fleeting, yet I was still present at nearly all of your games for the sole reason that I'd known they'd mattered to you. I expected the same consideration from you, but you were consistent about rarely showing up while I clung to the naive hope that someday, you would surprise me.

I all but stomped the six blocks back to your apartment, my heart pounding and my face hot. All I really knew was that I had to get away from you, even if it meant going back to my petty roommates in West Chester a half-day early.

I burst through your unlocked door a few moments later, ignoring your attempt to say hello to me as I made a beeline for your room, and for my overnight bag. I began throwing all of my crap into it without bothering to arrange things properly, intent on getting back through the door in as little time as possible. I would check the bus schedule once I was outside, but I really just needed to leave.

You followed me into your room, crouching down beside me as I tried to zip up my overstuffed duffel.

"Morgan, what are you doing? What's wrong?" you

asked frantically.

But I pushed you away, ignoring your question as I slung my bag over my shoulder and headed for your door.

"Morgan!" you cried, grabbing the strap and pulling me back. "Please, talk to me!"

"How do you not know? How is it not perfectly *obvious* to you?!" I yelled, my voice breaking against a loud sob.

I didn't have it in me anymore to flee; I was too wrecked, so I just stood there, staring at you through pools in my eyes like I was underwater.

"Hey, hey—I'm sorry," you said, your voice sincere but your sentiment tardy as you grabbed my arms, leading me toward your bed to sit. You took my bag from over my shoulder and dropped it on the floor, letting your hands come to rest on my knees.

"I had work to do, and I thought you understood that. If you had told me you really needed me to come to Mass with you, I would have. But I should have known, and I am sorry."

"Y-you d-don't know," I started, sniffling and gasping, "h-how hurt it m-makes me. Th-this is so imp-portant to m-me."

You reached toward your nightstand to grab a wad of tissues for me, and I blew my nose hard and crumpled the tissues in a ball. But you reached for them, never thinking twice about my gross snot all over your skin, and tossed them in the trash when I was done. Then you knelt, un-blinkingly, on the floor in front of me, your hands never leaving my knees and your eyes intently locked on mine. I could tell, then, that you had finally heard me. You nodded a succinct little nod, the way you always did when you'd absorbed the gravity of a matter, and repeated,

"Morgan—I am *sorry*. Really. I will be there next time,

no excuses, and I should have been there today with you." Then, looking down at my overnight bag, "You can still leave if you want. But I hope you'll stay."

The thing about me, Wade, is that I've always found forgiveness to be one of the most challenging aspects of my faith. I have trouble forgiving people over something as dumb as a simple, inconsiderate moment, let alone huge things like breaking my confidence or betraying my trust. You were slowly destroying something in me—maybe it was my hope—but all I could do was look at you, love you, and forgive you. God, it was so easy to forgive you.

I ended up staying, and when we climbed into bed that night, I convinced myself that I didn't care about anything except for the fact that I was curled in your arms, where I'd convinced myself I wanted to be forever.

TWENTY.

OUR FIVE-YEAR ANNIVERSARY arrived the following month, in April. I'd been thinking about it for weeks, occupying my mind with trivial thoughts of where we'd go for dinner and what I'd wear. Our anniversary was always, to me, an *occasion*—a celebration of the number of years we'd been together, and the fact that I believed I'd found the right person so early in life.

...In reality, it would be our last, truly happy anniversary.

The 25th fell on a Saturday, so we'd made a reservation that evening at an upscale Italian restaurant your parents had recommended in Old City. I'd worn an orange sundress that crisscrossed in the back, which had been a bit optimistic for early spring, and a pair of 4-inch Guess wedges that had rendered the act of walking a balancing routine, their stiff ridges digging against my feet as soon as I'd slipped them on.

We took an Uber to the restaurant, and as usual, you'd made small talk with the driver throughout the ride while I sat, quiet and content, beside you. To this day, I try to mimic your easygoing exchange with Uber drivers, asking them casual questions about how long their shifts last and whether it's been a busy day. It baffles me how nobody else seems to make normal conversation with people, the way you always had. Even the smallest of your personality traits had been attractive to me.

When we got to the restaurant, you held the door open for me, then stepped ahead to speak with the hostess as I glanced around, taking everything in.

The ambience was elegant, almost opulent. The walls

were reminiscent of Carrera marble, and a series of mounted lamps cast a romantic glow on the tables. The chairs were large and heavy, constructed of cherrywood with thick, plush cushions, and there was a brass sign that pointed toward a set of winding steps that led down to a wine cellar. The central theme among all of these details seemed to be *weight*; density.

When the hostess showed us to our table, we both struggled to pull in our chairs, barely getting situated before a waiter greeted us, asking whether we preferred still or sparkling water. The menus were thick as books as he handed them to us, my right wrist just scarcely able to support the weight of one.

We were always a bit out of our element at these types of places, but I thoroughly enjoyed each experience because fine dining made me feel just a little more *adult*, a little more worldly. We ignored, for one night, the gaping holes in our wallets after an anniversary dinner. We splurged each year, and it was always worth it.

"What do you think so far?" you asked, once the waiter had left us.

"It's beautiful," I said, trying to keep my voice to a whisper. I could almost hear a pin drop—it was like being in a library.

"We should check out the wine cellar later," you whispered back, and then the two of us started giggling because of how ridiculous it was that we were whispering.

"Not a salt-and-pepper fight kind of place, huh?"

"Definitely not," I agreed.

When the waiter returned, he came bearing a basket of garlic bread and pushing a fully stocked brass cart featuring fresh meats and fish, which we pretended to look over even though we already knew what we were ordering. A la carte was *definitely* out of our comfort zone.

When our meals arrived, we lifted our heavy silverware as delicately as possible to dig into our plates. You'd ordered a salmon dish, and I'd ordered a Marsala. The food was, as I'd expected, top quality.

"Dessert?" our waiter asked, after we'd polished off our entrees.

We decided on a chocolate lava cake—mostly your idea, as I was never a huge fan of chocolate—with a scoop of ice cream on the side, and it was brought out with a candle in the middle to celebrate our anniversary. We'd made a wish together, holding hands over the table, and I remember wishing for yours to be the hand I held fifty years later.

We strolled out into the evening air afterward, and I shivered as my body struggled to adjust to the drop in temperature. I hadn't wanted to bring a jacket with me, as none of the options I'd had in my closet had felt suitable enough for my outfit, or for the restaurant.

It was still somewhat light out, so the two of us walked through a nearby park that brought us to the edge of the Delaware. The sun had just slipped out of sight.

"Let's take a picture. We gotta document five years," you said, gesturing for me to stand beside you.

You tried to snap a good selfie of us on your phone with a view of the Delaware in the background, but all you'd managed to capture was a photo of our heads, our height discrepancy doing us in. Still, that picture got over a hundred likes on Facebook—all of our friends loved us together. Over the years, we had become the predictable, solid couple who would never break up. I'm sure no one saw it coming when we finally did.

It was borderline *cold* by the time we finally called for an Uber, and you wrapped your arm around me on the ride back to your apartment as a solution, your perpetual warmth a soothing antidote to the chill on my exposed shoulders.

As though on cue, almost as soon as we'd stepped through your door, your mother called with a slew of questions about what the restaurant had been like, how our food had been, what you'd ordered, what I'd ordered...and the list went on. I sat beside you on the couch as you talked, trying to be patient while I fought to keep my annoyance at bay. This weekend with you was mine, and I wasn't in the sharing mood.

"Sorry," you said apologetically, after you'd finally hung up. "I didn't expect her to talk for so long."

As a response, I padded into your room to retrieve the anniversary card I'd written for you, handing it to you as I settled onto your lap.

You and I had, for the most part, decided against anniversary presents while we were still poor, broke college kids, but cards were an expectation. Cards meant *a lot* to me. Your words were always the ultimate gift when they were sincere and thoughtfully-written.

You tore open the envelope and read my message. Smiling, you leaned over and kissed me.

"You will have your card, Morgan," you promised.

I frowned and scooted away from you on the couch, because I wasn't sure if I believed you. Most of the time, you were a hardcore procrastinator, and you'd often claim you would do things that never actually came to fruition. It was frustrating to me that you could be overwhelmingly thoughtful on a random Valentine's Day, but not on an important anniversary. Still, you'd promised me you would have a card for me, so I decided to give you the benefit of the doubt and let it go.

The following evening, we went to Mass together, and it had—pleasantly—been one of the more effortless times you'd joined me. Later, you caught up on homework while I made chocolate chip cookies from scratch in your kitchen, wearing one of your t-shirts as an apron and humming with the serenity of a good mood. I had just popped the tray into the oven when you claimed the couch at 8 p.m. to watch *Mad Men*.

"Babe," you said, patting the spot next to you.

"In a sec," I said, tossing the mixing bowl into your dishwasher.

"You're missing the first few minutes!"

"I'm *coming*. Goodness."

Mad Men was our show. We also watched a lot of *How I Met Your Mother* on Netflix, but you were always further along than I was in watching it. *Mad Men* was the one show we watched *together,* and we caught new episodes as they aired every Sunday night while I was visiting. When the cookies were ready fifteen minutes later, we ate them from a big bowl as we sat, engrossed in the episode, my feet resting on your lap.

Afterward, I got ready for bed, already anticipating the obnoxious buzzing of your intense alarm that shook the whole bed at 6:15 a.m. I'd have to catch the 7:10 train to be back at school by 8:30, an hour before my first class started. I crawled beneath the covers and fell asleep instantly as you finished the last of your homework.

I awoke to you gently shaking me about an hour later. "Morgan?"

I stirred, looking at you through beady, hostile eyes. "What?"

You held up a homemade anniversary card with the picture we'd taken in front of the Delaware River on the cover. My lips curled into a slow smile as I opened it to find a picture of a Shiba Inu dog—my favorite breed—on one side, and a beautifully-written message on the other.

"I love you," you told me, wrapping me in a hug. "I just didn't want the whole weekend to pass without giving you your card. I'm sorry it took a while to make."

"It's perfect," I told you. And then I handed it back to you to put on top of my overnight bag, already starting to slip back into sleep.

I felt you tuck me in and turn out the light before returning to the kitchen to finish your work.

TWENTY-ONE.

YOUR TWENTY-FIRST BIRTHDAY fell on a Friday, just before my first week back at West Chester as a senior. As always, you'd lived in Philadelphia through the summer, taking your classes on the necessary schedule to graduate within the five years that your program was projected to take.

All of our friends seemed to have done the same thing for their 21st birthdays—they'd gone out, gotten rip-roaring drunk on a barstool somewhere, and barely remembered any of it the next day. This was the standard for most college students. Then there was me—the girl who had celebrated her 21st birthday six months prior to yours with balloons tied to kitchen chairs, my immediate family surrounding me instead of drunken college kids. My mother had gotten me an authentic Chanel ring as a present.

I knew you so well—knew that your preference fell somewhere between those two extremes. I wanted to give you a memorable 21st birthday, with all of your friends present in a laid-back, comfortable environment. So, weeks in advance, I contacted fifteen of your friends from both high school and college, asking them to meet us at 9 p.m. on your birthday at one of our favorite little dive bars called The Blind Pig, just off the Spring Garden subway stop. You and I loved going there for Kobe beef sliders and fried Thanksgiving balls, which consisted of turkey, stuffing, and mashed potatoes, all wrapped in a fried outer dough and served with gravy and cranberry sauce.

Food aside, The Blind Pig was cool because it felt like the best-kept secret in Philly—*our* best-kept secret. Its retro atmosphere, tucked away from the mayhem of crowded bars and restaurants in Center City, felt attainable and intimately familiar, like a cozy living room lined with string lights or a library filled with all the right books.

I'd booked a large side room just off the main dining area for your party, which included a juke-box, a dartboard, and two long tables pushed together with barstools for chairs—something like our own personal party room. Most of your friends had RSVP'd that they were coming, and I was thrilled to be planning an event I knew you'd love so much. I was no hostess, but with your happiness in mind, I could convince myself of almost anything.

When I took the train into Philly on the afternoon of your birthday, I was carrying an armload of presents, cake, and beer, the beer primarily leftover from the homemade Guinness chocolate cake I'd made for you. I waddled off the train at 30th Street on three-inch wedge heels, peering over the top of the pile of gifts as I stepped carefully onto the platform. Luckily, you were right there waiting for me.

"All of this is for *me?*" you asked, a huge smile spreading across your face.

I loved that I could make you smile like that, Wade. I would've done anything to see you smile.

"Just wait. I'm kind of the best girlfriend ever," I bragged, unable to restrain myself as I pushed about half of my load into your arms, exhaling with relief. You handled the weight of the gifts with ease, grabbing my old weekend bag from off my shoulder and sliding it, like always, over your own without a hitch.

"So—what are you thinking you want to do tonight? Any ideas?" I asked, holding my breath and crossing my fingers that all of your friends had dutifully told you they were busy.

"I was actually thinking maybe we could do something—just the two of us. I only need you on my birthday," you said, squeezing my hand.

I felt my heart drop a little, thinking that it would have been nice to spend the evening completely alone with you…maybe even light some candles that *weren't* birthday candles and hole up in your room. But you had thirteen friends who would be waiting for you at one of your all-time favorite spots in Philly, and I knew that by the end of the night, you wouldn't be disappointed.

"I have an idea," I said, feigning spontaneity in an attempt to protect the party.

"What's that?" you asked, bumping my arm as we approached your apartment.

"Maybe I want to make it a surprise," I said.

"Hmm…I mean, it *is* my 21st birthday. If your surprise is bad, you will have ruined the whole day," you joked.

"Just trust me," I said.

We made a light dinner in your apartment that evening, your roommates joining us this time, and then I brought out the cake I'd made for you with a singing candle that exploded like a sparkler when it was lit. We all laughed at the way you jumped when it came to life, and when it wouldn't shut up after five rounds of "Happy Birthday," we finally tossed it in the trash room down the hall for the nearest tenants to enjoy. We ditched it, and proceeded to run away from the scene of the crime as quickly as possible.

"This cake is kind of amazing," you said, licking the cream cheese frosting off your fingers.

"Agree," your roommate, Evan, said.

I finished the last few morsels of my slice with a smug smile on my face, always content after making a good impression on your friends or family. For the most part, I liked your roommates. They weren't perpetually stumbling around intoxicated, and they weren't loud or obnoxious. Evan, your immediate roommate who practically always went home on weekends, was Indian, and your other two suitemates—Bobby and Jeremy—were Asian. We barely ever saw Jeremy, because he hibernated in his room on weekends, usually leaving his rice cooker out and retreating to his room after meals to play video games. Bobby was a social butterfly, so we rarely saw him except when he came back to shower, where he would, without fail, give us a private concert in his off-key tenor vibrato every time.

The two of us cozied up on your couch after eating to watch Netflix for a bit, but my eyes kept drifting toward the clock. I hoped you wouldn't notice. Evan and Jeremy, who'd left around 8:10 to get to The Blind Pig, had made up some lame story about going to a classmate's party, which probably already seemed suspicious due to the fact that Evan and Jeremy did *not* go to parties. In fact, I'd been shocked to see Jeremy in an actual pair of pants in lieu of his usual uniform: basketball shorts and a sweatshirt.

Around 8:30, you looked at me and said,

"Do we have to go out, babe? We should just stay in tonight."

"But…it's your 21st birthday! And I have a surprise for you," I said, inwardly cringing over the fact that I'd used the word "surprise" to describe your own surprise party.

"But I don't even feel that great. My head is kind of bothering me," you replied.

I hadn't accounted for this at all, and I scrambled for ways to convince you to get off the couch without blowing the whole plan.

"What if we just go out for an hour or so? Grab a drink

at the Blind Pig, just to celebrate? Come on—you *have* to go out on your 21st," I said, hating myself. The last thing I wanted was to force you to go out when you didn't feel well.

"I guess we could go for just one drink," you said reluctantly.

"Great," I all but exclaimed, grabbing my phone to call an Uber.

We fixed ourselves up before heading downstairs and climbing into the car that was waiting for us curbside. I let your friends know in the party's group chat that we were on our way, but I could tell something was really wrong when you failed to make small talk with the driver. It was so unlike you.

"Are you OK?" I whispered, leaning against your arm.

You shook your head.

"I'm trying not to get sick right now."

I cursed rugby, and that last concussion, for the thousandth time in my head.

"Let's turn around," I told you. "I'm sorry I dragged you out."

"There are people waiting...aren't there?" you asked, and I had no choice but to nod in surrender.

"I can tell them we'll reschedule for tomorrow night. I'm sure some of them will still be able to make it. Everyone will understand."

"I don't want them to know that I don't feel well," you said.

I couldn't imagine what else we'd tell your friends if we didn't show up at the restaurant, but as our car came to a stop just across the street from the Blind Pig, you grabbed my arm and pleaded,

"Please, please don't tell them. Just...text them that we'll be there in a few minutes," you said.

"Babe, that doesn't make sense. I'll just tell them the truth, and we'll go home."

"Morgan...please. Don't say anything," you implored.

So I stood with you across the street for a good fifteen minutes, rubbing your back and instructing you to take deep breaths as you tried to control your nausea.

"OK," you finally said. "Let's just go in. I think I'll be all right."

As insensitive as it was, I was a little relieved, because we'd kept your poor friends waiting for nearly an hour.

Alan and Webb had clearly been keeping an eye out for us, because as soon as we stepped through the door, they dutifully ran to greet us and bring us back to the room we'd booked.

"SURPRISE!" everyone yelled, standing to greet you and wish you a happy birthday. And I watched your face light up as you shook their hands and received affectionate slaps on the back, despite the fact that you weren't feeling well and would rather have been at home on your couch. You loved that your friends had all shown up for you, and I knew you appreciated that I'd planned the party.

You ordered a beer and jumped right into a game of darts with two of your friends, your earlier ailments swiftly and suddenly forgotten. I stayed at the table to chat with one of your friends, Alice, who was also in your engineering program, and Robbie, one of your old football friends who'd taken the train to meet us from Temple University that night.

You came back to check on me after three rounds of darts, squeezing my shoulders as you whispered with beer-scented breath,

"You're the best. I love you."

"I love you too. Happy birthday," I replied, giving you a quick peck. "How are you feeling?"

"A lot better. Could just be the booze, though," you said, smirking. I punched your arm lightly, but I was glad to hear that you were finally enjoying your big day.

We stayed at the Blind Pig for nearly three hours, causing only mild chaos by ordering practically all of the appetizers on the menu and messing with the jukebox every five minutes. The highlight of the party was the moment someone selected "Jack and Diane," and we'd all sung along obnoxiously, despite (and perhaps even because of) the stares we received from the tamer patrons at the bar. You were three drinks in, and I was two, but the night was still young and we didn't even know it yet.

When your friends started to leave one by one, then a few at a time, I turned to you and asked,

"Back to your place, birthday boy? How are you feeling?"

"I feel great," you said, shooting me a winning smile. I raised my eyebrows. You were, at the very least, tipsy.

"OK," I said, nodding my head in confirmation. "Back to your apartment."

Just as we were all dropped off in front of your building, your phone chimed, alerting you to a new message.

"That's Brendan. He wants to know if he can stop by. He said he couldn't make it earlier because he was at another party," you relayed, your eyes scanning the phone screen.

"Loser," I muttered under my breath. Then, to you, "Your call. Your birthday."

"Just for a little while," you said, and I rolled my eyes good-naturedly as we all trooped upstairs.

Brendan burst through your door like a whirling

dervish about fifteen minutes later, dancing into the kitchen just as the rest of us were starting to simmer down from the excitement of your party. He had his iPod on full-blast, and was—as always—drunk. Still, the song he was playing was a good one. I recognized it immediately due to its overplayed status on the local country station.

"Happy birthday, dude!" Brendan yelled, spinning over to you and slapping you on the back. "Sorry I couldn't make your awesome party."

"Mhmm," I said sassily from my chair, one eyebrow cocked in disapproval.

"It's cool," you said. "So you ditched me for another party on my 21st. Happens all the time."

"DUDE," he slurred. "I brought something to make it up to you."

Brendan held up a six-pack of your favorite beer, Blue Moon. My nose crinkled just looking at it.

"Ah, well. I guess it's OK then," you said, grabbing the pack from his hand and ripping into it on the table.

Brendan glanced down at his iPod just as the song ended, searching for a suitable follow-up, and what came through the speaker next had me out of my chair as soon as I heard the first familiar chords.

"No way! You know this song?!" I exclaimed, forgetting all at once that I'd been giving Brendan the ice queen treatment. I was too excited, already hopping around and whipping my hair from side to side in time to the beat.

"*Beers Ago,* Toby Keith. Classic," he replied, playing air guitar to the introduction before you tossed him a beer. Then you held one up for me, eyebrows raised.

"Why the hell not," I said, taking it and popping it open against the table as Brendan had while I sang,

"*And we spent what little bit of money we had on winter-*

green Skoal and Main Street gas, go get your girl, go make the drag, if you're lucky, you can take her cross the railroad tracks..."

I was pumping my arms over my head like a cheerleader for our own private party, and then—even though I was certain you'd never heard the song before—you started singing the lyrics a few seconds behind Brendan and me, repeating what we sang as I took your hands in mine, spinning the two of us around in circles.

"Seems like yesterday, even though...that was 1452 beers ago!"

That was the first and only time I ever drank a full bottle of beer, and you know that I think all beer smells and tastes like cat piss. But something about that magic mix of the song, and your kitchen, and that night made it palatable, laughing and singing and stumbling around at 1 a.m. with all the energy of invincible youth.

"I have an idea!" Brendan suddenly proclaimed over the cranked volume of the next song. "Let's go for wings!"

Despite the fact that we'd just spent three hours in a restaurant devouring no less than half the menu, I jumped immediately on the buffalo wing bandwagon, tugging at your hand as though the whole of Philadelphia were beckoning us. And so you, your roommates, Brendan, and I all ended up back on the streets of University City, a band of harmless brigands or typical college kids whose lives were temporarily dictated by impulse.

We ended up at our favorite place for wings—Sava's, a small pizza joint near your freshman year dorm—and Brendan declared boisterously,

"Table for four!"

The waitress looked at us like we couldn't possibly be serious before stating matter-of-factly,

"We close at 2."

"Aw, we only want wings!" Brendan all but whined.

"...All right. I guess we can accommodate that much. This way," she said, and Brendan turned to wink at us as though he'd just scored a major life win.

"What are we doing?" you whispered to me, and we both snorted indiscreetly, unsuccessful in restraining our laughter. We were out getting wings at 1 a.m. for no good reason other than the fact that we *could*, and there was something so damn liberating about the knowledge that we could invent our own rules.

I don't remember what we talked about as we waited for our food, but I remember sitting next to you, our ankles interlocked like always, our thighs touching on our chairs as we made half-drunken conversation and demolished a tray of thirty wings until the waitress all but kicked us out at 2:03 a.m. Poor Jeremy had gotten stuck with the bill, as he was the only one with cash, and the waitress had refused to take credit cards right before closing.

The five of us made our way back down 34th Street after our escapade, and Brendan bid us a slightly-slurred farewell as we approached his house. He turned backward down his walkway, sliding one foot behind the other like he was doing the moonwalk, and saluted.

"Happy birthday, Kernel!" he said, calling you by your old football nickname from high school.

"See ya, Brendan," you said.

Then, bumping my shoulder, you asked,

"Tired yet?"

I loved that, even when we were out with other people, you had your own private, easy way of speaking to me like it was just the two of us in our own universe. One minute, we'd be interacting with a group; the next, you'd completely tune everyone else out, addressing me like only you and I existed—like we were the only thing in your world that truly mattered.

"Not so much," I said, stifling a bit of a yawn. "How are you?"

"I'm perfect," you murmured, leaning your forehead against mine as you threw your arm around my shoulders, making me shriek with laughter as we went zigzagging, dizzy, across the sidewalk.

"I don't want to turn in yet," I said, your apartment building already looming ahead like a parent enforcing curfew. "Could you show me the patio area behind your room? I've never been out there, before."

The communal patio you'd mentioned previously was something resembling a courtyard; it was just underneath your bedroom window, and was elevated from the sidewalk by a set of stone steps.

"Hmm," you said. "I don't know if our badges will work for the gate at this hour. Ev, Jeremy—any idea whether we can get onto the patio?"

"Probably not," Evan said, but we all circled around the building to check, anyway. To our disappointment, your badges were ineffective in the wee hours of the morning.

"That's OK, though," you said. "Plan B."

"Plan B?" I asked, puzzled.

"I know what he's going to do," Evan said, a mischievous smile forming on his face.

A few minutes later, we were all back in your room, forming an orderly line to the window behind your bed and climbing out one by one. I crawled out last, your arms wrapped around my waist from outside as I slid onto the slab of roof overlooking the patio.

You let yourself dangle from the roof and landed on the

wall a few inches beneath your feet, and then held out your arms for me to follow.

"Uh-uh. I change my mind. No way," I said, despite the fact that the distance was actually quite short from the edge of the roof to the wall below. Evan and Jeremy were already on the patio, cheering me on.

"Morgan. Would I let you fall?"

"No?" I said, my voice rising a few notches as my answer metamorphosed into a question.

You rolled your eyes, stretched your arms out even farther.

"Come on, baby."

I eased myself into a dangling position, holding onto the rim of the roof until your hands were firm and low on my hips, and I let go with a little squeal just as you caught me.

"See?" you told me, planting a kiss on the top of my head. I pretended to dust myself off, straightening my blouse and smoothing my hair as though I'd just narrowly escaped death.

For all the trouble we'd gone through to get to that patio, there were only a few clusters of tables and chairs—nothing else. Still, the success of the adventure had made our efforts worth it, and the four of us made ourselves comfy at a table and struck up a game of *Would You Rather?*

"Would you rather," I started, "get stung by bees or slice your finger on a knife?"

"Wait, wait. Hold up. *Bees*—as in, multiple? Plural form? Because in that case, I'd rather slice my finger open," Evan said.

"What if it was only one bee?" I asked.

"I'd take *one* sting."

"Hmm. Your turn," I announced, sitting back and tipping my head up to steal a quick glance at the stars. But

I couldn't really see them. I seldom could, smack in the middle of the city against the glare of a thousand competing lights.

I looked back down just as Evan began his question, making accidental eye contact with you. You were looking at me the way you always did when you wanted me, but there was something a bit more particular in your expression this time. You were looking at me like I was something precious, something rare—like you were in love with me in a way that only your eyes could convey, because words fell short.

I tilted my head ever so slightly, as if to ask, *what?* But you just shook your head and smiled shyly, looking down the way you used to when you were fifteen years old and nervous around girls. I loved that I still had that effect on you, even five years later.

"...Punched with brass knuckles or held at gunpoint? "

"Dude, really?" Jeremy asked Evan, and you and I started cracking up over how much we'd missed.

"It's a legitimate question!" Evan insisted. "Obviously being punched with brass knuckles isn't as scary as being held at gunpoint. But I didn't say you'd get *shot*—it's just the threat of being shot that would be terrifying. So—bodily harm, or just the *threat* of bodily harm?"

"...You're so weird..."

"Seriously, Ev," you said, still chuckling.

It was 4 a.m. before you and I were slipping into bed, your mouth hot on mine as our legs intertwined beneath the covers.

"This was amazing," you told me. "The best birthday I could've asked for. I'll remember it forever."

"I'm so glad. That was the goal," I said, running my fingers through your hair and wishing I could dissolve into you, because close to you could never be close enough. But Evan was already snoring in the bed next to yours, separated only by a half-wall in the middle of the room, so we fell asleep curved into each other, your chin on my head, my leg thrown over yours.

Do you remember all of it the way I do? Do you ever let yourself think back to the unfiltered, spontaneous, unbridled fun that accompanied being young and in love in a city where we could so easily lose ourselves? Because, Wade—I remember every moment, and I had the time of my life with you.

TWENTY-TWO.

"I T ' S S U C H A N I C E N I G H T," I said, leaning over your windowsill as the pleasant September air swept over me.

The days were shifting gradually into autumn as they grew just a touch cooler, the golden afternoons slipping effortlessly into earlier, crisper nights.

You and your roommates had the TV on, priming for the second half of the Eagles game with a bucket of wings and a plate of nachos on the coffee table, donning your jerseys in support of your favorite players.

I was never one for watching football, save for the Friday nights that I watched you play from the stands in high school. That had been different, though—those games mattered to me because *you* mattered. I couldn't care less about a bunch of overpaid athletes throwing a ball around when I barely understood the technicalities of the game. As a result, I didn't exactly look forward to Sundays in the fall. I knew I'd lose you to a game, and the couch, for a good half-day.

You looked over at me, mid-chew, as I turned away from the window. I must've had a wistful look on my face, because you suggested,

"Hey…why don't we go for a walk?"

My eyebrows rose in surprise.

"But…the second half…"

"Eh, they're losing, anyway," you said, wiping your hands and standing from the couch. "Let me throw on my shoes, and we'll head out."

I smiled as you made your way to your room, apppreciating your consideration. It must've been a sacrifice for you to miss the rest of that game, but you'd been thinking of me as you grabbed your wallet, your keys, and my hand, and headed for the door.

"Where to?" I asked.

"Well...we never walk by the river at night. Bike path?"

"For sure," I agreed.

We made our way down Chestnut Street, turning onto a descending set of steps that led from the bridge to the bike path below. Without speaking about it or even fully realizing it, we set out for the art museum at the very end of the trail.

"Look at that view," you said, stopping to snap a photo on your phone of 30th Street Station, which was completely illuminated and reflecting in all its grandeur on the Schuylkill. You framed the photo the way I'd shown you in the past, capturing the turning leaves of a nearby tree in the forefront of the shot.

"Nice work, Kerns," I said, bumping your shoulder playfully when you showed me the picture.

"Well, I learned a thing or two from my girlfriend."

"Did you, now?" I asked, feigning curiosity.

"Mhmm," you replied affectionately, lacing an arm around my shoulders and kissing the side of my head as we continued on.

"So...this was really sweet of you," I said.

"What?"

"This. You knew I wanted to go out. You missed the rest of your game for me. Thank you."

"Ah, no big deal," you said. "Besides, like you said, it's a nice night. How many more of these are we going to have?"

I know, looking back, that you'd implicitly meant "until the weather gets colder," but your words were more accurate than you knew.

We walked on until we reached a fountain just before the museum, and you joked,

"Nice night for a swim."

Feeling spontaneous, I flung my flip-flops aside and climbed in, my bare feet slipping a little on the bottom as I struggled to hold my hands above my head, looking upward like there was rain falling from the sky. Another picture for your phone, for my mental photo album. I wonder how many moments you collected in yours.

"Come on in! The water's fine!" I said, half-serious as I did a lap around the perimeter of the fountain.

"That's OK," you said, amused but unwilling as you watched me like I was an unattainable sprite or a free-spirited hippie.

Once I'd had my fun, you took my hand and helped me out of the fountain, and I shook my feet of excess water before sliding my shoes back on.

We walked the rest of the way to the art museum in comfortable silence, and I soaked in the way that night felt, the way my Philadelphia always felt when you were holding my hand; young and alive, and so in love with you—the promise of our shared future just within reach. Few things could penetrate the happiness I felt when I was with you in the city, and they were things I willfully fought to keep at bay. The borders of this city were walls around the house we'd built, the backdrop and culmination of the grand love story we'd been writing since we were sixteen years old.

We climbed the steps to the top of the museum, which for once wasn't overrun with tourists and joggers. One of the most famous spots in Philly was suddenly exclusively ours, and it offered the most incredible view of the city's center, complete with the dome of City Hall—a miniscule William Penn peering out from the very top—and the tips of illuminated skyscrapers piercing the darkness.

"Everything sparkles here," I whispered, sitting next to you on the top step as I looked out in wonder.

But you weren't looking at the view. You were looking at me.

I turned to you under the weight of your steady gaze.

"What are you looking at me, for?" I teased.

But you weren't teasing when you replied,

"You're beautiful."

"You're biased," I said matter-of-factly.

"Damn right I am," you agreed. "I'm in love with you."

I saw forever in your eyes as I sat there with you, letting your words sink deep through my layers of insecurity. My body absorbed the weight of your sentiments differently this time—they added to the essence of who I was and radiated, warm and reassuring, like starlight through my skin.

I gazed back out at the skyline briefly before stating,

"I want you to propose to me here."

"Not on the Brooklyn Bridge, Lee DeWyze-style?" you asked, taking my hand in yours and stroking it with your thumb. "You love that song."

I shook my head.

"Not on the Brooklyn Bridge. I don't know anything about New York. My heart's not there. It's here in Philly—with you."

And you conveyed a silent promise with your eyes, nodding at me in your quick, concise way like you always did when you understood.

We stayed there a little longer, enjoying our fill of the view before walking back down the museum steps into the remainder of the night.

I spotted an ice cream truck on the trek back to your apartment.

"I haven't bought anything from an ice cream truck since I was a kid," I said, smiling as my childhood memories came flooding back.

Without missing a beat, you pulled your wallet from your back pocket and pulled me forward. The two of us ordered Magnum bars, which we ate on a bench overlooking the river.

"This was such a quality night," I said, licking the melting vanilla drops. "And just think—we would've missed it if you had stayed to watch the game."

"Don't get used to it," you said, bumping your knee into mine.

But I knew you would do it all over again if I asked.

TWENTY-THREE.

A L L   A T   O N C E ,   I   L E A R N E D that the idea of reaching a "breaking point" is not a figure of speech, or merely an exaggeration. Some decisions are gradual, but others are made in the swiftness and clarity of a single moment—a moment with no true significance other than the fact that it is the moment you make up your mind for good.

That was honestly how it started for me. The feeling, the *knot,* materialized all at once, when I woke up one morning and felt—inexplicably—that something was wrong. I couldn't pinpoint exactly what it was, but there was an anxiety, a desperateness that emerged when I started thinking about my relationship with you. Deciding that I was simply in a mood, I texted you all day, the same way I had for the last five years, and called you to say goodnight before I turned in. I chalked it up to an off day on my end, assuming that things would return to normal after a good night's sleep.

But when I awoke the next day, the feeling was still there—a distinct nagging that I couldn't place and couldn't seem to shake. It followed me to class, to the gym, to my friends' dorms, and everywhere else I ventured in an attempt to distract myself. It was discomforting and unsettling for me that something resembling doubt had emerged so abruptly, ostensibly out of the blue. Eventually, it began to interfere with the way I talked to you and thought about you, despite my best efforts to prevent my disquietude from affecting our relationship.

When it became clear to you that we needed fixing, you drove to West Chester to visit me one random Tuesday night, despite the fact that you had to wake up early for work the next morning. You were participating in your university's co-op program that term, so you kept your car in Philadelphia rather than at home for an easier commute.

I met you on my university's main campus, just up the hill from my apartment, when you pulled into the lot behind the music building.

"Hi," I greeted you, standing on my tiptoes to give you a quick kiss.

"Hello," you said, wrapping me in your arms.

I was immediately comforted by the familiar sensation of your hug, but there was a stiffness between us that I couldn't control and didn't understand. I could tell you felt it too, solely by your uncharacteristically ramrod-straight posture.

"How was your day?" I asked, as we started up the hill toward town. The plan was to talk things out over dinner and call it an early night, but even with the encouraging warmth of your hand in mine, I wasn't sure we would manage to resolve in one night the concerns I'd been hoarding for weeks.

"It was all right," you said, sighing like something was already on your mind.

I didn't push you just then, so we continued on in silence for a bit until I could no longer take the tension. Despite the fact that the timing was wrong, I had to voice the thing that I'd pinpointed recently as the problem, though I broached the topic in a roundabout way.

"Wade...do you...admire me?" I asked.

You looked at me a little funny, like, *where is this coming from?*

"Of course I do," you said. "What gave you the idea that I don't?"

It was a valid question. You and I had been perfectly content only two weeks earlier, talking about our prospective engagement and ordering ice cream from a truck on one of the best nights I could remember. Now, here I was, bringing up a phantom issue that had materialized seemingly out of nowhere. But the feeling had taken root like a stubborn seed in the pit of my stomach, and it prompted me to wonder—perhaps for the first time ever—whether you actually loved or appreciated some of the most vibrant aspects of who I was. It stemmed from the fact that, on a subconscious level, I'd finally acknowledged that you loved me in spite of my faith rather than because of it, and if that was the case, it was a monumental problem.

I, of course, had no idea how to articulate any of this, and perhaps was even afraid to.

"I don't know," I said, grasping instead at other applicable examples. "You've said some things that have made me feel like maybe you wish I could be...different. Like, not too long ago, you suggested that I should run in a 5k, but how do you not understand after five years that I'm just not cut out for that?"

You threw your hands up, flustered.

"Seriously? All of this is about that? It was an innocent comment, Morgan. I saw online that there was a 5k happening in your hometown, and I just brought it up as a suggestion. It wasn't meant to be an insinuation of anything. I just...it would be cool to have running in common."

But we don't. I have asthma, I thought reproachfully.

I ignored your explanation, because of course, that wasn't really the issue. Instead, I floundered for another surface-level issue, continuing,

"And then over the phone a few days ago—Wade, I can't

believe that when I asked you not to use the expression, 'Christ on the cross,' you called me a hypocrite. Really? As if I don't have enough Catholic guilt," I mumbled.

We'd had a bit of a passive-aggressive fight that particular night on the phone when you'd called to say goodnight, and I'd been audibly upset. I had denied it so emphatically—mostly for my own sanity, because I was still sorting through my emotions—that the conversation had quickly escalated to a heated argument, culminating in your highly offensive, extremely insensitive use of such an expression.

Looking a bit dazed, you nodded in acknowledgement.

"I agree. That was wrong. I don't know why I called you out like that, and I don't really have an excuse."

Still, I kept going, because it felt good to ascribe more blame to you.

"And you've told me multiple times over the years how difficult it was for you to wait for me, as though I put you through hell. Geez, Wade, we were sixteen years old when we first got together. What did you want me to do? Jump down your pants? And did you ever stop to consider that it was a huge deal for me to make that decision *at all* before marriage?"

This commentary broke your stride, almost causing you to stop completely in the middle of the sidewalk.

"...Where is all of this coming from? That literally came out of left field," you said.

"I just...you wanted to know what's been bothering me. And things have been piling up over time. Unspoken things," I replied.

"Well, we really should have resolved them before it got to this point," you said, clearly exasperated.

By the time we arrived at the restaurant, neither of us was hungry, and neither of us was speaking. When the hostess seated us, it felt like we were two strangers sitting across from each other, and I could hardly believe that such awkward tension could really exist between us.

After we placed our orders, we proceeded to stare at everything, anything, other than each other. You pretended to be captivated by the baseball game on TV, while I took extra sips of wine to make it look like I was actually engaged in doing something.

When you were tired of the distraction, you finally set those beautiful blue eyes on me and cut to the chase.

"So, why exactly am I here, Morgan? Is it really because of all those things you mentioned on the walk up here?"

I'd been dreading this moment. All I wanted was a simple conversation to settle my uncertainties, but from the way the evening was going, it wasn't likely that an entirely honest conversation would end well. Neither one of us was in the right headspace for a productive dialogue.

"I mean...how was work? You seem a little quiet," I began.

Questions were good, I reasoned. Questions gave you a chance to speak without feeling like I was attacking you any more than I already had.

"I'm tired. That's what happens when you work nine hours," you said. And you didn't say it with an attitude, exactly, but it still came across as extremely patronizing. My stomach did the giant rollercoaster-dip like always when something was really wrong—a feeling of dropping and contracting, as though even my intestines were wincing at the remark you'd made.

We reverted back to a loaded silence after that, as I had already expressed all of the easily-solvable things that had been on my mind, and wasn't ready to delve into the core of those issues. To get into anything further, anything heavier, just didn't feel right, even though I knew it was an area we'd eventually need to address.

When we were finished eating, I asked you if we should request separate checks. You said yes, and blamed it on the fact that you hadn't gotten your paycheck yet.

"You know I love buying for you," you said, trying to be sweet. I handed my debit card to the waitress and tried to believe you.

That night was supposed to fix things—it usually helps to talk things over in person rather than argue over a phone call—but nothing had been resolved. There I was, out for no good reason, spending $16 on an unnecessary meal when I had plenty of good food in my fridge. If anything, this dinner had put us in a more tenuous place than we'd been before.

"Cheer up," you implored, as we stepped out of the restaurant into a light drizzle.

But I couldn't. I was already reeling, spiraling with the knowledge that I was ultimately dealing with an unsolvable problem. It was impossible for me to continue to overlook the fact that, as much as we loved each other and quite possibly had more fun together than any other couple we knew, we had serious and unalterable differences that could break our relationship. Addressing this, however, would take time. I had to be emotionally ready before I could pull the trigger.

We walked back down the hill to the lot where you'd parked, and as we drove back to my place, you asked, clearly irked,

"Why are you so quiet?"

"I just...feel that we didn't resolve anything. You weren't interesting in listening to me, you were interested in defending yourself," I said spitefully.

"*I came out here to listen to you in the first place,*" you said, your voice the equivalent of the calm before the storm. I detected the slowly-rising anger in your tone immediately, but I wasn't intimidated.

"I know you did, and I appreciate that, but we didn't actually talk through anything. So many things you've said and done have just been weighing on me recently, and—stay in this lane—"

"I know where I'm going," you snapped, nearly running a red light as you swerved into the correct lane.

And then I stopped talking. I hated when you were short with me.

"What were you saying," you said, trying to keep things even-keeled. I raised my voice anyway.

"See! That's exactly what I'm talking about! How you reacted back there—you upset me so much sometimes—"

"You upset me ALL the time!" you yelled.

I was so outraged by your irrational response that I couldn't even find the words to respond. Instead, I clutched my purse against my body as though I were about to fling myself from the car. At the time, it hardly seemed like a worse fate than sitting beside you for a moment longer.

"I am sorry," you backtracked, carefully emphasizing each word as your hands tightened around the wheel. "I meant that you upset me *sometimes.* You expect me to be someone I'm not—to love something that I just don't—and when I'm not exactly who *you* think I should be, it's like I freaking devastate you."

The reality of your words crushed me, and I knew that suddenly, we had arrived at the issue. It had taken us the entire evening, but the truth had finally reared its ugly head.

"It's just...you know how important my faith is to me. And I know I've put it on the backburner for a really long time, because I wanted to make you happy, Wade. I know you don't love that I'm so devout, and I know it's not something we share. But...is it maybe something we can work on moving forward?"

"Listen," you began, pulling into the lot across from my apartment and killing the engine. "I know you have this great hope that someday I'll change. That I'll wake up and suddenly be different—more like you. But it's not going to happen." Then you added more quietly, "I can respect your faith, though. Is that enough for you?"

I sat in silence for a few moments, thinking, before I replied,

"But you don't respect it."

You sighed and rubbed your forehead, annoyed.

"That's not true."

I was too tired at that point to continue arguing about it, so instead, I stared through the windshield and said very calmly,

"I think you should leave."

But you shook your head.

"We both know you don't want that. You're saying that because you're upset, and because you're trying to hurt me. You want me to stay, so I intend to stay. Unless you really, honestly want me to go."

You were right. You knew me too well, and I temporarily resented you for it. My words didn't deter you.

I didn't say anything else as I opened the car door and walked toward my apartment, you trailing dejectedly behind me. I knew I had upset you on top of the fact that you were already exhausted from work, and I felt guilty that I'd put you in this position, but I couldn't tiptoe around feeling so torn anymore. My heart had been burdened by this weighted thing for long enough, and it wasn't right for either of us if I continued to hide it.

We turned in a little after midnight—we'd stayed up talking for several hours, and the conversation had helped set my mind at ease. Still, I was appalled that after maneuvering through such a perilous emotional minefield, you would still try to touch me, to be intimate with me, as soon as we turned out the lights.

I rolled away from your advances toward the edge of the bed, indignant, and I heard you grumble to yourself and sigh loudly. Next thing I knew, you'd taken your pillow to the floor, and the blue glow of your phone screen was piercing through the darkness of the room.

"What are you doing?" I asked groggily.

"It's too hot. I'm trying to cool down," you said stiffly.

You were mad because I wouldn't sleep with you. I didn't need to be an expert in the field of all things Wade to accurately interpret your moodiness.

I closed my eyes and tried to relax enough to fall asleep, but I was consumed by fury and guilt as it became clear that your current frustration with me had nothing to do with the issues we'd discussed earlier. Simply: I wasn't giving you what you wanted.

After you decided that you'd sufficiently made your point on the floor, you came back to bed, though the two of us were careful not to touch. I lay awake for hours while you slept, feeling sick as I listened to the sound of your soft snores.

Early in the morning, I rolled over and, still half-asleep, rested my arm on your chest. A small sound of pleasure emanated from your throat in response.

Physical intimacy was the last thing I wanted, but

somehow I convinced myself that it might improve things between us. I reasoned that it might make you gentler with me, more sensitive to my needs. Maybe I could even manage to forget everything I'd been grappling with over the last few weeks if I just submitted to what had been one of the most central aspects of our relationship for the last three years.

When I knotted my fingers in your hair and pulled myself close to you, you reacted instinctively, wrapping your hungry arms around my small torso and kissing me in ways that would ordinarily liquefy me. It only took a few seconds, though, for you to realize that this time was not like all the other times—that it was fueled by something cold, like strategy, rather than the usual ardor to which we were accustomed.

You tried to tell me between kisses that we should stop—that you were going to stop—but I kept my legs clamped around your waist, determined. You didn't exactly try hard to extricate yourself.

It was 6:45 a.m. when I glanced at the clock afterward, and I was the kind of numb that accompanies the early stages of frostbite—a decaying cocoon, beneath which I could conceal everything and through which I could feel nothing.

"Did you actually want that?" you asked, your voice small and cracking with a question that came half an hour too late. But I couldn't blame you, couldn't be bitter, because I'd initiated it. Yes, you'd been a five-year-old about not getting your way the night before, but I hadn't *had* to do this. I was responsible for my own burning eyes and hollow chest. I couldn't keep piling everything on you just to allow myself the capacity to breathe.

We dozed off for a while longer before it was time for

you to get ready for your day. I made you scrambled eggs and coffee while you were in the shower, but it turned out you didn't want my Keurig brew—it apparently had nothing on your Aeropress.

You came into the kitchen after your shower, your hair still damp after being towel-dried, and I handed you the hot plate.

"Thank you," you said, and I recognized the same stress that had been present in your voice the night before. You scarfed down breakfast and threw on your jacket, checking your watch as you laced up your boots.

"Shit," you murmured, tossing the last of your toiletries into your athletic bag. "I shouldn't have slept in. I should have gone earlier so I could be on time."

"I'm sorry. That's probably my fault," I joked with sad eyes.

You shot me a half-smile and admitted,

"Yeah, you're right."

Another small blow.

I walked you to the door and planted a brief kiss on your chapped lips.

"Don't drive too fast getting there," I said.

"I won't," you said hurriedly, and then you were out of my apartment and headed for your car.

I retreated back inside and stared at my empty, rumpled bed. A torrent of sorrow washed over me, the first wave of emotion to penetrate the thin walls of my chrysalis, and I took the sheet and stretched it over the pillows that still smelled like you.

At least I have class soon. I won't have time to dwell on this.

There are no words for what I felt and what I kept from you that morning. We never talked about it. I loved you so much, but there was no question that you could destroy me in any way you so chose—even by way of an un-touched cup of coffee. Still, the wreckage had always been worth the reward of your affection.

I cried violently for approximately five minutes before taking a cup of yogurt from the fridge, wiping the evidence off my face as though nothing had happened at all. I ate slowly at the countertop, staring at my cell and willing it to light up and buzz with the promise of a message from you.

I didn't hear from you for the rest of the day.

~

A MONTH LATER, absolutely nothing had changed, and I'd come to accept that things wouldn't get better if we continued on like this. After having been so attached to you for nearly six years, this wasn't something I had ever anticipated—this feeling that maybe, quite possibly, we could be wrong for each other.

The truth was that I wasn't exactly who I wanted to be when I was with you. You didn't encourage me to grow in the ways I so desperately wanted to, but that wasn't really your fault. You hadn't changed—*I* had. I'd once chosen our lifestyle, had submitted to it with at least half my heart, or perhaps an even larger proportion. Really, I'd chosen a permanent state of separation from my faith—from an identity I deeply valued—for years, and I'd thought it wouldn't catch up with me. I'd once believed that I could somehow reconcile the choices I was making with the promptings of my conscience, but now I understood that such polarities couldn't coexist.

The weekend before homecoming, I decided that I

needed to talk to you seriously when you visited. I knew what I had to tell you, and that it was long overdue. I revealed my decision to Brie, who'd remained close friends with me throughout college, on the way to class.

"Wow, Morgan—you sound so sure," Brie said. "I'm happy for you. I can tell you've been struggling with this for a long time. You definitely plan on telling him this weekend?"

I nodded, but the more I thought about it, the more the knot in my stomach grew. I knew that everything about our relationship could change once I told you that I couldn't continue living this double life—that I couldn't subject myself to feeling constantly split in two just for the sake of sex. I knew that no matter how hard it would be, making this decision was the only way of potentially saving our relationship. I knew I couldn't continue to be with you if I continued to feel torn in my identity.

But when you visited that weekend, I couldn't find the words. I didn't want to ruin the fun days ahead. It was my favorite time of the year; the weather was beautiful, and we had pumpkin patch outings and haunted hayrides planned. Why should all of that be spoiled with bad timing?

It wasn't lost on me, though, that I was being a coward about it.

Next time, I promised myself.

For yet another month, I buried my decision. What I quickly discovered was that nothing ever felt like "the right time," and I frequently tried to deceive myself into believing that my decision wasn't one that had to be made with any urgency. Thus, I defaulted to a false, surface-based happiness that enabled me to be content without actually experiencing true peace, but it was peace that I ultimately yearned for.

Then came the weekend that everything changed for good, unbeknownst to you. You visited West Chester in early November—November 8, to be specific—and we spent the weekend together as we normally did: half in bed, half not. Dog park visits, restaurant dates, Netflix on the couch and bar-hopping with my friends. The usual things.

The safe things.

When I walked you to your car on Sunday afternoon, I felt the usual prick of tears at my eyes, and I blinked rapidly against the golden autumn sunlight, trying to hide my emotional side that always emerged when I was around you.

But you knew me too well. Wrapping me in a long hug in front of your car, you asked,

"Are you OK?"

I nodded, head buried in the soft fabric of your sweater. You smelled like your musky Degree deodorant and a mix of some cologne your parents had gotten you for your sixteenth birthday—I'd been there when you'd opened the box.

I wanted to hold onto you and never let go, because every time I did, I felt like it could be the last time.

"I'll be OK," I finally murmured, taking a step back and sniffling as you unlocked your car.

"I love you. I'll call you once I'm on the road. I'll see you in five days," you promised.

When you drove away, I sat on the curb that bordered the parking lot and exhaled, allowing more unwanted tears to flow freely.

Another Sunday at Mass where I'll have to face myself.

A few hours later, I dressed and headed for St. Agnes

Church in the borough of West Chester. I could have just gone to a later Mass at the Newman Center, but I loved the solemn darkness and the gothic architecture of the cathedral in town. It was a meditative atmosphere, one that inspired prayer and spiritual transcendence.

I walked inside and made my way on pattering tiptoes to an empty pew. There were only a few elderly men and women with their heads bowed in prayer, and a few families waiting for the Mass to begin—no one my own age. I was early.

I sat in the very back of the church, and although I had time before Mass started, I couldn't bring myself to my knees to pray the way everyone else was. I felt hardened; desolate. I didn't have the heart to attempt a conversation with God. Instead, I sat and stared blankly at the tabernacle.

It wasn't long before several of the overhead lights flickered on and the entrance hymn began. I stood, tired and robotic, and watched as the priest processed down the aisle. He said the opening prayers, and Mass began as it always did.

I'd thought this would be just another Sunday of feeling trapped in my own guilt and hopelessness, or perhaps a case of feeling nothing at all. And then, midway through the Mass, something happened very suddenly as the congregation rose and began to recite the Nicene Creed.

A thought entered my mind—a very firm, very adamant thought:

I'm not going to be this person anymore.

Before I could lose my nerve, I slipped my phone out of my purse and texted you:

`Hey...I love you so much, but I can't do`

**this anymore. We have to stop sleeping togeth-
er.**

I knew once I sent the message that I couldn't mess with your head and continually change my mind. This solidification meant that I was certain about my decision, and never had I been more certain of anything. Looking back, the only thing to which I can attribute that kind of strength is grace.

More tears slipped down my cheeks, but they weren't of a sad, desperate nature this time. Instead, I knew something certain about myself for the first time in over three years: I was choosing to embrace the person I'd always wanted to be. There would be no more contradictions in what I believed, and in the way I lived my life.

I chose my identity in Christ at that moment. I chose to be Catholic, to stand rooted in my faith, for more than just the reason that I was raised with it or because I shared it with my family. I chose it not because I was afraid of the potential of Hell, or because I was afraid of God Himself.

I chose my faith, and all that it taught, because I'd finally realized that it was the only authentic way I could truly love both Christ *and* you.

...And myself.

I hit "send," and dropped my phone back in my purse. Peace flooded in.

TWENTY-FOUR.

I H E L D M Y B R E A T H F O R the remainder of that Mass, struggling to refrain from checking my phone every two minutes for your response to my text.

You replied about half an hour later with three words:

No problem, beautiful.

...And I'd thought that I was so lucky to have someone as amazing as you in my life, who could recognize what was important to me and respect it enough to work toward the goal of chastity with me. What I didn't know at the time was that you'd assumed it would just be a phase—that was something that came out later, in the heat of one of our final arguments.

I won't pretend that you didn't have reason to doubt my personal commitment, because chastity was something I'd tried and ultimately failed to practice long term. Without your help or understanding, I was always going to fail to live my faith as vibrantly as I wanted. I hadn't had the emotional strength before, and hadn't been firm enough in my resolve those other times, the way I'd been when I texted you that night from church. But that wasn't something you could have known, so you'd played along, believing that my request didn't actually carry any weight. It must've been similar to the way I'd learned to nod and smile each time you relayed that you wanted to do something crazy, like run a marathon or take the Polar Bear Plunge in Sea Isle City. Most of the time, I knew that if I just played along, there was a good chance you'd simply forget all about it.

A few weeks after I'd amended the constitution of our relationship, you came to visit me in West Chester just before Christmas break. As always, we slept in the same bed, but this time—when you crawled on top of me and began kissing my neck, your face already buried in my hair—I chose to fight for a more perfect love.

I looked up at the ceiling, and I prayed.

You, of course, had no idea what was going through my mind; I was far too timid to tell you. So you proceeded with skilled hands and lips to work my senses, the way you always had and the way you still did.

By the time you whispered, moments later, that you wanted me, looking more irresistible than you ever had with your stormy, smoldering eyes and your messed-up hair, my breathing was erratic, my heart was on fire, and my skin was burning with the inextinguishable white heat that only you could ignite.

This was what I'd surrendered to so willingly, so powerlessly, over and over again for the last three years. How can you prevent a grenade from detonating once it's thrown? How do you stop a firecracker from exploding once it's lit? I'd once believed that you couldn't. I'd once even tried to convince myself that the destruction caused by the explosion was justified if the match was lit with some version of love. But in those moments, lying on my bed like a sacrifice that wasn't mine to offer, I pulled back just enough to look at you through new eyes, and kissed your forehead with all the gentleness and patience of grace.

"I want you, too. But there's something else that's more important."

Someone else.

You rolled off of me then, defeated. "This isn't going to happen, is it?"

And when I looked directly into your eyes and shook my head, I think it finally registered with you that I was serious. That this time, my resolve meant something.

It was hard, Wade. Maybe you think it was only hard for you—that it came easily for me—but every time I was with you, it took every shred of willpower to resist from slipping back into our old habits. We were wildly attracted to each other, used to each other, and it made no sense for me to have done a total 180 after having a sexual relationship with you. In some respects, you'd been dating a different girl, and then I'd gone and changed overnight. It must've been frustrating for you beyond what I could imagine.

…But I'd hoped, till the very end, that there was enough love between us to make it work.

When you were truly upset, you didn't always come right out and say it. In fact, you often hid the ugliest of your totally human emotions until I forced them out of you, begging and pleading with you to be honest with me when I noticed a major change in your demeanor, and in the natural rhythm between us that was usually easygoing and comfortable.

You tried to hide your true feelings about my pursuit of chastity, the way I'd once tried to stifle my desire for it from you. You tried to conceal your distaste when you called me at night and I answered, breathless and cheery, after walking back from a Bible study at my university's Newman Center. You tried to understand, tried to accept. Ultimately, you couldn't.

We were intrinsically different in a way that shatters, Wade. We always were, but it was never more apparent than when I started living in a way that was conducive to my beliefs. The gap between us grew wider and wider, and sometimes I felt a thousand miles apart from you, even if you were standing right next to me. I know you felt similarly, because in the end, you told me that without sex to bridge the gap between us, it took that much more work for you to feel loved.

Our arguments became more frequent, causing rifts in our perfection and in my heart. The worst that I can remember happened on New Year's Eve. I spent the evening with you and your family over your family friends' house, as usual, since your mother's birthday fell on New Year's Day. When the clock struck midnight, we always brought out a cake for her and sang "Happy Birthday." It was more than a little unfair for me to have to spend every New Year's Eve with your family simply because your mother's birthday overlapped with two holidays rather than one; still, it was a sacrifice I gladly made over the years for you. I was never there to kiss my parents and my grandparents when the ball dropped, and it hurt not to be there with them, but I'd always reasoned that you were my family, too—my entire future.

That particular New Year's Eve, you'd proposed that I go back to your family's house and sleep in Leigh's room so that you wouldn't have to drive me home. My own house was about twenty minutes away, down the bypass, but neither of our parents liked that we were on the road at all on New Year's Eve. I'd packed an overnight bag in preparation, but at the last minute, I found myself begging you to drive me home.

"I know it's a pain, and I know it wasn't the plan," I said, stealing a moment alone with you in a quiet corner. "But I miss my family. I want to at least be able to hug my mother goodnight. Please drive me?"

Honestly, I didn't think it would be a huge issue, or I wouldn't have asked at all. You seemed annoyed, but "annoyed" was quickly becoming your default resting state when you were with me. What else could you do but agree?

It wasn't until we were in your car, driving in total silence down the vacant streets, that I realized something was very, very wrong. I could practically feel the tension in your set jaw, in your white knuckles that gripped the steering wheel. You stared, unblinking, straight ahead. For once, you didn't reach for the radio.

"Wade?" I asked anxiously, shifting toward you in my seat. I tried to lean my head on your shoulder, but you not-so-subtly shrugged me off.

"...Are you really that upset with me?" I asked.

"It's fine. Whatever, it's fine. I had more than I should have had to drink, and I don't think I should even be on the road right now."

I stared at you incredulously, unsure of where to even begin in formulating a response.

"Why the hell didn't you tell me that before we got in the car? Pull over, I'm fine to drive," I said, already unbuckling my seatbelt.

"No," you insisted. "We're nearly at your house. Five minutes isn't going to make any difference."

"Wade," I said quietly. "You would've had to drive back to your house, anyway. Why did you drink too much when you knew that?"

You didn't really respond. Your answer came as an unintelligible grumble.

When we pulled into my driveway—the house still lit with ironically festive Christmas lights—we both stepped out of the car, and you pulled my overnight bag from the backseat and handed it to me. I stood on my tiptoes to kiss you.

"I really did have a fun night," I said, squeezing your hand as I began to turn away.

When I was about two steps from the walkway, you yelled after me,

"I guess you don't want me physically *or* emotionally, anymore."

I turned in shock to face you, overcome with anger and frustration that you were blowing the circumstance so ridiculously out of proportion. You were standing in what was technically a confident stance—feet spread apart, tall as ever. But if the moment hadn't been so charged, I would have noticed the way your shoulders slouched forward. Would have noticed the pain in your eyes, like you needed me to say a magic word and release you from the perpetual ache you'd felt every single day over the last two months.

I dropped my bag on the ground and walked straight back to you, already on the defensive.

"How? *How* do you get that from the fact that I just wanted to go home at the end of the night?! I spent my entire New Year's Eve with you, just like I always do. All I wanted was to say goodnight to my mom before bed. And you think that means I don't want you?" I cried, my voice escalating and breaking.

"It has *nothing* to do with tonight," you said, your own voice taking on an ugly, impatient tone that I rarely heard you use.

"Then tell me, Wade. Because I'm dying for you to actually speak to me. I'm just *waiting* for the passive-aggressive brooding act to finally end, so that we can have a normal relationship again."

"Ha! Normal? *Normal*, Morgan? We *had* a normal

relationship! We were in love! We were sleeping together! That's what couples do—that's a normal relationship! And *I'm* the one who has the problem?" you yelled, your eyes flashing with furious tears. Then, you said quietly,

"I'm not the one who changed. You made a decision for yourself. Great, awesome, I'm glad it's working out for you. But it involves me, too, and I don't understand it. I can't understand it. All I know is that you wanted me before. And now, I'm the only one left in the relationship who wants *us*."

There was so much I wanted to tell you, Wade—so much I wanted to explain—but I didn't how without rubbing salt in the wound. I wanted to tell you that I wanted you more than ever. That I'd never stopped loving you, but in fact had learned how to love you *more* and *better*, because I'd finally chosen to put God first in my life.

But you didn't love God—I'm not sure you even believed in Him, at all—so all I could do was stare at you and shake my head.

"That's not true," I murmured, taking a step forward in an attempt to bridge the distance between us.

"It is true! What other possible explanation is there? You've always had faith—you've always prayed, and gone to Mass—but that was a separate part of your life. You can't honestly be telling me that after all of this time, it's suddenly a real priority?" you guffawed.

"It is," I said, taking your hands in mine. "It is, and it's beautiful. I wish you could see it. I wish I could make you understand."

"But relationships are supposed to be give and take. Shouldn't this be a compromise?" you asked.

I shook my head.

"Wade...I've compromised for pretty much the entirety

of our relationship. Compromise is about considering the other person's opinion about what color to paint the walls, or about what movie to watch on a Friday night. But…I can't keep compromising myself for you."

You must've known I was right, because you didn't respond directly. Instead, you told me,

"It's not who I am. I'm never going to be religious, Morgan. I mean, I can try—for your sake. But I don't think I'll ever be Catholic—not in the way that you are. I'm just not…like you."

"But you *can* be," I said, my voice urgent and hopeful in the dense blackness of the night. The winter air cut against my hands, stung at my cheeks, but I was already numb to everything except the possibility that you might still change. I wanted to be your savior—wanted us to share this great, spectacular faith together. I wanted to show you its radiance, the beauty of its truth.

I wanted you to chase after God with me.

But I'd set you off again, because you glanced up at me with a new resentment in your eyes.

"You want to change me," you said matter-of-factly.

You were right. I wanted you to change more than anything.

"Wade, I love you for you," I began. "But I believe that you could be so much more if you were just…open to it."

We stared at each other. I waited for your reaction. And when it came, I was more taken aback than I'd ever been over anything you'd said to me before.

"Screw you," you said. And then you got in your car without another word, slammed the door, and backed up my driveway, leaving me standing there without really knowing what had hit me.

I burst through my kitchen door moments later, the

warmth of the house melting the bitter chill beneath my skin, but nothing could've felt like relief that night.

"Sweetie?" came my mom's voice from the family room.

I walked directly to her, threw my arms around her, and sobbed. And then, when I was calm, I told her everything.

"I'm going to delete my Facebook relationship status," I said, already reaching for my phone to declare myself 'single.' But I didn't follow through—my statement had been a knee-jerk reaction, seemingly the quickest way I could get you to care or respond.

"Honestly," my mom said. "Do whatever you think is best."

She was usually on your side, Wade. If I took offense to something you'd said—if you'd screwed up somehow, or made me mad—my mom was the first to argue things from your perspective. She loved you like a son. So when she told me that I should do what I thought was best, I knew I had grounds to break up with you—that I would be justified in ending something as beautiful and as promising as what we'd had.

I've always been glad I didn't act impulsively that night, much as I'd wanted to. Looking back, I've found peace of mind in knowing I never made any rash decisions when it came to our relationship. As high as our emotions ran, I always took time to consider what would be best for both of us in the long run.

Instead, when I woke up on New Year's Day, I decided to pour my heart out to you in an extremely long email. I was always better at verbalizing my feelings than vocalizing them. You responded by texting me a few hours later, as though nothing at all had happened.

I tried to remain calm, but the hurt from the night before stayed with me throughout the day, and we talked about it in bits and pieces over text. I tried to express the effect you had on me when you were mad or upset with me—how my whole body started shaking, and how it became impossible to breathe. I told you I'd felt that way since you'd left me standing alone in my driveway the night before. You'd apologized, telling me that you never wanted to hurt me.

I recalled your sweet, 16-year-old promise as we'd sat on the wall behind the movie theater eating Take 5 bars: "*I would never hurt you, Morgan.*"

And I wept.

I went to Mass that afternoon by myself, selecting a pew just before a break in the aisle. The slant of the setting winter sun shone through the stained glass on the marble floor, and I sat in its narrow strip of light, envisioning it to be an extension of God. I cried throughout the Mass, blowing my nose obnoxiously between responses and hymns.

Who am I without him? I asked God.

The strip of light shone wider and brighter around me, enveloping me like an embrace.

Mine. You're mine.

I looked up at the massive wooden sculpture hanging on the wall above the altar. It depicted the glory of Heaven, with God the Father crowning Jesus as the Holy Spirit hovered above, surrounded by a host of trumpeting angels. Some might call the sculpture intimidating—it portrayed the severity of God the Father, and the magnificence of the world that awaited those who loved Him. But from the time I was a young girl, it never scared me.

You're worth it. You're worth this, I thought, fighting back the tears as they threatened to fall again.

That small beam of sunlight managed to hold me together for the remainder of the Mass, and when I left the church, I texted you that I wanted to take a break. I thought it might be a good idea for you to spend a few weeks thinking about what you wanted—about the fact that we could be all wrong for each other, and that I might not make you happy in the long run. I told you it might do us both good to miss each other for a little while.

You responded:

But I miss you already...

And I promptly fell apart again.

Still, I insisted that we take time away from each other until my birthday at the end of the month, adding that you were welcome to come to West Chester to celebrate it with me. You'd asked me if I was serious, telling me that three weeks was too long to wait. But my decision was final—God knew, I needed the time to heal from our blow-up on New Year's Eve.

The next night, I was still trying to adjust to the feeling of not being able to reach for my phone to text you as I prepared to go to a small gathering at my cousin's house. He'd invited some extended family over while it was still the holiday season, and I wore a sleek, black turtleneck paired with my favorite pair of heels and a colorful skirt. I pinned a section of my hair to the side and slung my Kate Spade purse over my shoulder. My father and I drove to Joseph's house, and my mother, who was feeling tired, decided to stay home.

I spent the evening eating one too many cannoli, and getting warm on laughter and sweet wine. By the end of the night, I was starting to feel much better about my decision to take a break from our relationship for a few weeks, even though the mere thought of it had seemed unbearable at first. I felt, in some ways, renewed—like I could start over without the weight of your disappointment in whom I'd become constantly taking its toll on me.

When my dad pulled into our driveway around 10:30 that night, though, I immediately recognized your Ford Explorer parked along the street.

"That's his car," I said, more to myself than to my father, who already knew.

You were sitting at the kitchen table with my mother when I walked through the door, and I felt a little like I was looking at a stranger. There was already something inside of me that was beginning to shut down, possibly to protect myself and possibly because I'd already made up my mind about you on New Year's Eve.

"Let's go talk," I said, leading you away from the kitchen into the more-private dining room.

"I'm sorry if I wasn't supposed to come," you started, pulling your chair closer to mine. "But Morgan, I couldn't wait three weeks. Three weeks is too damn long."

You took your hands in mine.

"I want to fight for you. I want to go to Mass with you. I need to be in your life. What's important to you should be important to me," you said, and I searched your desperate eyes for validity in your words.

I was touched by your gesture, and moved that you'd been courageous enough to show up at my house. You hadn't known if you'd be walking into a hostile zone, but you'd come, anyway—with a big bouquet of flowers and a scented candle, no less.

I can't deny that the gesture and the gifts were too little, too late for me, but I wanted to give you a second chance. I wanted to believe that you'd fight for us the way you'd sworn you would. So, we called off our break, and I allowed myself to hope—just for a while—that things might still change, but there was also a part of me that couldn't wait for you to leave that night.

"There was something different in your eyes when you walked through the door and saw him," my mother remarked, after you'd left.

I tilted my head in disbelief over the truth of her observation.

"You caught that?" I asked.

"I took one look at you and thought, 'Shoot—she doesn't care,'" she said.

And you'd seen it too, because later, you told me that when you first saw the look on my face, I'd seemed disgusted.

Neither was true. I did still care about you, more than you knew, and I wasn't *disgusted*—could never be disgusted at the sight of you. It was simply that I'd already begun training myself to move on. When you'd shown up that night, you'd disrupted the process, and I'd been annoyed at the prospect of starting all over again.

Of course I still loved you. How could I not? You can't separate yourself from a feeling. But my mind was beginning to grasp something that my heart was still struggling to accept: if we stayed together despite our myriad differences, we would risk unhappiness for the rest of our lives. The difficult part was trying to determine whether I'd rather be unhappy with you, or unhappy without you.

By the time you left my house that night, I was already beginning to convince myself again that it was worth being unhappy sometimes if it meant I could hold onto you forever.

TWENTY-FIVE.

YOU MADE THE TRIP TO West Chester for my birthday weekend in January, despite the projected blizzard starting on Friday night that would likely last until Sunday morning. We fully expected to be snowed in together for at least two full days, and I was a little nervous about what we'd do with all of the time spent alone. I figured it would be make-or-break for us, and though that terrified me, I wanted to move forward. I needed more clarity.

"Happy birthday, baby," you said, stepping into my apartment when you arrived with two handfuls of shopping bags. You'd brought all of the ingredients necessary for a steak-and-potatoes dinner, and we had the place to ourselves since my roommates had holed up in their boyfriends' apartments or at home. You began unloading the food, turning on my oven and moving about the kitchen like it was a shared domain, and suddenly, I was choked up with overwhelming feelings of tenderness toward you. Moments later, I was closing the space between us, coming up behind you and wrapping you in a backwards hug.

"Thank you for coming," I said, my voice muffled against the fabric of your shirt. You turned in my arms to face me.

"I could never miss my princess's birthday," you replied, kissing me softly amidst the scattered pans and grocery bags.

I knew, after such a genuine display of affection, that the next forty-eight hours would be *hard*.

We did everything we could to entertain ourselves after dinner. I pulled out several of my favorite DVDs, and we proceeded to make popcorn and have a movie marathon, watching *Ghost* with all the lights turned off for added effect. You'd taken the opportunity to dryly point out that Patrick Swayze had gone to Heaven despite the fact that he'd had premarital sex, which was the first indication that your good mood from earlier in the evening was beginning to dissipate. I was, once again, the "bad guy"—the villain who'd interrupted the natural and easy flow of our partnership.

Post-movie, I gave you a late yoga lesson in the living room, pushing aside the couches and coffee table to make room for two mats. You'd been complaining about neck stiffness ever since your final concussion, and I swore by yoga as a cure for all things, so I thought that some of the stretches and poses might help. Instead, they acted as a stimulant for you, and our "lesson" ended with you scooping me up off the floor and carrying me to the bedroom.

Between kisses, I placed an apologetic hand on your chest and murmured,

"Wade…no…"

You set me down on my feet and sat on the edge of my bed, lacing your hands over your head as you stared hopelessly at the floor.

"I'm sorry…" I started, but you shook your head as I began to speak, still avoiding my gaze.

"Just…let me cool down," you said, exhaling like it was the end of the world.

I padded back to the living room, rolled up the yoga mats, and waited.

When it became clear that you weren't coming out, I made my way back to my room where I'd left you, and found you lying on your back, staring up at the ceiling. I knew you were livid that, with all of this time we had to ourselves, we weren't spending it the way we would have in the past. *I* was even livid—at times, it felt like a torturous test to be completely alone with you and have to treat you like little more than a best friend.

"Wade?" I said in a small voice, sitting gingerly on the bed beside you.

"You sure are willful," you chuckled sadly.

"Hey," I said, and snuggled into the side of your arm. "I'm sorry."

"I'll get over it. I'll adjust at some point," you said.

"How can I help…?" I asked, but I already knew there was little I could probably do.

"You can't. There's nothing you can do. I guess…just… Morgan, maybe you'd be better off with someone more like you. I've told you that I don't think I'll ever be religious, but that I'll always support you. Could you live with that?"

I flashed back to all of the times in years past that it had felt like pulling teeth just to get you to go to Mass with me—even when we *were* sleeping together, and things were more solid and stable between us. When you did accompany me, you usually acted like it was an agonizing ordeal, stretching and yawning obnoxiously throughout the service. You couldn't even find it in yourself to make the sign of the cross or genuflect upon entering a church, not to mention that you'd expressed your disdain for God and faith on more than one occasion.

I didn't know how to work with any of that. None of it was evidence of "support," and the fact that our relationship seemed to be hanging by a thread as I lived out my faith more and more only proved that my beliefs and our relationship were incompatible.

We were incompatible.

I decided to be completely honest with you, and was the

first of us to exhale after too much time spent holding our breath.

"...I need to be with a Catholic man," I said, the words tumbling out like poison from a spilled vial. It was the first time I'd articulated, acknowledged, the truth of the statement since I'd begun to realize it.

You covered your face with your arms in an attempt to hide your tears. When I finally dug through that mass of biceps, triceps, and flannel, your face was blotchy and red, and I held you as tightly as I could, as though I could hold the two of us together by sheer will when we were so treacherously close to unraveling. We lay there quietly for a long time, individually processing everything that the conversation implied while sharing the heartbreak collectively in devastated silence.

It is such a strange feeling, like an out-of-body experience, to love someone and want them so much once you've realized that you're wrong for each other. There was a part of me that wanted to revert back to everything I'd been when things came easily for us—before I started taking my faith and all that it taught seriously. But I knew that my old lifestyle was no longer conducive to this person I'd become—wasn't even conducive to true love. You and I had loved each other as much as we could, but never entirely selflessly.

"Where does this leave us?" you finally asked.

"I don't know," I said. "I do know that I love you. I'm hurting a lot, but you are, too. I don't know how to make something work that...doesn't have a solution."

"I'm not enough for you," you said quietly, more to yourself than to me.

"It's not that you're not enough," I insisted. "But God, Wade, it would be so nice to see eye-to-eye with you on these things that are so important, without having to constantly butt heads and feel at odds with you all the time. I don't know if I can live like that my whole life, and you probably don't, either."

You took a deep breath and switched gears.

"We've been having the same conversation for too long. I think we need a break. I have something for you," you said, crouching on the floor to dig through your athletic bag.

You pulled out a small box, kissed the side of my head, and said,

"Happy birthday."

I opened the box to find a miniscule, handmade book, constructed of cardboard and tiny pieces of paper that you'd painted, meticulously glued, and tied together with a little pink ribbon. It hung on a chain to be worn as a necklace, but you quickly pointed out that it could also be used as a keychain. It must've taken you forever to make that book—especially with your large, masculine hands—and it meant so much to me, Wade. I still have it in the back of my drawer beside my bed, because I refuse to part with something made with such devotion and care.

"This is...kind of incredible," I laughed, wrapping my arms around your neck in appreciation.

"You like it?" you asked hopefully, as though this tiny talisman could fix all our problems.

"I *love* it," I corrected. "Thank you so much."

"I love you," you murmured into my hair, turning to rest your head on my shoulder like a lost, little boy.

I held you a little tighter to internalize your scent, to memorize the way you felt against me. I knew it wouldn't be like this for long. I knew we only had a matter of time.

When we climbed into bed an hour later, the snow was

falling constantly and steadily outside, already piled up to my bedroom window on the first floor. As we snuggled under the covers, you placed your hand on my side and kissed me, and because it was never just a simple kiss with you, it escalated almost as quickly as it began before I placed a hand on your chest and forced myself out of your embrace.

You rolled onto your back after that, blinking into the darkness. I could sense that you were even more upset than you'd been earlier, the tension filling the room until the air felt oppressive.

All of a sudden, you were up and out of bed, pulling on a sweatshirt, your snow boots, your gloves.

"Where are you going?" I asked, startled.

"To clear my head," you replied.

I guess I was afraid that I would lose all six feet of you in a snow drift out there, so I got up and threw on some layers, too.

"Seriously, I need to be alone," you said, but I'd insisted on accompanying you into the arctic wilderness.

Outside, we were the only two people to be found. It was midnight and freezing, and the wind scraped frosty fingers across our faces and blew snow up around us, making it hard to see. I tried to tuck my chin into my coat and drag my hat down over my eyes. You walked in front of me to take the brunt of it.

We threw some snowballs, made snow angels. You chased me, tackling me playfully to the ground. For a moment, we were figurines trapped inside a snow globe, captured in a moment of time that kept us young and secure and happy in a bubble of hope.

It was the most beautiful moment of falling apart I've ever known.

The next morning, when the snow finally stopped, you got out of bed early to dig both of our cars out of the powdery rubble while I slept. My roommates reemerged later in the morning with their obnoxiously egalitarian boyfriends, who'd insisted that they help shovel.

...I remember thinking how lucky I was, even then.

~

TIME PASSED, but nothing changed. We were stuck in an exasperating limbo where our minds knew something that our hearts couldn't reconcile, and every day was a struggle to stay optimistic about our relationship. You weren't coming to terms with the way I'd redefined the nature of our relationship, and it weighed heavily on your heart and manifested in your frequent brooding and pouting. Every single time I was with you—every time we went on a date—we plastered fake smiles on our faces and pretended that nothing was wrong, even though we couldn't relate to each other anymore. We consistently went through the motions, trying to move past this gaping hole in our relationship but never quite figuring out how.

In February, there was a presentation—a conference of sorts—taking place in my hometown specifically for fallen-away Catholics, and my mom called to suggest that I mention it to you.

"I wouldn't be able to go with him," I told her. "I have an evening class I can't skip."

"What if Dad took him?" she asked.

"I mean...would that be really weird?"

"You can at least ask," she suggested.

So I did. I mentioned it to you, wincing as I waited for your response, but Wade—you went. Do you know how much I appreciated that? The fact that you were still trying to work through our impossible circumstance meant that maybe, you still believed in us. I was so encouraged, so uplifted, by your willingness to attend something so blatantly out of your comfort zone for me. At a minimum, I hoped you'd hear something that night that might help you understand where I'd been coming from all this time. The advertisement for the presentation had stated that confessions would be heard immediately following the conference, and I couldn't help but pray that it was an idea you'd consider.

It had felt like holding my breath for three hours as I awaited a call from my dad at the end of the evening. I knew he'd give me the full scoop, whereas you were more likely to give me a neutral response that lacked all detail—the CliffsNotes. Mostly, I wanted to know whether you'd gone to confession.

"He said he'd go on Sunday," my dad told me, clearly taking your word for it—but he didn't know you the way I did. It was clear to me that you wouldn't go to confession; attending the conference had been one thing, but penance was quite another. If you hadn't gone when you'd had a prime opportunity that night, you definitely wouldn't go when you never even made time for Mass.

I think whatever hope I had left died that night—not because of anything you'd done or hadn't done, but because I finally realized that even if you attended a million more conferences that led you to gradually resent me, you would never be what I truly needed. You would never experience a full conversion of heart. This wasn't something I could bring myself to relay to you, or even fully grapple with, yet.

Later that week, while I was sitting on my bed IMing you as I worked on an essay, you spontaneously typed,

Hey I'm sorry we don't agree on a lot of important issues, I know it makes things very hard on you and I wish I felt differently, but I do know that I love you so much and need you in my life.

My heart rate sped up, and I knew this meant that I was going to respond completely truthfully. I didn't have to think about it before I replied,

I love you too Wade...I will always love you. I need you to understand though that there is a very good chance that if we stay together, we will end up in a fairly unhappy marriage (if neither of us changes, which I don't think we will)...we are constantly at odds with each other and that is a major problem.

The little chat box alerted me that you were typing.

I'm just not interested in the religious aspect of things, I just get the feeling that's like 90% of who you are now.

It is, I typed simply.

You took a few minutes to respond to my assertion, but when you sent your response, it was immediately clear why.

**...But there is so much more to you than that.
Why not tone it down to like 50%, which is
still a huge amount?**

I am still shocked by those words, Wade. I couldn't believe that you would actually ask me to tone myself down when I was finally at peace with who I was.

**This is what I love. Would you have ever advised me to tone down our relationship to 50%?
I can't tone down who I am — that's what you're
asking me to do.**

You typed,

Ok...I apologize, I didn't mean it like that.

But I was already shaking, and my tears had begun to fall with the reality that we were rapidly coming undone.

Wade...I think we need to let each other go.

I disagree wholeheartedly with that statement,
you replied, as I'd known you would.

I had to ask:

**Why? Why do you want to stay with someone you
are no longer happy with? Who you feel inadequate with? Who you don't understand? Who you
want to "tone down" for the sake of being comfortable? What do you see in me other than the
fact that you're attracted to me? I'm tired of
arguing...we shouldn't spend our whole lives**

**compromising who we are just to try to make
something work that might not, in the end.**

I was sobbing onto my keyboard at this point, reaching for the tissue box as I waited for your response.

**I think letting go of something this great is a
very bad idea and something we will both regret
for a lifetime. Even with all of this shit,
Morgan, you're the only person I'm completely
comfortable with and the only person I can call
my best friend.**

I took a deep breath and stared wistfully at the conversation that was unfolding in front of me. I couldn't believe it had come to this, but we'd had so many back-and-forth moments—moments in which we'd circled the possibility of breaking up without allowing ourselves to go there fully. We were both disconsolate at the idea of life without each other.

And then you messaged me:

I love you so much, Morgan.

I took a few steps from my bed and collapsed into a sobbing heap on the floor, the rough carpet scraping my bare legs as I curled into a ball. In those moments, I allowed myself to feel everything that I was going to feel for you—for us. About what it would be like to not know you, to not love you anymore. And my throat closed and my heart collapsed through my rib cage onto my stomach, and I was a mess of caving in and sputtering and leaking like something broken. I wrapped my arms around my torso as though it were the only way I could hold myself together, and I remembered all of the things that you're not supposed to remember when you're breaking up with someone you love—things that should have been irrelevant, obsolete in the face of irreconcilable differences, but were somehow still everything.

I thought about our shortcut to your apartment from 30th Street Station, walking diagonally through the same parking lot hand in hand on Friday evenings with the whole weekend stretched out ahead of us. I thought about the way I would always reach my arms up, opening and closing my fists when I wanted you to hug me, like a toddler who wanted attention, and about all of the high school formals, football games, and movie dates we'd shared as teenagers. The bookstores, the coffee shops, the dinners and cookies we made together, joined at the hip no matter what we were doing; Halloween and matching Barbour jackets and *Mad Men;* your little sister, your father's corny but lovable jokes, and the way you hugged and kissed my family hello and goodbye like they were already your family, too. The way you changed the presets in your car to include the Philadelphia country station, which you immediately switched on whenever I was riding shotgun in your Explorer. Your arms around me at the Luke Bryan concert, wearing your cheap, black cowboy hat and singing "Crazy Girl" in my ear.

...Every dark night spent alone in your room with you, little electronic tea candles flickering on your nightstand while your hands tangled in my hair and made a home on my hips, claiming all of it—all of me—as sacred territory I'd relinquished in exchange for the rights to yours.

I thought about how I'd given myself fully to you so long ago, not just physically but emotionally. You took up the most space in my heart, and in my future. You were my husband from the second month into our relationship, when I told you I loved you curled in your arms in Jenny's pool. In truth, I'd thought I would marry you even before then.

You were the only thing I'd ever consistently wanted.

Mostly, I thought about the fact that you, as a person rather than a place, were home to me. That I could be lost, overwhelmed, in a crowd of strangers, but if I caught a glimpse of your face in that same crowd, I knew I wasn't alone anymore—I was safe and loved, and all was right in the world.

How was I supposed to lose my best friend, the one and only love of my life, *and* my home, all at the same time? Could I bear a loss like that? Would I ever recover from it?

We didn't break up that night. In fact, we would stay together for another three months, but a large part of my heart let you go that night as I fell apart on my bedroom floor—my rock bottom. It was the last time I ever cried over you that way, even after we broke up. I'd already accepted what perhaps you wouldn't learn to accept until months following our break-up.

That entire last year with you, I learned that the process of letting go can begin long before goodbye.

TWENTY-SIX.

S P R I N G O F T H A T Y E A R was the finale of our relationship, and on a subconscious level, I was already aware of it. Despite my prescience, I won't pretend that I wasn't still grasping at straws, desperately trying to hold onto you however I could, even as we began to drift.

We celebrated our six-year anniversary with a dinner reservation at another sumptuous restaurant, which had been equal parts intimidating and enchanting. Barclay Prime is a self-described "world-class steakhouse," situated in the perpetually-charming Rittenhouse Square—a modern edition to an otherwise historic neighborhood. From the moment we pushed through the immense brass doors, I was thoroughly impressed. The restaurant's ambience was undoubtedly the swankiest I'd ever encountered in Philly. Upon checking in, we were swiftly escorted to an intimate table with white leather seating, just along the deep mahogany walls with their charming, built-in bookshelves. I was enthralled by the antique books, by the stylish chandeliers, and by the candlelight that flickered romantically in every corner of the dining room.

As we were looking over the menu, trying to decide which $75 entree might justify draining half the funds in our bank accounts, you murmured,

"Morgan...I still don't feel right..."

I sighed, placing a concerned hand over yours on the table.

"Are you going to be OK? Should we leave?"

Shortly before our original reservation time, which had initially been much earlier in the evening, you'd fallen prey to another nauseating headache—one of many you'd accumulated since your last concussion. We'd called the restaurant, and had managed to secure a later reservation in the hopes that you'd feel better over the course of the night.

"Nah," you said, pressing the tips of your fingers to your temples and smirking. "I can always throw up on the books."

We both began chuckling then, a pair of awkward college students dressed so obviously in our "Sunday best" and still managing to miss the mark in this lavish place, where all of the women apparently owned Louboutins and the men sported Rolexes. Famous people probably dined here, and now you were about to get sick all over their rare manuscripts.

...Thankfully, you didn't.

We caught an Uber back to your place after, your headache miraculously cured by your bone-in fillet and asparagus spears. Snuggled against you in the backseat, the reassuring weight of your arm draped around me like always, our energy should've been higher, more positive. Instead, we were both quiet, our minds far away as the sound of rain against glass improvised a pitying conversation on our behalf.

Earlier that weekend, I'd presented you with an anniversary card in which I'd taken the time to articulate everything you still meant to me. When I'd handed it to you, you'd assured me—much like the year before—that you'd have a card for me by the end of the weekend, but this time, I doubted. As I leaned against you, sans seatbelt and jeopardizing my own safety in exchange for the scent of your skin, I wondered what would even motivate you to follow through this year.

Like a disappointed child on Christmas morning, I was

crushed when Sunday dawned and faded without your promised card. By nightfall, I was all but begging for your sentiments, desperately afraid that you didn't love me enough anymore to even spend ten minutes wooing me via the written word. Finally, because my reaction had probably seemed so overblown to you, you exasperatedly grabbed a plain piece of computer paper, folded it in half, and scrawled a few half-hearted words on one side of the fold. When you handed it to me, refusing to even meet my gaze, my eyes were fogged over with tears. I unzipped my overnight bag just enough to cram your failed attempt at appeasement inside.

"Why did I even bother," you mumbled, your mood clouded over the way it usually was after a weekend passed without intimacy.

From West Chester that night, I called you in the blackness of my room, whimpering like a wounded animal beneath the covers.

"I don't understand. I wait for these occasions just for an opportunity to hear how you feel about me. Our anniversary doesn't have to mean a big gift, but it *should* mean a card—something picked out and written thoughtfully once a year."

"Hey," you murmured, your voice muffled with the thickness of sleep, "I'm sorry. I'm sorry, Morgan."

I blew my nose into the phone, and the line fell silent. The two of us nearly fell asleep like that—just like the early years of high school, with phones pressed between ears and pillows in the small hours of the night—before you finally whispered,

"I love you."

"I love you too," I said.

And those words, always our temporary bandage, made

it OK enough for me to hang up with some amount of peace before allowing the dream world to pull me under.

~

THE LAST MEMORY I have of the two of us together in Philly is a decade-themed party we'd been invited to over your friend's place, two weeks prior to my graduation. I donned a 70s-reminiscent, marigold suede mini dress and a pair of tan ankle boots with wool-blend socks bunched up around my legs. I completed the look with stick-straight hair, thinly-lined cat eyes, and pale pink lipstick.

"You're channeling Megan Draper from *Mad Men*. I like it," you said, after I emerged from your bathroom.

Changing clothes had now become an excruciatingly awkward ordeal for us. I always attempted to slip out of your bedroom and into the bathroom with my intended set of clothes without you noticing, but you inevitably always did, rolling your eyes as if to say that modesty at this stage in our relationship was the craziest thing ever.

"That's what I was going for," I said, stopping before your mirror to fix a stray hair.

You were wearing your Johnny Bravo t-shirt with your hair completely slicked back, like a character out of *Grease*, and you threw on a pair of black, fingerless gloves as an added touch.

"You look tough, dude," I said, and you bumped your hip into mine as you walked past me. Your relaxed attitude made me smile, and I found myself growing more optimistic about the rest of the evening. Maybe we could pretend, just for one night, that nothing at all had changed.

"Come on, *Megan*," you teased, grabbing my hand as we headed for your door.

The walk to the party was a short one, just a few blocks away, and when we stepped through the door fifteen minutes later, we discovered we were pretty much the only two people dressed in costume. Apparently, the "decade" theme had been more of a suggestion than a requirement.

"Aw, what is this?" you asked, slapping Webb on the back as he made his way around the makeshift beer pong table. "No costume?"

"I wanted to look my most dapper for you, Wade. No costume for me," Webb said. Then, "Morgan," he greeted, nodding in my direction.

"Webb," I returned, feigning seriousness before breaking into a smile.

"So, I want in on this beer pong game. When can I face off against you?" you asked.

"Get in line. And get a drink, first," Webb replied.

The two of us made our way to the kitchen, where a group of people were pouring flavored liquor into red solo cups before mixing it with juice or soda.

"Any beer?" you asked, and someone tossed you a can of Miller Lite. You made a face when you saw the brand. I reached over the table and poured some orange-flavored vodka into a cup, filling the rest with orange soda before we headed back into the living room for your round of beer pong.

"Morgan," you said, gesturing to the unoccupied space beside you. "Come be my teammate."

I raised my eyebrows and took a slow sip of my drink.

"You don't want Miss Uncoordinated on your team."

"Never mind that," you said, waving your hand as

though it didn't matter. So I made my way to your side, and the two of us faced off against Webb and some dude from Switzerland, with whom I tried to converse in French before realizing that his native language was German. He seemed determined to beat us after that, taking offense to my assumption, but you and I won handily, high-fiving each other over our still mostly-intact triangle of red solo cups.

"Ah, you just got lucky," Webb insisted, retreating with us to a corner of the room as other people took their turn at the game.

"Excuse me," I murmured, darting around you and making my way back to the kitchen for round two of my drink.

When I walked in, an unfamiliar frat boy with a backwards baseball cap was preparing shots of Jaeger on the table, and he and four others were getting ready to do a round.

"Want one?" the guy with the bottle asked me.

I shrugged. "Sure, I'll do one with you guys."

He poured me a shot, and the five of us raised them in the air before tossing back the warm, bitter liquid.

"Another!" one of the girls yelled, and the others all agreed. I had just finished pouring my mixed drink when another shot was handed to me.

"Bottoms up," the guy said, and—perhaps because it felt like a reprieve to not be so tightly-wound while I was with you—I participated in the second round.

You emerged a few moments later, clearly looking for me, just as I had begun to turn back toward the living room.

"There you are," you said, taking my hand in yours. "Was starting to think I'd lost you to a bad conversation."

"Just a couple of shots," I said, raising my cup.

"A couple of shots?" you asked, concerned. "That's not like you."

"Eh, it's a party. Why not," I replied, shrugging as I took a sip of my drink.

"Feel OK?" you asked, studying me more closely than usual.

"I feel fine," I said, rolling my eyes. "Come on. I want to win another round of beer pong."

We found ourselves back behind the table for a second game, and for a while, the two of us were the reigning champs before more guests arrived and began challenging us. By the time we finally lost our hard-earned title toward the end of the night, I was friends with nearly everyone in the house, my buzz enabling me to socialize more freely without my usual inhibitions. When the host of the party started talking about an old Cascada album—an early 2000s group known for the pop-disco song, "Every Time We Touch"—I even burst into song with him, singing lyrics from each song on the track list as I remembered them from my childhood. Afterward, everyone clapped for us as if we'd just performed at the Grammys, and we took a bow from the fourth step of the carpeted staircase that had acted as our stage.

"That was kind of awesome," you told me, as we stepped out into a steady drizzle and headed back to your place.

"What?" I giggled, leaning into you to try to escape the rain.

"That you're the life of the party when you open up. When you want to be," you said. "Seriously. You should do that more often. People love you when you just put yourself out there."

I snorted. "Yeah, but that takes too much effort, usually.

If you haven't noticed, I'm a little drunk."

"A *little*?" you asked, amused.

"Are you *judging* me?" I accused, feigning shock.

"No," you said, interlacing your fingers with mine and squeezing my hand affectionately.

When we stepped through your front door, shaking ourselves off like wet dogs and pounding the water from our shoes in the entryway, it was clear that your room-mates were already asleep. We tried to tiptoe down the hallway to your room, but I exaggerated how tipsy I was by throwing my hands against the walls for balance, prob-ably causing a disturbance in the process.

"Geez," you said. "You really are drunk."

I shook my head playfully. "Nah...I'm just messing. Look, I'll walk in a straight line."

So I set off down the hallway again to prove my point, placing one foot in front of the other until I finally stum-bled off-balance, launching myself into your arms and laughing at the weightlessness I felt, at the goofiness of the moment.

You smiled down at me.

"What?" I asked.

You shook your head.

"I just like you like this."

I raised my eyebrows. "Intoxicated, you mean?"

"Just...free," you said.

I knew, even in my inebriated state, that you were refer-ring to my faith, and who I was when I wasn't living up to it. But I'd had too good of a time that evening and wasn't in the mood to sour the rest of the night, so I towel-dried my hair, slipped into my PJs, and crawled into bed beside you.

"I had fun tonight," you whispered, stroking my cheek with your fingers.

"Wade," I started, moving closer to you and closing the space between us under your sheets. "...Am I enough for you?"

"What do you mean?" you asked softly, your hand still on my face. "You've always been enough."

I stared at you then, the moonlight pouring in through your blinds and landing on your eyelashes as you blinked innocently at me. The realization that you and I were still inevitably doomed to end came flooding back, even through the protective shield of my intoxication and the high of what had been such a great evening.

I laced my fingers in your hair, trailed my free hand onto your stubbly cheek.

Those eyes.

"You're going to have beautiful children someday," I told you.

"We're going to have beautiful children," you corrected.

And I fell silent, letting you kiss my forehead and hold me as I fell into a deep sleep.

TWENTY-SEVEN.

Y O U C A M E T O M Y college graduation in May, finally making up for the graduation nightmare I'd experienced in high school. I wore two cords that day over my robe: one for the English Honor Society into which I'd been inducted, and one to indicate my status as a Summa Cum Laude graduate. I still remember the elated feeling I'd experienced when they called my name and announced that I'd graduated with highest honors. I also remember that the only reason I really cared was because, even six years into our slowly-dying relationship, I wanted to show off in front of you. I still wanted to impress you.

Despite everything, I still had the biggest crush on you.

You met me afterward in front of the bleachers, bearing a bouquet of roses and an umbrella to shield me from the light drizzle that had begun midway through the ceremony. My dad snapped a few pictures of us, and then we all drove to one of our favorite spots near home, Ted's Montana Grill, for a late-afternoon meal.

The table conversation was a bit stiff, and felt more than a little awkward. You were always uncomfortable when my family started talking politics, because you were more or less apolitical in comparison with my family's and my staunch views and passionate opinions. I tried to change the direction of the conversation, shifting the focus to something a little less heavy than the upcoming presidential election. Still, it was annoying for me to have to do that—to have to worry about "protecting" you from beliefs or ideals that didn't exactly align with your own, for fear that you'd make me feel guilty about it when we were alone together later.

When we returned to my house that evening, I was standing at the sink washing my hands when you came up behind me, wrapping your arms low around my waist and kissing the side of my neck.

"Congratulations," you said. "You look beautiful."

I turned to kiss you, sliding my arms around you, and you deepened the kiss, grabbing my waist and pulling me closer.

"I want you…" I said, breathing the words against your lips.

And it was like I'd started a frenzy, because you crashed your mouth back against mine, holding me tighter than you had in so long and making me dizzy with the rush of desire.

…But my parents were home, and I wouldn't have given in after so many months of living a chaste lifestyle, anyway. I'd *chosen*. There was no going back—I knew that and appreciated it with my whole heart.

When you finally pulled away, it was almost like you knew what I'd been thinking—that even if we'd had the house to ourselves, it wouldn't have changed the outcome.

"What?" I asked, trying not to let your disappointed countenance affect me.

"Nothing," you said uselessly, moving away from me toward the kitchen table.

"Babe…let's talk…" I implored, already feeling helpless. You sighed, placing your head in your hands.

"There's nothing to talk about," you said. "It's just…you confuse me. You shouldn't tell me you want me when it doesn't change things."

I shook my head, amazed that you couldn't seem to understand the simple concept of self-control, or that *wanting* and *giving in* were two very, very different things.

"Just because we're not sleeping together right now doesn't mean I don't want you, Wade," I said. "I thought you knew that."

"I don't know what to believe, anymore. It doesn't feel like you want me," you said dejectedly.

"But I wouldn't be human if I didn't want you. Sex is good. Our feelings are normal and natural—they're not bad. But we can only act on them under the right circumstances."

"Marriage," you finished, sighing. "I just...I feel like I'm putting so much into this, and I'm not getting anything out of it."

And although marriage had once been the only thing I'd ever wanted—to commit to you forever, to start a family with you—I wasn't so sure anymore, standing there at the kitchen sink and watching you indulge in another pity party over a lifestyle change that wasn't going to last forever. Did it matter to you at all that you still had *me* back then? That I was standing right in front of you, loving you and willing your good, even if we were going through a major adjustment? Or were you really, honestly so dependent on physical intimacy that when it was removed, you actually felt like you weren't "getting anything" from me? Wade, that must have been the case, or we would have been able to figure things out.

Based on all of our differences, and based on your increasing hostility toward everything I believed to be good and true and right—as well as your growing hostility toward me—I had little hope that we could have a successful marriage. How was I supposed to be with someone who couldn't see or appreciate truth? Who couldn't even acknowledge it? If we started a family in the future, would I be able to depend on you to be the spiritual head of our household? Would you ever pray with me, and for me? Could I count on you to help me raise our children in a way that taught them to value their faith? And would I ever be able to freely reference God's beauty in the sunlight, or the ocean, or the stars and expect you to understand?

I believed the answer to all of these was negative.

I couldn't marry you.

So what were we doing?

"Wade...I know I changed...but you changed, too. When I started dating you, you were more or less Catholic. You identified as Catholic. You went to Mass with your family. I was under the impression that your faith meant something to you. And as the years went by, you just became more and more hardened, without even a reason. Why?"

You were quiet for a moment as you sifted through your thoughts.

"I just don't trust the Church. I don't believe exclusively in Catholicism. I think religion can be good in that it instills values and morals into a person from a young age, but it can also be extremely flawed."

"But faith is...everything. It's sacrifice. It's mercy. It's authentic love—it's the whole reason why we were created," I said.

"Well, it's not for me," you said abruptly.

After such an abrupt proclamation, all we could do was settle into the inevitable silence that followed, wondering how things had turned so ugly so fast.

"I'm going to go," you finally said, sliding back your chair and reaching for your jacket.

"Oh," I replied. "OK."

You didn't say anything else, and I didn't argue with you. The truth was that I wanted you to leave, though I'd always historically wanted you close at the height of a conflict so that we'd be able to work things out more quickly. I'd reached my breaking point—I knew there was nothing left to figure out. My heart was throbbing from your abrasive words and startling display of detachment—you'd so suddenly decided to give up, walking out of my house like you were only running out for groceries.

But I didn't realize it would be the last time I'd ever see you. If I had, I would've kissed you like I meant it when I walked you to your car, rather than barely touching my lips to your cheek. I would've held onto you a little longer before you climbed in and started the ignition. I would've told you, even after the brutal honesty of that last conversation, that I loved you. I would've looked into your eyes to better memorize them for the lonely years that followed.

I wanted you to go—was ready for you to go—but it would've broken me knowing that it was our last goodbye. It turns out that not-knowing is one of the universe's most merciful gifts.

You backed up my driveway and out of my life that day, and I watched you go, breathing a sigh of relief as your car rolled out of sight.

~

YOU TRIED TO TEXT ME the next day, and again two days after, but I didn't respond. I was too busy thinking. If you would have called, I would have answered. If you would have called, Wade, I don't think I would have broken up with you the way I did.

But you didn't call. You knew that something was irrevocably wrong, but you were too afraid to pick up the phone and have a conversation about it. So you hid behind half-hearted texts, asking, **Are you still not talking to me?** like I had randomly decided to give you the cold shoulder.

After a solid week went by without so much as a call—without a visit from you to check on me—you sent me an email. *An email*, Wade. As though you hadn't had my phone number for the last seven years. As though it hadn't been etched into your memory forever.

When I opened my inbox and saw that *that* was how you'd chosen to communicate with me, I wrote you a strongly-worded email in response, too livid to worry about how it would look or how it would make you feel. I was insulted, enraged, that you'd let the whole week go by without attempting to make things right between us, and the fact that you'd emailed me to try to solve it just pushed me over the edge.

In one sitting, I wrote a 1,433-word break-up letter, touching on every point that I felt I needed to address, and hit "send" without a second thought. Truthfully, I'd been ready to end things since February, and my words were the culmination of four months of constant guilt and rejection. You were never going to understand me, or even attempt to understand or appreciate the fullness of my identity. You would always resent me for it, and I would spend my whole life waiting and hoping for you to accept the person I'd chosen to be.

It was no way to live.

When you finally wrote back to me three days later, you expressed that you'd understood a lot of what I'd said, but that you were disgusted that I'd chosen to break up with you in an email. You tried to convince me that our differences, in fact, completed us, and that our relationship wouldn't have lasted as long as it had if we'd been exactly the same. I promptly responded that all of the hurt and bitterness between us, which emanated from our differences, hardly "completed" us.

...And then my inbox was quiet.

About a week later, a friend of mine from church, Felicia, invited me to go on a retreat with her to Maryland. I had the whole summer ahead of me, with no boyfriend and no real job to speak of, so I packed an overnight bag and met her at her house on somewhat of a whim. The two of us went speeding into the early summer twilight, blasting her music with the sunroof down as the Philadelphia skyline winked goodbye behind us.

It was impossible not to miss you.

Felicia and I arrived at her friend's house three hours later, who was running the retreat directly from her home. I got so little sleep during those few days, and my heart was aching as it struggled to adjust to life without you, but the events that unfolded over the course of that weekend were desperately needed. God must've known that I needed that retreat for some amount of peace—for some amount of closure—because, when I went to confession that weekend, I mentioned our relationship to the priest.

"Father...I broke up with my boyfriend of six years in an email."

He took a long time to respond, the silhouette of his face outlined against the illuminated screen in the dark confessional. When he finally spoke, he said,

"You know you basically wrote him a Dear John letter, right? I mean...six years...that had to have hurt so much."

He confirmed what I already knew, but I'd needed to come all the way to Maryland to hear it. So when I arrived back home when the weekend was through, I waited for a quiet evening, and then proceeded to do one of the singularly hardest things I've ever had to do in my life: I picked up the phone and called you.

You didn't pick up, and I was convinced you probably wouldn't call me back, so I left you a voicemail. I told you that nothing had changed, but that I was sorry for the way I'd ended things. I told you that I missed you—that I still loved you, for whatever that was worth. I truly believed I'd never hear from you again.

Half an hour later, your name lit up my phone screen.

"Hello?" I said, picking up the phone cautiously, as though you would bite me from your end of the line.

"Hi," you said.

"…Did you get my voicemail?" I asked.

"Yes…it made me sad," you said.

"I'm sorry, Wade," I repeated. "I'm so, so sorry for the way I handled it. I was just…so mad at you. And there was no solution, you know? Things wouldn't have gotten better. And you let the whole week go by without calling to make sure I was OK, and that hurt, on top of a mountain of other things, but it's still no excuse. I'm sorry."

"It's OK," you told me.

"…How are you?" I asked.

"I'm OK, Morgan. I went biking today, actually not too far from your house. I'll have a whole summer to just…focus on school. Stay on track."

My stomach turned as I listened to you try to convince yourself that everything would be all right. In truth, I was already internally doing the same thing.

"Well, that's good," I sighed, sliding my knees under my chin on my bedroom floor. Then, "Wade…I really don't think we had a choice."

You were silent for a few moments. Then you asked,

"Is it important?"

I will never, ever forget that you asked me that question, Wade. I knew that you already knew the answer—knew that my faith was important, was the center of my life—but the way you asked...it was like you were finally recognizing its significance.

"Yes," I whispered, knowing that it was the last time I'd have to choose between you and my values again.

"OK," you replied. And even over the phone, I could picture you nodding in your quick, succinct little way that meant you understood.

"Well...I guess I should probably go. I haven't slept for three days. I was on a retreat," I explained, already yawning into the phone. "But please...don't hesitate, ever, to text me. Or call me. I'd like to be...friends..."

"Me too, Morgan," you said, and I cringed, because I never wanted to be that person who uses lines like "we can still be friends." For me, though, it wasn't a line.

"So...I'll talk to you soon?" I asked.

"Sounds good."

And there was another moment—an unspoken moment—that I'll always remember. It was the moment right before goodbye. The moment where we had, for six years, always said *I love you.*

It hung there between us, unarticulated, but conveyed in the silence.

"Bye."

"Bye, Morgan."

It was the last time I ever heard your voice.

DEAR WADE,

AFTER WE BROKE UP, I ATTENDED healing Masses in an attempt to relieve my heart from the ache of letting you go. I said a 54-day rosary novena for you—for all of your intentions, and for your ultimate happiness. I sat in front of the Blessed Sacrament for hours, talking to God about you when I felt your absence the most, imploring the Blessed Mother to keep you under her mantle and protect you since I couldn't be in your life anymore.

...Then, I did my fair share of young and reckless things, like cliff-jumping, midnight pool-hopping, and skinny dipping at the Jersey Shore at 2 a.m., trying to eject you from my mind before realizing, ultimately, that I never would. I pursued new skylines, chasing adventure on the streets of exciting and exotic cities like New York, Los Angeles, Vienna, Prague, Budapest, Florence, and Rome, trying to override the memories we'd made in Philadelphia. I dated Catholic men, and came home at the end of each night with the sad realization that no one measured up. I got my first job in the corporate world, then built and managed my own business. I cultivated new and inspiring friendships, started graduate school at an Ivy League college, wrote four books, and published an album of my original songs. I did anything, everything I could to try to fill the gigantic hole in my life that you'd left behind.

I don't know if you remember, but when we broke up, I told you I was going to spend some time alone, working on myself to become the best person I could be. I meant that—and I *became* my best self. My best self led me to all of my goals, to everything I accomplished...and then, inevitably, back to you.

Seven months prior to Open Mic Night, I'd been thinking about you and missing you so painfully that I'd sent you a long message, telling you:

I know this message comes after a year and a half of not speaking. I really struggled with whether to send this to you at all, because the last thing I want is to cause any confusion or disruption in either of our lives, but I decided I couldn't risk never sending this to you and never knowing what could have come of it.

In the two years we've been apart, I've worked every single day on building a life for myself based around my faith, and my interests and passions. I am more myself than I've ever been, and I'm so proud of that, Wade. But when it comes to dating, I can't find a single person who can make me feel half of what you made me feel when I was with you, and I'm starting to think that maybe, there's a reason for that.

If this isn't reciprocated, then you can totally disregard all of this. I might be way out of line here, but I had to at least tell you. I'm guessing nothing has changed much for either of us in terms of our convictions or lifestyles, and that the same issues that caused us to break up remain unchanged. Still, since I can't be certain that this is the case, I'm choosing to reach out to you. I need you to know that I still miss you and think about you often. And I think that no matter what happens in my life, I'm always going to have feelings for you on some level, and it hurts so much knowing that this probably doesn't change the reality of the situation. I just couldn't live the rest of my life wondering, "What if I had just asked him?"

If you believe we'd still hurt each other with our conflicting beliefs, and that nothing would be any better if we tried to work things out (or if you're simply not interested), then please be straightforward with me about your feelings. I would really appreciate the honesty. If, however, something has changed on your end—if you've had any change of heart in regards to your faith, or if you're even slightly more open to it than you were before—well, I had to at least ask. I'm fully aware of how that sounds, but I just had to ask one more time, because if we saw even slightly more eye-to-eye than we did two years ago...well, you just have to know that you're still my first and only love, and that I don't really know where to go from here.

I hope with all of my heart that you are well and happy. I'm so sorry for reopening this chapter if it is one that you would prefer to keep closed. Again...I just couldn't risk not telling you how I felt.

A week passed after I sent that message without a response. Then a month. Then two months. I finally came to the realization that you were never going to write back, and that your lack of response spoke clearly to the fact that you wanted nothing to do with me. I carried the weight of that disappointment around for some time, and eventually made whatever peace I could with it.

Then, Wade—the morning after that Open Mic Night, in a city that had the power to break me open—I heard from you. Seven months later, you found it in your heart to respond. I'd love to know what inspired you to think of me in the first place when you finally reached out, but the point was that you had, and your response was simple:

Hey Morgan, I'm sorry it took me over 6 months to respond. I appreciate your reaching out and telling me how you feel. I know that took a lot, and it was very unfair of me to not respond to that (for both of us). I've been seeing someone for a while now, and she makes me really happy. I just thought you should know that. I hope you're happy and I wish you all the best.

When I saw your name flash across my phone screen for the first time in years, my gut clenched and dropped. But then I read your message, and I realized it wasn't nearly as painful as I'd expected it would be. The fact that you were happy—the fact that you'd chosen to respond at all—brought me so much peace. I was able to respond afterward, completely honestly, that I was healing, and that I was beyond glad you were happy. For so long, I had prayed for your happiness above all else. Still, a part of me will always wish we could have found that happiness together.

God, or the universe—whatever your idea of destiny looks like—operated in such a meaningful and deliberate way in our lives and in our relationship, Wade. From our innocent beginnings all the way through our poignant end, something unstoppable was set in motion to ensure our paths would cross in a way that would render me incapable of ever forgetting you. When I stood on that stage and sang "Can't Help Falling in Love" in the presence of old ghosts, I hadn't realized that it was the second and final time I'd be singing it to you. The recording I'd given you for Valentine's Day so long ago had been a romantic gesture, and—though I hadn't realized it that night— singing it onstage in the city where I'd fallen so completely for you was my goodbye. Your response the following day to my old message had been your goodbye to me, in return.

I've always been torn between two very distinct mindsets: at least part of me has always believed that if things are meant to be, they will work out seamlessly, effortlessly—exactly as they are supposed to. However, as I've continued to learn and grow, I've begun to feel differently. It seems that nothing will ever fall into place without action—unless I am brave enough and convicted enough to take my life into my hands and make things happen.

Now, looking back on that final weekend—the weekend I healed and got my heart broken all over again by your bittersweet goodbye, and the weekend that, seemingly by coincidence, you chose to contact me after a period of endless silence—I believe that God actively works. Usually through the choices we make, yes, but also in the moments we least expect it—in the moments we are least cooperative. And maybe you'll never believe in that type of destiny or grace the way I do, but I hope, after this extremely long love letter, that you can appreciate the way all of our little moments fell together in the type of perfection I had once believed I'd only read about in books.

I regret nothing, and despite having turned into someone very different than the girl you'd once expected to know your whole life, I'd do every bit of it all over again if given the chance. Staring at your name on my phone screen—at your response crafted from feelings I believed you'd long ago filed away—I understood why I finally had the peace I'd lacked before.

Your happiness was all the closure I'd ever needed.

ABOUT THE AUTHOR

Lindsey Todd began writing at age six, and is now a young adult author who is passionate about encouraging a new generation of Catholic fiction. She holds a BA in English from West Chester University, and is pursuing her Master of Arts degree at Dartmouth College. Lindsey is a blogger for the Chastity Project and Thought Catalog, and her work has been endorsed by *New York Times* Bestselling Author Elizabeth Marcolini, famous speaker and writer Jason Evert, and speaker Pam Stenzel. Lindsey has been featured on Nashville Catholic Radio, the Catholic Feminist Podcast, and a variety of other platforms to speak about her passion for writing and Catholic morality. She runs her own content marketing business, and works with clients all over the world to create inspiring content for businesses and influencers. When her nose isn't buried in a book (and when she's not writing), Lindsey enjoys fitness and yoga, singing and music, hiking, art, Eucharistic Adoration, and adventures of all kinds! She has traveled extensively through the U.S. and Europe, and is always planning a new escapade. *Closure* is Lindsey's debut novel. You can learn more about her work at: www.lindseytodd.net.

If you enjoyed *Closure,* add it/rate it on Amazon and Goodreads! Follow my bookish endeavors on Instagram: @veritaswords.

Made in the USA
Middletown, DE
03 December 2020